Thief of Words

Thief of Words

JOHN JAFFE

WARNER BOOKS

An AOL Time Warner Company

This is a work of fiction. All of the characters, incidents, and dialogue, except for incidental references to public figures, products, or services, are imaginary and are not intended to refer to any living persons or to disparage any company's products or services.

To Phyllis Richman for her big heart and wise words

I would like to thank the following people:

Richard Jaffe and Beverly Reifman for their early and enthusiastic first reads.

Jenny Bent for her keen comments.

Annie Isaac for her memories of Atlantic City.

Ben and Sam Shepard for sharing Internet access.

Steve Hunter for saying I could use his name to pitch this book to Esther Newberg.

Esther Newberg for placing this book with Jamie Raab.

Jamie Raab, one hell of an editor and a nice person to boot.

Phyllis Richman for reading as many drafts as I threw at her and always making it better.

Steve Proctor and the *Baltimore Sun* for his and its generosity.

And finally to Laura Lippman for Operation Muncie, without which this book would have never been.

Thief of Words

A flimsy curtain separates memory from imagination.

Elizabeth Loftus

PROLOGUE

(1982)

If you like rooting for the underdog, Annie Hollerman would have been a fine choice.

She came from nowhere, she knew no one, and her clothes were all wrong for everything. Yet she'd talked herself into a reporting job at a well-respected newspaper in North Carolina, talked herself ahead of fourteen other applicants, including a Cliffie and two Yale grads. She even talked herself over a prep from Princeton, which was the most astonishing part because every morning the paper's managing editor slipped his navy blue Princeton belt through the loops of his pressed khakis.

Maybe the M.E. liked underdogs, too. Maybe he liked the fact that Annie was eager, energetic, and bright. Maybe he liked the set of her jaw as she tried to seem tougher than her twenty-six years. Maybe there was something in her xeroxed clips that reminded him of how hard and exhilarating it was to be starting out with nothing but potential.

Whatever the reason, the man in khakis stood up at the end of the interview and stuck out his hand. "Welcome aboard, Ms. Hollerman," he said. Then he assigned her to the health beat and added, "I expect you to make page one in three weeks."

Annie made page one with four days to spare.

Who would have thought the daily rounds of a chicken farm inspector could read like a detective story? The underdog, it turned out, could write like a dream. She had an eye for character and an ear for conversation. She could transform the most mundane tragedy into something that would turn your morning coffee salty with tears.

In less than a year, Annie was on the feature writing staff. And six months after that, the man in the khakis called her into his office again. They chatted a few minutes about her progress and his satisfaction. Then, because he was a man who liked ceremony and flourishes, he stood up and, once again, extended his hand.

"Congratulations, you've got a new assignment," he said.

And so Annie Hollerman became the youngest reporter in the history of the *Charlotte Commercial-Appeal* to join the paper's special projects team. Until then, the team had consisted of veteran reporters. Three years before, it had won the paper's only Pulitzer Prize for its investigation into brown lung disease.

If this were a movie, Annie Hollerman would be spunky, leggy, and pretty and drive a secondhand convertible. And she'd be from New Jersey.

Annie had plenty of spunk, but she also had a temper, hated her thighs, drove a white Honda hatchback, and was as leggy as five foot three can be. She was, however, from New Jersey, and she was friendly and funny. Within two weeks, everybody in the newsroom liked her—everybody except the food editor, a lonely and hateful spinster whose only friend was the gay chef she was in love with.

As for pretty? Annie was more interesting than pretty. Her nose was a little too long and her eyes were set deep with shadowy circles underneath. But you could tell she had a face that would wear well. Her strong cheekbones would push out even more prominently over the years. And the laugh lines, now temporary, would radiate around her eyes.

Everything about her would sharpen. The softness of youth would give way to a kind of carved elegance that gets more beautiful with each year. And her carriage would change. Her hands, which often hid behind her back, would someday find an easy resting place on her hips. One day, she would walk into a restaurant wearing a clingy black dress and a man at a window table would nearly spill his wine trying to get a better look.

But that would be years from now. At this point, Annie Hollerman was no great beauty. Her hair, however, was another story. It was, and always would be, a showstopper. Long waves of red, gold, and blonde tumbled around her face and down her back. It was the kind of hair that drove Botticelli and Rossetti to canvas. And it was the first thing anyone noticed about her, usually providing the opening line for men who found her almost-beauty appealing.

"Wow, great hair," was Andrew Binder's opening line. He blurted it out as she walked past his desk on her second day in the newsroom. It had been a long time since Annie had heard anything that inept (once in high school: "Hey girl, your head's on fire!"), but she didn't mind, this was Andrew Binder, the star reporter, the hotshot writer, everybody's pick for the next Pulitzer. Her hair had stunned Andrew Binder into an incomplete sentence.

Within weeks Andrew and Annie were known in the newsroom as A-Squared. They seemed destined not only for each other, but also for greatness—or at the very least, the *New York Times*. They were wunderkind bookends, full of talent and drive. Friends could picture Andrew and Annie reporting from the White House or pontificating on Sunday morning talk shows. And, in truth, A-Squared could picture it, too.

Life was good for Annie Hollerman.

Until.

These underdog stories always have an "until." This one came on an uncharacteristically cold spring day in the Queen City of Charlotte, North Carolina. It was so cold that the new red tulips lining the city's main streets seemed to be shivering in the morning wind.

Annie got to the paper at 9:15. First she stopped at the cafeteria where she bought coffee, and joked about the cold weather. She seemed even more buoyant than usual. If the cafeteria ladies had thought to ask her why, she might have told them that the night before she and Andrew had talked seriously about moving in together.

Up in the newsroom, she saw a small box on the keyboard of her computer. Inside, resting on a pillow of white cotton, was Andrew's house key. "For you, Annie," the note said. "Always and forever."

But before always and forever could even start, before she could tuck the key back into the box, three editors were standing by her desk.

"Step into my office, please." It was the man with the navy blue Princeton belt. To his right was the projects editor, Annie's direct boss; to his left was the executive editor, everyone's boss.

Only one person besides Annie and the three editors know exactly what happened that cold spring morning. The food editor, whose desk faced the executive editor's glass-walled office, was very good at reading lips. But it seems she wasn't as hateful as everyone thought, for she refused to tell anyone why Annie Hollerman bolted from the editor's office, her eyes as red as those shivering tulips.

Annie never even came back to clean out her things. It was the food editor who finally tossed the little white box with the key inside into a trash can. Soon after, she asked for a new desk, away from the glass offices, and they gave her the desk where Annie Hollerman, the wunderkind, had once sat.

CHAPTER 1

(2001)

What you need, Annie Hollerman, is a man with a good ass."

Laura Goodbread scrolled down to the bottom of her message, added her usual "xoxo," and hit the send button. Just as her words disappeared, Jack DePaul's cute butt appeared a few feet away. Jack was standing by the music critic's desk, his back to her.

She wondered what he might look like underneath those pleated black Dockers. She'd never know firsthand, she was a (happily) married woman and wanted to stay that way. Not to mention that Jack was her boss and morally, legally, and many other "ly" words, forbidden to do anything but edit her.

Anatomy aside, she liked Jack DePaul as a person, which was not something she could say about many editors at the *Baltimore Star-News*. He was funny, smart, and fair—or as fair as an editor could be. He only asked her to cover the annual City That Reads festival every other year. Well, "asked" might be the wrong word, but Jack made it seem like asked, rather than assigned.

But the best part of him, as far as Laura was concerned, was his passion for good writing. There was only one other person Laura knew who loved words as much as he did, and that was her best friend, Annie Hollerman.

Annie, who ran her own literary agency in Washington, called her at least three times a week just to read lines from manuscripts she'd gotten in. "Laura," she'd say, "I know you're busy, but you've got to hear this." And she dragged Laura to innumerable book readings just so they could hear writers deliver their words personally. "As they were meant to sound," Annie would say.

As many times as Annie had called Laura about the next Jane Austen, Jack had read to her from the latest *New Yorker* or novel he was reading. He loved simple language and cadence. He had lots of favorites—F. Scott Fitzgerald's short stories, Ian Frazier's sketches, David Quammen's essays, Raymond Chandler's pulp. At least fifty times, he had peered over his glasses and said, "Goodbread, if you could write a lead like Chandler's 'Red Wind,' you could win a Pulitzer." (To which she inevitably replied, "If I could write a lead like that, I wouldn't be working for you, Jack.") She'd even known him to quote poetry. Poetry in the newsroom!

She'd also known him to call reporters crybabies, knuckleheads, and whiners. When someone didn't want to do a story, he'd say, "You don't have to like it, you just have to do it." That didn't bother Laura. She knew Annie could handle him. The crybabies Jack dealt with were minor leaguers compared to Annie's prima donnas.

Aside from their mutual love of words, Jack and Annie needed each other. Or so Laura thought. Laura didn't know much about Jack's personal life beyond newsroom gossip and the fact that he'd stopped wearing his wedding band three years before. Rumor had it, he'd left his wife for a dark-haired woman who broke his heart in eighteen pieces. Half the newsroom was still trying to guess the identity of his Madame X.

Laura's money was on the ambitious assistant city editor, Kathleen Faulkner, an attractive brunette with boarding school bones. The joke was she had the biggest balls in the newsroom. One time at a party, Laura overheard the managing editor tell the business editor that Faulkner "clanged when she walked." She was particularly tough on her female staff, who called her Captina Queeg behind her back.

Rumor also had it that Kathleen and Jack had hooked up at a management skills conference in New York City. That was a month before Jack stopped wearing his wedding band. Kathleen never took hers off.

In any event, something had changed recently, because twice in the past three weeks Jack had asked Laura if she knew of any women he could meet.

She figured Jack was lonely; she knew Annie was. They were perfect for each other. Almost. There was the journalist part. Annie could barely talk to Laura about their days together as reporters at the *Charlotte Commercial-Appeal*.

Getting Annie to agree to a blind date would be hard enough. Except for a brief affair with an energy analyst, Annie had been moldering around solo since her divorce two years ago. Getting her to go on a blind date with a journalist would be nearly impossible. She'd tried before and Annie had dug in her heels deeper than Laura could dislodge. And if anyone could dislodge anything, it was Laura Goodbread, generally regarded as the pit bull of the *Baltimore Star-News*'s Features department.

Laura knew why Annie refused. She didn't want any reminders of her past. When Laura had pushed so hard a few months back, trying to fix up Annie with the new city hall reporter, Annie had finally slammed the phone down and refused to talk to her for three days. When they started talking again, Annie said, "It's too painful to date someone who has the life I used to have."

Uncharacteristically, Laura gave in. She wished she hadn't, though. Annie was becoming a hermit. This time, Laura wouldn't take no for an answer; she'd even enlisted her daughter—Annie's goddaughter—in the mission. Sure, Jack was a journalist, but he was also funny, smart, and soulful.

And when he walked away, the view was good.

The phone started ringing. "This is Laura Goodbread, *Baltimore Star-News*."

"And this is Annie Hollerman, agent to the stars. Is Becky all set for this weekend?"

"Set? Are you kidding? She's rolled and rerolled her sleeping bag a million times. You know what she's told all her friends? That she's going camping with Xena, Warrior Princess! She can't wait. I could hardly get her to school this morning. I can't tell you how glad I am that you're doing this. You know how I feel about peeing outside. However, I do have the perfect thank-you present."

Annie laughed. "I bet it involves a man, right? Some guy you want to see naked but never will so you want me to tell you what he looks like. Right? Am I close?"

"I guess this means you haven't read my e-mail yet."

She could hear Annie groaning on the other end of the line.

"Stop it," Laura nearly shouted into the phone. "You need this. You need something."

After the groan came the sigh. "Laura, I don't need anything. Especially a man with a big butt."

"Hold on, girl, I've never said anything in my life about big butts. Great butts, yes. Big butts, no."

"I know your taste. I've known your taste for the past twenty years. Every man you dated, from John Gilliam to the man you married, they all look the same from behind. I don't care if it's big or great or flat or whatever. I'm not interested. Not now."

"When, Annie? When you lose your looks? You know, that's not a perpetual flame on top of your head. Someday it'll go out. You'll go gray and then you'll get wrinkles or vice versa. Let me tell you, Annie, it's time to start living before you start dying."

"Laura. Stop. Tell me about Becky. Tell me what wonderful new things my goddaughter has written."

Laura looked up to see Jack DePaul walking her way, motioning that he needed to talk to her.

"Annie, I'll tell you Friday when you pick up Beck. Your future husband's coming over. Gotta go."

Laura hung up the phone and turned toward the man standing by her desk. "Jack. Do I have the woman for you."

CHAPTER 2

As soon as Annie put the phone back in the cradle it started ringing again. Mondays were the worst. She was so busy she barely had time to eat lunch. Authors. Editors. All pulling at her thirty-seven different ways.

Right off, it was bad. First call of the morning. The publicist from Simon & Schuster saying the *Today* show people were apoplectic after Lynn McCain's on-air tantrum. "Do something," the publicist had said. "She's got three more interviews this week. You're the only one she sort of listens to."

McCain, Annie's most successful mystery writer, refused to be called a mystery writer and got nasty when anyone did so. She thought of herself as a Reynolds Price, so when interviewers compared her to Sue Grafton, she came back punching.

This morning, Katie Couric had interviewed McCain about her new book, *Shadow on the Shenandoahs*. "I can't remember when I've had so much fun figuring out who the murderer was," Couric had said, flashing her Kewpie-doll smile.

Annie almost spit out her latte when she heard McCain's response. In an exaggerated Appalachian twang and a look that could make a baby cry, McCain said, "And I bet you figured out who done it in the Bible, too?"

Unfortunately for Annie, Couric was just one of many McCain

had offended on her latest book tour. At its start, the head of Simon & Schuster publicity told Annie she was through mopping up after McCain. "Five book tours of abuse is enough. I just don't have the staff or budget to make nice after her anymore. She's your client, handle her."

And so Annie tried. So far, Annie's assistant had sent $780 worth of flowers to irate bookstore owners, radio reporters, and magazine writers.

As if that wasn't bad enough, Monday morning got worse. The editor at Scribner's backed out of the auction on a book by an author Annie was sure would be the next Alice Hoffman. And just when she thought things had bottomed out, she learned that her hottest author, Eda Royal—aka the She-Devil—had gotten arrested the day before in Nashville, Tennessee. She'd taken off her underwear at the Centennial Ladies Club luncheon and set them on fire.

Now Laura had some guy at the *Star-News* she was trying to pawn off on her.

She felt as stretched as saltwater taffy, the kind she used to eat on the Boardwalk in Atlantic City. It made a pop when it broke apart if you stretched it too hard, what she thought her brain might do any second if she had one more problem with an author or an editor.

She tried not to think about snapped taffy or finicky authors or lying editors. Instead she thought about the Mr. Planters Peanut Man who used to strut back and forth across the sea-grayed planks of the Boardwalk, tapping his top hat with the tip of his black cane to all the ladies in their spike-heeled shoes. Once, her mother got her heel stuck in a crack, and it was Mr. Peanut who so gallantly pulled the glossy black patent shoe back from the Boardwalk's unforgiving bite.

Saltwater taffy. Mr. Peanut. Summers in Atlantic City. Days on the beach. Singing Sam the Ice Cream Man and his nickel chunks of dry ice. Her mother baking in the sun; Annie frying on the sand. Her father? She knew what memories came next. Sitting on the steps crying. Her father on the sofa crying. Thank God the phone was ringing.

"Annie Hollerman."

"Xena? Warrior Princess, is that you?"

"Yes, my faithful subject, it is I," Annie said. "All ready for this weekend?"

Annie heard a giggle on the other end. "Yeah, sorta. But Mom called me to tell me to call you to tell you to read your e-mail right away—whew, I can't believe I got that out. She also said that you have no choice. If you don't do as she says, she'll make your life miserable. And Annie, she can do it, believe me. I know better than anyone."

They both laughed because they knew how true that was. "Okay, I'll check it. Now, tell me who you're reading these days. Moved out of the horse books yet?"

"Sort of," Becky said. "Does *The Horse Whisperer* count? It's not completely about horses."

"Ugh," said Annie. "Stick with *Black Beauty*, it's better written. For the life of me I'll never figure out what it is about girls and horses."

All the other lights on her phone were blinking, but Annie ignored them. She didn't have an auction today. So much for the next Alice Hoffman. To hell with them all, she could afford the luxury of ten minutes with her goddaughter.

When they hung up, Annie turned away from the blinking phone and looked through the little round window near her desk. Her office was the second floor of a small art deco building on P Street in Dupont Circle. The building's theme was nautical, hence the portholes and the stone-carved ropes at the entrance. On the first floor was Diego's Hollywood Barbers and the Firehook Bakery, and on the third floor the National Hellenic Society.

Annie thought about the last time Laura had tried to fix her up with a man from the *Star-News*. She'd lost it. She'd acted like a jerk, slamming the phone down, and refusing to talk to her. Annie felt like such an ass that she showed up at Laura's door three days later with two bottles of Yoo-hoo and a half dozen sticky buns from Firehook. "Forgiven?" Annie had said.

The funny thing was, after she'd made Laura back off, she wondered if she'd made a mistake. When she was married, she thought it was worse to be lonely with someone than without. Now she wasn't so sure. Her nights were blurring into one long run of gym, take-out dinner, and books.

When Monday night salsa-boxing class became the most exciting part of her personal life, she knew things were seriously out of balance. But Washington isn't an easy place to meet single men, especially where she lived: Dupont Circle—the Fruit Loop, as her gay friends called it.

A few of her friends had met men on the Internet or through the classifieds in *Washingtonian* magazine. One time, Annie even circled three of the ads but couldn't bring herself to call.

So now that Laura had started in on her again about going out with someone from the newsroom, a part of her wanted to say yes. But there was always another part, a bigger part, that warned her to steer clear of her past and anyone who might pry it open. And if that weren't enough to keep her away from journalists, there was the good-bye scene with Andrew Binder to make her say no to Laura's fix-ups.

It wasn't particularly dramatic. A big blowup would have been better. That way, there would have been a definite end, a border, a knife's edge delineation between A-Squared and A-Alone.

They were sitting at a corner booth at the Park Road Deli. Pastrami for him, a Reuben for her. She'd driven in for the weekend; he had tickets for a Leon Redbone concert at Spirit Square.

She'd been living at her mother's house in Greensboro since that horrible morning at the *Charlotte Commercial-Appeal*. For the first week, she and Andrew talked every day. He said all the right things—"I'm with you Annie"; "You can work your way back"; "We'll be fine." But she'd heard it in the silence when she first told him what happened, and she heard every time he called—he was already gone.

Over the next few weeks, they talked less. He was busy working stories. In the past, they'd talked shop for hours. They'd give each other blow-by-blow descriptions of interviews; she'd pull out her reporter's pad and read him quotes; he'd describe the flattened *a*'s of his source's Michigan accent; she'd tell him how she unearthed a slumlord's fraudulent tax returns.

Now she had nothing to tell him.

"Could I get another cherry Coke?" Andrew said to the waitress who'd just brought their sandwiches. He'd been fidgeting with the straw, looking for something to do with his fingers—and his eyes. Only a few sentences had passed between them while they'd waited for their food, mostly about a news show WBTV had pulled because it had zoomed in on two men holding hands.

Annie looked at him. As always, he was weeks overdue for a haircut. Brown curls looped down his face. When he wasn't noodling the straw, he was pushing the hair from underneath his wire-rimmed glasses. His eyes were the most surprising pale blue she'd ever seen on a Jewish guy. The glacial blue of a Siberian husky.

They ate their sandwiches. They'd been going to the Park Road Deli since they'd met. It reminded them each of home, her of the Forum 6 Diner in Paramus, New Jersey, and him of Hymie's Deli in Bala Cynwyd, Pennsylvania.

Three-quarters of the way into her Reuben, Annie couldn't stand it any longer. "Heard anything from the Inkie?" she said.

Andrew looked down, as if his pastrami sandwich had the answers. Annie took his hand in hers—did she feel him pull back just a little?—"Andrew?"

He kept looking at his sandwich and said, "Yeah, they offered me a job. It's the Montgomery County bureau, but it's a start."

The Inkie, the *Philadelphia Inquirer*. At that time it was regarded as a Pulitzer Prize factory. A month before everything came crashing down, they'd both applied for jobs there.

He left two weeks later. She never heard from him again.

Damn Andrew Binder and his downturned eyes. How long was she going to let what happened in Charlotte control her life? Or, at the very least, whom she had a glass of merlot with?

Maybe she wouldn't fight Laura this time. Maybe it was time to stop pushing back. Annie was tired of pushing people away. Truth be told, she was getting tired of her Monday night salsa-boxing class.

She typed in her password on the computer and listened to the modem's chipper little song.

Laura's e-mail, entitled "Great asses of civilization," said the following:

"What you need, Annie Hollerman, is a man with a good ass. And I have just the one, I'm watching it as we speak. But there's more to him than that. Trust me on this one. And stop scrunching your face up. You'll get even more wrinkles. Really, sweetie, this guy is fabulous. He's smart, funny, screams across the newsroom, 'Hey, Goodbread, are we gonna edit this fucking story or not?' AND. . . . he actually improves my brilliant copy on occasion. You know there aren't many people I willingly let fondle my words. This guy's good. He's divorced, has a grown son and the gossip around here is that his heart's been tromped by a woman meaner than Cruella DeVille. He needs you. But more to the point, YOU NEED HIM, you just don't know it. It's time to get past this journalist bullshit. Andrew was an immature little asshole. Jack, on the other hand, is a mature asshole (only when he cuts my copy), so why would he care about something you did when you were a kid?

"Besides, he's kinda cute. Looks like Richard Dreyfuss or Steven Spielberg, one of those gray-haired bearded guys. I know I promised I'd never try to fix you up again. But you didn't really believe that did you? Please go out with him as a personal favor to me. And to Becky. I swear this is the last fix-up from me if you do it. We all want to see you happy.

"xoxo Laura

"P.S. It's too late to say no. I already gave him your e-mail address and told him you couldn't wait to hear from him."

CHAPTER 3

Jack DePaul eyed Laura suspiciously. "Goodbread, I know your tricks; you're trying to divert me. You know exactly why I'm here. It's City That Reads time and guess whose turn it is to cover it?"

He paused, then said, "What do you mean, 'Do I have the woman for you'?"

"You asked me if I know anyone you could meet. Remember? It was just last week. Early Alzheimer's is a terrible tragedy, Jack."

"Oh, yeah. I'd forgotten . . . about Alzheimer's. So, who's the woman?"

"Her name is Annie Hollerman. She's a literary agent in D.C. She's great. She's smart and funny and has fiery red hair that goes down the middle of her back. She got divorced a couple years ago from the world's most exacting and unpleasant man. I told her about you and she said she was very interested. By the way, she's my best friend. If you mess with her I'll break every one of your appendages—and your glasses."

"Mess with her, or mess around with her?" said Jack, leering.

"You know what I mean, buster."

"She said she was interested in me?" asked Jack, the bantering tone suddenly absent. "What did you say about me?"

"I said you were nice—for a slime-sucking editor type."

"Laura!" exclaimed Jack. His horror was unfeigned. He knew Laura's general position on the subject of editors.

"Oh, relax, Jack. I just told her who you were and what you did. And she said she couldn't wait to meet you. So e-mail her right away. Right now, this very morning. She's waiting to hear from you."

"Did you really say I was nice?"

"Do I really have to cover the City That Reads festival?"

CHAPTER 4

It wasn't until 3:45 that afternoon that Jack DePaul summoned up the courage to send Annie the following e-mail:

"Annie,

"Laura Goodbread tells me you're fabulous. I trust her in these matters, she is a very careful reporter. If you, too, trust her in these matters, would you care to meet for lunch? I know this e-mail stuff is pretty impersonal, but it's also less embarrassing if you just want to say no. In any event, I'll now have to read the authors you represent to show you what a great guy I am.

"Jack DePaul"

Laura had called Annie three more times that day, asking if she'd gotten anything from Jack. Finally, on the fourth call at 5:30, Annie reported that indeed she had gotten something from a jdepaul@aol.com.

He was funny, Annie gave him that. But what would she tell him when they got to the résumé part of the lunch? She couldn't tell him everything. With other dates, it was easy. She'd say, "I used to be a reporter," and they'd smile and move on to another subject—themselves. But a fellow journalist would want to play Journalist Geography: Where, when, who owned the chain, and why'd you leave the calling?

What to do? A polite no, or should she take a chance?

The nagging voice in her head started again. But then she thought about Monday night salsa boxing. Plus, it had been more than eight months since she'd gone on a date. And worse, her underwear was getting tattered and she didn't even care.

She hit the reply box in jdepaul's e-mail and a blank form appeared. She put her fingers to the keyboard, but they didn't move. Should I answer him? Maybe I'll just lie, never mention I was a reporter. He doesn't have to know every minute of my life.

It wouldn't actually be a lie, more like an omission. Hell, it's lunch, not an interrogation. Maybe it won't even come up. Where's the damn J key anyway? For that matter, where is the A, or the C, or the K?

Her hands poised over the keyboard. Should I, shouldn't I? Twenty years ago, her fingers had hesitated the same way over the send button. One push of her finger had sent a story to her editor, a story that changed her life.

Should I, shouldn't I?

Her index finger found the J key.

"Jack,

"Yes, I trust Laura about most things. And yes, you must read my authors. I suggest starting with 'Confessions of a She-Devil.' Would you like to call to make arrangements?

"Annie"

To which Jack replied:

"I will read 'She-Devil.' Why don't we make arrangements this way: I like the notion of meeting you sight/sound unseen/unheard. It'll force us to set up a rendezvous involving black fedoras or pink carnations in the lapel and secret passwords. Don't sit down to lunch with anyone who doesn't say: 'There are storm clouds over Lisbon.'

"Jack"

Sight/sound unseen/unheard. He was a romantic. Annie liked that. She replied:

"Jack,

"There are many wonderful things about being in my 40s, one of them is not memory. So if a woman with red hair comes up to you and says in a fake cockney, 'The Rain in Spain Falls Mainly on the Plain,' do not call the police; all she could remember of the passwords is that they had something to do with weather in Europe. If you want to make Laura a fulfilled person, lead this woman to a table and order lunch. If you're curious to see what I look like, you can check my agency's web page.

"Annie"

Within minutes of receiving her e-mail, Jack DePaul wrote back.

"Annie,

"Alright then, meet me Wednesday at Donna's at the Baltimore Museum of Art, 12:30. You'll know me in this way: I'm of average height, maybe on the short side. Short brown beard and hair shot through with white. People say I look like Steven Spielberg. I'll be wearing the newspaper editor's uniform: tie undone, sleeves rolled up, cheap sport coat slung over a shoulder. Friendly smile, wary eyes. I'll say: 'If you're not Annie Hollerman, this is very embarrassing.'

"I haven't visited your web page yet. I probably won't before we meet. Why have preconceptions? Though, truth is, I already have at least one: this will be fun.

"Jack"

Just as Jack hit the send key he heard a familiar voice.

"Hey, DePaul."

Jack, startled, looked up from his screen a little guiltily. Standing by his desk was the regal figure of Kathleen Faulkner. She was carrying a black briefcase in one hand and a gray jacket in the other.

"I'm heading out a little early today. Wondered if you had thought any more about that Washington lobbyist story."

He appraised her coolly. She looked down at him with brown eyes that hinted at absolutely nothing.

"I want it for next Sunday," said Jack. "But it's going to take some work. The concept of illuminating details hasn't made it to the D.C. bureau yet. And you know my feeling about illuminating details." He curbed his desire to glance ostentatiously at Kathleen's ring finger.

"That's what I've always liked about you, Jack—you know what you want." She said this with a slight smile. "I wish I could be so certain." She placed her coat across the briefcase and, as she moved past him toward the exit, touched him lightly on the shoulder with her free hand.

"I'll ship the story over tomorrow," she said. "By the way, Alex Beyard called. He's not going to this year's management conference. His paper's cutting back on trips, and everything else. He couldn't believe the *Star-News* was still sending us all. Anyway, have a good evening." Kathleen walked briskly away.

CHAPTER 5

Jack stared at Kathleen Faulkner's back as if trying to read hieroglyphics. What the hell was that all about? It had been six months of peaceful nothing. Now this sudden bit of ominous innocence.

Three days ago, she had offered him a piece from the Washington bureau. A day later she had e-mailed him: "Need to talk to you about the lobbyist story and other things." From anyone else, it would have been completely normal newsroom business. But this was how it always started and restarted with Kathleen, when she wanted to worm her way back into his life.

He watched her disappear around a corner. Why do I feel like I'm back in the soap opera from hell?

Jack turned to his computer, thankful for work to take his mind off Kathleen. He called up the master list of unedited stories. First up was something by feature writer J. R. Thelman slugged "Firehouse 773." He opened the file and began reading.

"It was a hot, dusty August day. The noon sun had burned away the shadows and when they came back eight hours later they brought no relief." Jack reread the sentences on his screen, made a whimpering noise, and slumped in his chair.

Arts editor, Mike Gray, looked up from the adjacent desk. "That doesn't sound good. What's up?"

"J. R. Thelman," Jack replied.

"Let me guess," said Gray. "His story starts: 'It was a dark and stormy night.' "

"Close. 'It was a hot, dusty August day.' "

"Why does J.R. begin every story with a weather report?"

"I don't know, but I can't take it any longer," Jack said. "I'm going to kill him."

"Good thinking, Jack," said Gray. "I can see those management training classes have really paid off."

Gray's phone rang and he turned away, leaving Jack to face the hot, dusty August day alone. He glanced at his watch (wasn't it time for a meeting?) then at his coffee cup (it was full), then checked his bladder (it was empty). He forced himself back to the screen. The problem, he knew, wasn't the lede of J.R.'s story. In fact, the second sentence wasn't half bad.

The problem was thirty years in the business, a twenty-year marriage he didn't mourn, and three years of promises from Kathleen Faulkner. Six months ago, she'd made her choice: she'd moved back in with her husband while she was still sleeping with Jack. Jack swore he was finished with her and her lies, as he'd sworn many times before. Now she was back.

Problems. His neck was getting wrinkles; hair was sprouting from his ears; his right shoulder ached; words wouldn't come, names were lost; rock and roll was dead. The problem was middle age.

The problem was Willoughby Treffle.

Jack remembered it more clearly than he remembered last week, though it had happened thirty years ago. It began when a rich dowager from Oakland, California, had bequeathed $100,000 to the city for public art. The municipal arts council spent $50,000 of the money on a commission for a statue to be placed in a prominent spot downtown. A local artist named Santino proposed a huge work—nearly twenty-five feet high—made from twisted steel girders. He called it *Civic Duty*.

It was a piece of modernistic claptrap; naturally, the arts council loved it. A year later, it was erected in an open square facing the courthouse. Howdy Doody, as it came to be called because the girders grinned like a big set of choppers, soon became the target of graffiti artists and snide newspaper columnists. It also became the soapbox for Willoughby Treffle, the city's favorite gadfly.

Every day, Willoughby stood on the base of Howdy Doody and harangued passersby. Willoughby was against everything from the city's housing policy (he had once been denied a housing voucher) to vegetarians (Willoughby liked steak). Aside from his oratory, Willoughby had other distinctions: he had a barfly's thick red mottled nose, he always wore a black business suit covered with campaign buttons, he sold miniature American flags (three for a dollar), and he was vertically challenged. Will Treffle was a dwarf.

In 1972, the city council voted to disassemble the statue. They claimed that if radical war protesters booby-trapped *Civic Duty* the resulting shrapnel could kill hundreds. The fact was, no radical had ever considered the statue a target. The fact was, all the judges at the courthouse hated the thing. However, the day workmen showed up with trucks and cranes, war protesters did, too. They knew a photo op when they saw one.

Enter Jack DePaul, eager young metro reporter for the *Oakland Tribune*, who knew a story when he saw one. The courthouse square that morning was a pandemonium of protesters, workmen, cops, news crews, and innocent citizens called for jury duty. In the midst of the confusion, a tie-dyed protester climbed the statue and began shouting something through a megaphone. Immediately the TV cameras turned. Not to be outdone by TV, Jack climbed up after him. But he didn't get far. About five feet up, Jack felt himself losing his grip. He reached out to grab on to the protester's foot, but the man kicked him away. Down Jack fell, right on top of the flags, buttons, and diminutive body of Willoughby Treffle.

"The Midget Mash," as it came to be called, was all over the TV news and for a few weeks afterward Jack was a minor celebrity in the Bay Area. His account of the statue protest led page one in the next day's *Tribune* (Will Treffle wasn't mentioned) and became his prize barroom tale for years (it once got him into the bed of a San Francisco anchorwoman). It was an exhilarating time to be a journalist: the world teeter-tottered every day between upheaval and possibility. The air seemed charged with extra oxygen. No one sneered in those days at a passion for truth or justice or peace, love, and understanding. In those days.

Jack scrolled down to the end of J.R.'s story and read the last paragraph. Then he checked the story's length. At least fifteen inches too long, no matter how well written. He returned to the lede again with a sigh. It had been a long time since he'd knocked over a dwarf. The problem, he knew, was Jack DePaul, not J. R. Thelman.

CHAPTER 6

Great, this Jack DePaul guy'll think he's having lunch with Rocky Raccoon." Annie examined the dark circles under her eyes as she looked in the bathroom mirror and cursed herself for staying up so late.

She'd read until 1:20 the night before because she'd stupidly promised three different authors she'd get back to them today. Rick Kantley wanted to know if he should agree to his editor's changes on his new military thriller. That would be affirmative. And if he were really lucky, the editor would rewrite the whole damn thing. Kantley made Tom Clancy read like Hemingway. But his books hit the best-seller list and he was a dream to deal with. The other two authors were first-timers with solid, salable proposals.

"Well," Annie muttered as she reached for the little blue tube of concealer, "that's why God put Estée Lauder on the earth."

Most days it took Annie twenty minutes from the time she rolled out of bed until she was out the door. This morning, Wednesday morning, Annie was still playing Barbie doll with herself forty-five minutes after she'd put on the concealer.

She stood backwards to her bedroom mirror, holding a small mirror before her eyes. She wanted to see if her butt looked big in a pair of charcoal linen pants. On her bed lay three other pairs of pants and two skirts, all of which had failed the butt test.

She knew she was being stupid. Just pick something, she told herself. You'll be sitting down; he won't even see your butt. Suppose he did, though? And suppose he was really as terrific as Laura had said and she showed up in something that announced, "I have saddlebags."

With her eyes still focused on the small mirror, Annie took two steps to see how the pants moved when she did. Okay, so she was being stupid, the truth was she was having fun. She'd never been on a blind date before, and now that she'd broken the journalist barrier, she was getting more excited about the notion.

"Looks like Richard Dreyfuss or Steven Spielberg," Laura had said. Well, that's promising, she thought, I've had a crush on Richard Dreyfuss since *The Goodbye Girl*. The playful tone of Jack DePaul's e-mails was promising, too. She liked that he wanted to be surprised when they met. "Why have preconceptions?" he'd written. It was a good beginning.

Then it struck her—this really was a beginning. Wednesday, May 29: the first day of the Dating Journalists Era, Part Deux. No one knew where it would lead. The lunch could be horrible— nowadays, Richard Dreyfuss looked like a paunchy sofa salesman (and there was that *People* magazine story about his rehab). It could be wonderful—she pictured Dreyfuss walking toward the *Close Encounters* spaceship. Either way, some kind of relationship was going to start today. And if it didn't, apparently there was a whole newsroom of men to think about.

She smoothed down the sides of her charcoal pants and brushed back her hair with her fingers. She thought about her relationships past. How less than a year after she left the *Commercial-Appeal* in disgrace, she'd met Thomas Harrington Boxer III, or "Trip" (for triple), eventually her husband, eventually her ex.

She'd felt like damaged goods, and Trip, six feet of steadiness and solidity, seemed like someone she could hang on to through every storm. Someone who would stay. Unlike her father, Milt Hollerman. Unlike Andrew Binder.

It took her years to realize Trip was never there to leave.

At first she thought he was the opposite of her father. She called it the Anti-Milt theory. Trip seemed to be everything her father wasn't—responsible, loving, caring, hearing. But it turned out that Trip out-Milted Milt, right down to hearing loss.

Whereas Milt Hollerman had lost his hearing ducking mortar shells in World War II, Trip's diminished auricularity resulted from too much skeet shooting and duck hunting as a boy. And what Annie had mistaken for steadiness turned out to be a deep coldness that made her father's inept attempts at affection seem inspired. Annie's mother called Trip "the Cardboard Box."

To add insult to injury, Trip was even cheaper than her father, though Milt had an excuse—he could never make a living. Trip, on the other hand, had been a highly paid lawyer before he retired at age forty-six to live off what he called his "welfare checks," the $400,000 he received annually from the family's pharmaceutical business.

Despite his wealth, he always frowned when Annie came back from Sutton Place Gourmet with a bag full of cardamom seeds to put in their morning coffee. "I admit it tastes better," Trip would say, "but at two dollars an ounce, I just don't think it's worth it. That's almost a hundred dollars a year if we use two seeds a day."

Their marriage got sick and died long before it arrived at the emergency room. On a mild fall Saturday morning when Annie picked up the phone to make a call and instead heard Trip arranging a tryst with their neighbor across the street, she realized she didn't care. She wasn't angry, sad, or even hurt. She felt nothing but the sudden urge to buy as many cardamom seeds as she could find.

When Trip went to meet his paramour, Annie went to Sutton Place Gourmet. With their Platinum Visa, she charged $347—the largest sale of cardamom seeds ever, the salesgirl told her. She drove back to their Bethesda home, packed three suitcases, and left one of the four large plastic bags from Sutton Place on their kitchen counter with the following note: "Trip, here's something to remember me by, Annie."

That'd been two years ago. She was pushing forty-five now, and her hormones were shouting "Last chance" so loud, all her body wanted to do was procreate. But other than the energy analyst, there hadn't been anyone around to make Mother Nature think she was trying. And Mother Nature wanted her to try again. Maybe this Jack DePaul would be the answer. Or maybe he'd be an arrogant jerk or maybe he'd be boyishly charming or . . .

The possibilities were limitless.

CHAPTER 7

At 12:15 that Wednesday afternoon, Jack DePaul parked his maroon Pathfinder in the empty parking lot of the Baltimore Museum of Art. Inside, there was no one by the entrance to Donna's with fiery hair, just a guy wearing a blue-and-white seersucker and a bad combover.

The last time Jack had been on a blind date was in high school. Thirty-five years later and he was still feeling nervous and goofy. He took a deep breath and told himself to relax. To kill time he went to the museum store. He circumnavigated the handcrafted earrings and painted silk scarves and found himself by the art books.

Thinking about hair, Jack picked up a twenty-pound coffee-table book called *The Pre-Raphaelites* and began thumbing through. Dante Rossetti's women were there, in abundance. Elizabeth Siddal, Fanny Cornforth, Jane Morris, Alexa Wilding—all those models (and wives and lovers) Rossetti had turned into pouty icons of pseudo-medievalism. One hundred and fifty years later they were still sexy, with their fog-fed complexions and their great waterfalls of hair cascading down in colors of copper, wheat, and polished heartwood. Rossetti and his earnest band of young Victorian rebels had gotten it just right—the sleepy, sensuous look of passion about to be uncaged.

Jack looked at Lizzie Siddal as Dante's Beatrice. Her ecstasy did not appear religious. Wavy locks of sunset hair spilled down her shoulders like lava. If this Hollerman woman looks anything like Elizabeth Siddal, Jack thought, I'll give Laura my next three paychecks. Hell, make it the next ten paychecks.

He checked his watch: 12:20. He was starting to turn back to the Pre-Raphaelites when something caught his eye. By the front of the store, looking at the racks of arty postcards, stood a woman with her back to him. She wore a black linen jacket and loose charcoal pants. A green suede bag was slung over her shoulder. Flowing down to the middle of her back were curls the color of chestnut, if the chestnut was lit by a summer sun at, say, 7:30 in the evening.

She pulled a card from one of the racks. Just as it began to seep into Jack's brain that she might be Annie, she walked off in the direction of Donna's. Jack rushed to the card racks and peeked around the corner. The woman was leaning on the hostess stand. Jack still couldn't see her face. She was turned toward the restaurant and the sculpture garden beyond the tables.

He stepped back into the store, out of sight, and looked into a small mirror with a wildly colored Haitian frame. He never thought it would happen to him, all that white hair. But then again, he never thought any of it would happen to him. That his marriage would shatter and fall. That the image of a long white shirt on a tall brunette would keep fluttering through his imagination like a nightmare bird. That he would live half a century and come up dry, the years behind looking more and more passionless in the rearview mirror. Nothing to paint a picture about.

With a shake of his head, Jack banished the memories. He slung his jacket over his shoulder, rolled up his sleeves a couple of turns, and loosened his tie. He thought of the once-and-future Lizzie Siddal. The wave of self-pity ebbed away; in its place, he was surprised to discover, came a fluttery feeling in his chest. He briefly flashed to junior high and Carol Davidson's gap-toothed smile. To hell with age, he said to himself. Then he walked toward the woman who, from the back, looked as if she'd just stepped out of a Rossetti painting.

"If you're not Annie Hollerman, this will be very embarrassing," said Jack.

The woman turned. She wasn't Pre-Raphaelite. She didn't have the bee-stung lips, the dreamy British curves. This woman had bones. Good, strong bones from the old country. Her cheeks slanted slightly up and out; there was peasant stock in her, and exotic fragments of the far steppes. The wild red hair framed the lightest of olive complexions. Pre-Raphaelite by way of Minsk.

"So. You must be Mr. Dreyfuss," said Annie. "Are there storm clouds over Lisbon?"

Jack grinned. "Not anymore."

CHAPTER 8

By the time the coffee came, Jack had scored at least 100 points. He'd lost one when he was abrupt with the host, who didn't have the outside patio table he'd reserved, and another when he dropped some *farfalloni con fungi* on his tie. Actually, the fungi bumble was funny. And Annie would've been the last person to fault someone for messiness. Besides, he'd spilled it because of her. Call it 100–1.

Laura deserved some points, too. She'd been right about the funny, smart, and brash part. But she forgot to mention how Jack DePaul's bottom teeth were in a cute jumble with the middle one tucked slightly behind.

When Laura had told Annie she thought Jack was around fifty, that had sounded old. She'd never dated anyone out of his forties before, and she'd worried that Jack DePaul would look like someone's grandfather.

Jack DePaul looked like no one's grandfather. Yes, his hair was gray and he had well-worn eyes, but he also carried himself with a tight, coiled energy. And even though he wore baggy pleated pants, she could see the outlines of what she knew must be a great rear, just as Laura had said.

As the waiter poured their coffee, the words "What you need,

Annie Hollerman, is a man with a good ass" rang through her
mind.

"Something funny?" Jack said.

Annie hesitated, then she pictured Trip's scrunched face and
heard his familiar critical words: "You're just like a ten-year-old,
always blurting out whatever's on your mind."

So she said, "Yes."

"Okay," Jack said, "I give, what's so funny?"

Annie remembered how Trip carefully measured every syllable
he spoke. Then she gave Jack a sweet smile and said, "Laura's first
words to me about you were, 'What you need, Annie Hollerman,
is a man with a good ass.'"

That's when Jack had fumbled the *farfalloni con fungi*.

CHAPTER 9

By the time the coffee came, Annie had put up so many points that the scoreboard was broken. It wasn't just the cool hair or the way her slim body skimmed against her loose clothes that attracted Jack. Annie turned out to be as smart and bold as Laura had told him.

Lunch had been easy and fun from the start. Jack felt as if they'd jumped onto an inner tube and were shooting merrily down a snowy slope together.

Just after being seated, Jack opened the menu, peered at Annie over the top of it, and said, "So, who's Annie Hollerman, and why does Laura Goodbread think she's so great?"

Annie didn't miss a beat. Without even looking up from the menu she replied, "Because Laura refuses to pee outdoors and won't take her daughter camping. So I do it for her."

"I bet there's more to it than that," he pressed her. "Laura told me *Publishers Weekly* thinks you're a big deal. And you *are* Eda Royal's agent."

Annie made a little shrug.

"So it's true," Jack said. "If it weren't for you, *Confessions of a She-Devil* wouldn't have been on the *Times* best-seller list for eight zillion weeks."

"Only four zillion."

"I see. So your agency specializes in hacks?" said Jack, insulting her before they'd even had a chance to order.

Annie straightened up in her chair; her mouth began to form a little O of surprise before she realized Jack was smiling. He could see her relax.

"You could say so," she said, glancing back down at the lunch entrees on the menu. "I've signed three of your friends from the *Star-News*."

Now it was Jack's turn. Oh.

"And by the way, Mr. DePaul, tell me again: Who's your agent? And which house is it that publishes your books?"

"Ouch!" said Jack, pulling an imaginary arrow from his chest. "Okay, Annie, I guess the gloves are off."

Chapter 10

Two strangers meet over lunch. Nothing revolutionary about that. It's as common as a traffic jam. In this case, the strangers were a man and a woman. They were single; they were searching; they were wary, but wanting; they had opened the windows, if not the doors, to themselves; they had grave doubts about romance, but believed in it anyway.

What Jack and Annie brought with them to lunch was not uncommon: broken marriages, haunting mistakes, roads not taken. But they also brought assuredness. When you're twenty-five you know what you want; when you're forty-five you know what you need.

When Jack and Annie met, the possibilities flickered and flared, as hard to follow, at first, as fireflies. But these two strangers had come with a cautious hope. It was just possible they might catch lightning in a jar.

The first course of lunch—nervous badinage—was quickly consumed and Jack and Annie moved on to more substantial fare.

Annie went first, giving Jack the résumé version of her life, carefully editing out her years at the *Charlotte Commercial-Appeal*: graduated from the University of Colorado ("I majored mostly in hiking"); worked in a bookstore; met Thomas Harrington Boxer III, aka "Trip" ("My mother still curses the day she fixed us up");

moved to Washington; met Trip's friend, power agent Greg Leeland; became Leeland's assistant; married Trip ("I was forty-five minutes late to my own wedding—that should have told me *something*"); started the Hollerman Literary Agency; bought a big house in Bethesda; divorced Trip; lost the big house in Bethesda; moved to Dupont Circle.

"There you have it," Annie said. "Annie Hollerman as sound bite."

"What happened between those sentences?" said Jack.

Soon she was telling him about growing up in New Jersey, her summer weeks in Atlantic City, her father leaving when she was ten. "That made me the only kid with a single mom, the only kid with a mom who worked," Annie said. "This is going to sound stupid, but for years the thing I wanted most were waxed floors."

Jack looked puzzled. "Waxed floors?"

"If I'd had waxed floors that'd meant my mother was like all the mothers on the TV commercials, the ones that stayed home and waxed their floors."

She smiled. "Now you know what's between the sentences—a yearning for floor wax."

Then it was Jack's turn. He marched Annie through his newspaper career: *Oakland Tribune, Rochester Democrat, San Diego Tribune, Baltimore Star-News*. He talked about his son, Matthew; bragged, in fact. Of his marriage he said, "After twenty years it was like we didn't know each other. Nothing dramatic. We just bored each other." But even as he said it, he knew it sounded lame and incomplete. All he said of life after divorce was this: "I've had one relationship. It was pyrotechnic—and disastrous. I should have had the good sense to stay away from her."

Eventually he brought out the well-polished tale of Willoughby Treffle. He finished off his story with a sigh. "Now I'm just a guy in the comma factory," he said.

"You're not getting off that easily," said Annie. She knew he was being modest. He was features editor at one of the country's top papers. Plus Laura had said he'd actually improved her stories.

That, from any reporter, is a mouthful; that, from Laura, was a whole Thanksgiving dinner.

"I told you my stuff between the sentences, now it's your turn. For example, why Pablo Neruda?"

For the first time since they sat down, Jack didn't have a snappy comeback. "What do you mean, Pablo Neruda?"

"Why'd you go halfway around the world to see where he lived?"

"How'd you know?"

"Laura said you were a Neruda nut. She told me you'd won an award for a story about him."

Jack gave her a sheepish look. "It's true. A girlfriend gave me a book of his poetry in college. It was the first time anybody ever gave me poetry. I loved him right off. He has a great appetite for life, a great passion for everything—from women to the windows in his house. I'd have given anything to have met him. Second best was seeing where he lived."

He looked down at his plate. "I still have it. That book. I took it with me on the Chile trip."

Poetry. That was 60 points right there for Jack. Another 30 came when the waiter passed by with the pepper mill. "Pepper?" he'd asked, and started grinding after Jack said yes. He was about to stop when Jack looked up at him with the smallest pleading in his eyes and said, "I like a lot of pepper." That's when Annie saw it, in the most trivial of moments, the flash of a hurt so deep it made her wonder what could have happened to him and why it looked so familiar.

The salads and pastas came and went. The dialogue moved rhythmically; long thoughtful answers followed short peppery quips. Their list of mutualities surprised and delighted them: the secret joy of dissing Raymond Carver, the shame of homelessness, the brilliance of Gabriel Márquez, the brilliance of Lyle Lovett, the brilliance of fresh basil, Peer Gynt's onion soliloquy, the deliciousness of Shakespearean insults—"Hang ye, gorbellied knaves!"—and the most memorable line in *Goodbye Columbus*, which startled them both as they said in unison, "His hair stopped smelling like raisins."

Somewhere in the second hour, they reached the topic of religion. Annie said she discovered hers at Camp Reeta, where on Friday night she'd dress in white shorts and a white T-shirt and sing the prayers of her Jewish ancestors alongside the boys from Camp Arthur. "They were the happiest days of my childhood. The only time I ever felt like I belonged to something."

Those two unguarded sentences disconcerted Jack as if he'd been given a surprise Christmas gift and had nothing in return. He switched the subject—but not too far to be obvious—and asked if she'd ever been to Israel.

She shook her head.

"Hell, Annie, I'm a better Jew than you are and I'm not even Jewish. I lived on a kibbutz for six months."

"When?"

"Twenty-five years ago. I mostly picked grapefruit. I'm proud to say that Tony Prickett and I were personally responsible for picking one-tenth of one percent of the entire export crop to Europe that year. Oh, and also I sexed chickens."

"What?"

"Finally, something Laura didn't tell you. At one time I was a serial chicken sexer." Jack explained that chicken sexers determined the sex of newly hatched chicks. He also explained that the two things he loved most in the world—his true religion if he were to confess it to her—were playing basketball with Matthew and traveling. Along with his Israel and Chile stories, he told her of a summer bumming around Europe and a trek in Nepal.

"I wish my passport had as many stamps," said Annie. "We—I've been to France and Spain. And a lot of ski places in the U.S. Trip—that's the ex—wasn't much of an adventurer."

"Funny name for a guy who doesn't like to travel," Jack said.

"You're not the first to say that," Annie replied. "Trip had to control every situation—including me, his most difficult situation. He couldn't stand not knowing the language, so that's why we didn't go abroad much."

"That's too bad. Not knowing is half the fun."

Annie slapped the table like a lawyer in summation. "That's right. I loved trying to bargain. I loved trying to talk to little old Spanish men in cafés. It's amazing what you can do with a phrase book and a smile."

"At least you got to Spain. Trip couldn't have been that bad, could he?"

"Well, you be the judge," Annie said. "Our first trip outside the U.S. was Spain. Trip spent most of the time looking at phrase books and maps. When we got to Jerez, the man at our hotel couldn't stop talking about how lucky we were to be there because Renatta Vega-Marone was going to be in town that night. Turns out she's one of the most famous flamenco dancers in the world and was going to perform at a music festival in the central square.

"The hotel man kept telling us not to miss it, that we were truly blessed to have arrived then because it would be her only performance there for years. But she wasn't due on stage until about midnight, and Trip wanted to be in bed early. He'd planned a long drive the next day and said he wanted to be 'fresh' to navigate the roads. I could have gone on my own, but what's the fun if you don't have someone to share it with?"

Annie made a small, rueful smile. The same kind of smile, though Jack didn't know it, that he'd given the pepper mill waiter.

"Oh well," she said. "You can't rewrite your past, can you?"

Somehow they'd found time in their long conversation to order dessert: one sunken chocolate mousse cake and two forks. When it arrived, Jack said, "You know something, Annie, this may be my first blind-date lunch. How am I doing? What do you think?"

For a second Annie was confused. Blind date? Blind date! My God, I'd forgotten, just ninety minutes ago this man was a complete stranger. And now he's Jack. What do I think? Well, I talked nonstop for an hour and half to a journalist and I'm not dead. In fact, I even had fun. I talked about what I love and what I hate and about New Jersey. I talked about waxed floors and I talked about my missed night in Jerez.

What do I think? I think it was a mistake to fight Laura so hard in the past. This blind-date stuff isn't so bad. I think I wonder what that other *Star-News* guy was like; maybe I should've gone out with him, too. I think I'm tired of sitting alone reading books. I think a million things and about 979,000 of them are how Jack must look without those dumb pleated pants and smoky-gray shirt.

"Oh hell, Annie, that was a stupid question. You don't have to answer," he said, the fingers of his left hand dancing along the ghost keys of the invisible piano he'd played throughout their lunch.

"I don't mind," said Annie. She caught two of those fingers in hers. "For a beginner, you're doing very well."

CHAPTER 11

A long day at work followed Jack's long lunch. Afterward, the music critic had dragged him to Meyerhof Hall, where the symphony was performing Mahler's Second under the baton of the new conductor. Dinner had been coffee and carrot cake in the symphony hall foyer. He hadn't gotten home until close to midnight.

But when the lights were finally off and before the tide of fatigue pulled him under, Jack replayed the moment, feeling again the cool, dry fingers, the gentle pressure. Annie's fingers on his. They had held him for several heartbeats.

He decided he should have looked deep into her eyes, holding her with his piercing gaze, while projecting a soulful world-weariness, and replied, "I guess it's just beginner's luck." Or "What do I have to do to become an intermediate?"

But of course he hadn't done anything like that. Instead he had looked down in embarrassment, his two fingers, freed from Annie's grasp, still pointing toward the invisible piano. Who knows how long they would have stayed that way if the waiter hadn't stopped by?

"Anything else, sir?"

Jack looked at his hand hanging in midair, then up at the

waiter. For a second he couldn't find the words in his brain—or his brain.

Annie stepped in. "I think we're fine," she said. "Just the check, please."

Jack was certain he'd made a fool of himself. But then she smiled at him, and he knew it wasn't the smile of a reduced evaluation.

"So," she said, "what's on your agenda this afternoon?"

And for the first time since they'd met, Jack looked at his watch.

"Oh my God," Jack said. "It's two forty-five! I have a meeting with the restaurant critic in ten minutes. If I'm late and he's missed his meds he'll probably hold my assistant hostage with a knife at her throat. And I'm not kidding."

That made Annie's smile even broader.

"If you hear sirens going toward Calvert Street," he said, "you'll know I've gotten there too late. I'm sorry I have to rush." He pulled some bills from his wallet and tossed them on the table.

He started to rise, but Annie motioned him to sit. She raised her glass to him and said, "Here's to Willoughby Treffle." Jack raised his glass to her and said, "Here's to floor wax."

He wanted to say more, say something about how easy Annie was to talk to, how he wished the afternoon could stretch into evening, but an image of the throbbing veins in the restaurant critic's neck stopped him. "Oh man," he said, "I'd love to stay, but . . ."

Again she did it. She touched him. She reached her hand to his right shoulder and gave it a light squeeze.

"Me too," she said. "But I've got my own psychopaths to deal with."

As they rushed out, Jack tried to think of a clever way to say good-bye. But when they got to Annie's old red Mustang convertible, the only words Jack could find were these: "Lizzie Siddal's got nothing on you."

"Lizzie Siddal?" Annie said, the left side of her face crunching up in question. "Who's that?"

Jack turned and started to run to his car. "Look her up."

At the time it seemed like a clever thing to say. But replaying that conversation hours later, he knew how stupid it must've sounded. Lizzie Siddal. Lizzie Siddal? What was I thinking? She probably thinks I'm a jerk for bringing up another woman. Why couldn't I just have kept things simple? Simple and to the point, like, "Would you like to go out again?"

Or . . .

Jack fell asleep practicing all the lines he should have said.

Chapter 12

Forty-seven miles away Annie Hollerman was also musing, but not about Jack DePaul.

Not at this particular moment. She'd already worked and re-worked the lunch enough to rewrite it the way it should have been—if she wasn't such a blabbermouth. Someday she'd learn the art of mystery. Someday she wouldn't tell a man twenty minutes into meeting him every last detail about her father. Maybe Trip was right, maybe she was a "pathological revealer."

But then again, maybe he was wrong. She hadn't revealed anything about her years at the *Charlotte Commercial-Appeal*. She'd actually held something back. She almost felt like calling Trip to tell him. But that would involve caring about what Trip thought, and it had been a very, very long time since she'd felt that way.

It had also been a long time since she'd cared about what a man thought of her. Sure, she'd wondered if Martin the energy analyst thought her thighs were fat when things got steamy between them nine months ago. But that's pretty much as far as her musings went. Their affair wasn't much more than a biological release for her. After three weeks, she'd told him it was over.

After just one lunch with Jack, Annie found herself caring about whether she'd said too much or worn the wrong thing or . . . just caring.

But now, as much as she would have preferred thinking about Jack, all she could think about was her mother and the inquisition. She'd just called. Not that an evening call from Joan Hollerman Silver was unusual. Or an afternoon call. Or a morning call.

She called all the time. "Just checking in." "So what's new?" "Had your Pap test this year?" "How's the weightlifting coming?" Anything. She was like June Cleaver on steroids. Now. Now that Annie was an adult. But when Annie had been the Beav's age, the only June Cleaver was on television, making birthday cakes for Wally or Ward or the Beav. Annie's mother had never baked a cake in her life, nor much cottoned to the concept of mothering little kids. Annie always felt like she had to go way beyond the normal kid stuff to get her mother's attention. No Annie-original drawings were ever taped to the refrigerator in the Hollerman house. It wasn't until Annie won the sixth-grade poster contest that Annie's mother even noticed her daughter could draw.

But now. Now. NOW. Annie had become her mother's project. Her last project, after she'd moved from Hackensack, New Jersey, to Greensboro, North Carolina, had been law school. Never mind that she didn't have a college degree. So at age forty-six, Annie's mother became a coed. She'd even convinced the dean to give her college credits for the years she worked as a bookkeeper when Annie was a little girl. And at age fifty-three, Joan Hollerman Silver became the oldest graduate of Wake Forest University Law School.

Their conversation, just minutes before, went like this:

"So, how was the date?"

"Oh hi, Mom, and how are you?"

"The date? So, it was fun?"

"What date?"

"Oh, Annie, stop it. I know. Laura called me."

Annie groaned into the phone. "Is there anyone who doesn't know?"

"Hmmm, let me think. Judge Foster. I didn't get a chance to tell him—yet. Maybe tomorrow. Give me all the details."

Annie's mother then shouted, "Geri, pick up. Annie's going to tell us about the date."

Geri was Joan Hollerman Silver's paralegal and best friend. They dressed alike, looked alike, and, thanks to six packs of Virginia Slims a day between the both of them, talked alike. In the same raspy, nicotine-coated voice of Annie's mother, Geri said, "So how was the date? Laura says he's got a cute butt. Darn, I wish I were your age."

"God, you two, stop it," Annie said. "It was just a lunch. It wasn't a date. A date is dinner, a movie, some kind of good-night where you're worried about whether you should kiss or not. This was just pasta and coffee."

Geri laughed and broke into a cough. Annie was just about to say good-bye when Geri stopped coughing and said, "I hear it in her voice, Joan. She likes hirn. We're looking at a second date here. At least."

"Geri, stop it," Annie said. "You're worse than she is. Does the whole building know?"

Annie's mother answered this time. "You could say that. Betty's got a little pool going, she thinks this one might be a keeper."

"Betty? Betty Blackthorn, the process server? You told her? God, Mom. It was just lunch. Besides, what do you mean she thinks this one might be a keeper? How would she know? Wait, don't tell me. I remember now. She's that nutty woman who uses a Ouija board and spirit guides to find the people she's serving, right? You told *her*? She's probably going to post it on the psychic hotline. Mom, I can't believe you told her."

"Annie, everyone cares about you here, you know that," her mother said. "They all want to see you happy, as in happy with a good man who appreciates you. Not like the Cardboard Box you were married to. I always get asked, 'What's new with that beautiful daughter of yours?' I had to tell them about your date. So tell me, is Betty right? Is he a keeper?"

Annie rolled her eyes, shook her head, and took a deep breath—all the things she'd been doing since her mother went into Mother Turbo-Drive. Some days, days like this, Annie wished for the old Joan Hollerman Silver, the one who was either too busy talking on the phone with her girlfriends or too tired from work to notice the little redheaded girl wanting to play Scrabble or Barbie or anything with her mother.

"Okay, Mom, Geri, you win. I give up. Christ, you two are worse than Laura. I'll tell you. Not that there's anything to tell. He's very nice."

"Nice?" It was Geri. "Nice? Like he takes his mother to church on Sunday nice? Or nice like you couldn't take your eyes off him nice?"

"I don't know," Annie said. "He was nice. N-I-C-E. Nice. We talked. We laughed. Actually, we laughed a lot."

"He made you laugh?" Annie's mother said. "I haven't seen you laugh around a man since you-know-who. That gonef. He should never laugh again for what he did to you."

Oh God, here we go again, Annie thought. "Mom, that was a million years ago. We were both young and stupid. I probably would have done the same thing if the situations had been reversed."

Annie said those words every time her mother brought up Andrew Binder. She said them not only to make her mother stop talking about him, but also hoping one day she'd believe them.

"There you go again making excuses for him. Ach, enough about him. So this one's name is Jack. I don't suppose he's Jewish."

"Not exactly," Annie said.

"Could you please explain to me what 'not exactly' means? As far I've ever understood it, you either are or aren't."

"Well," Annie said, "he lived in Israel for six months."

"So he's a goy. Okay. Okay. I gave up on having full Jewish grandchildren a long time ago. Is he smart at least? I want smart grandchildren."

"Mom, I'm ending this conversation now. Asking me about the date is one thing, asking me about breeding is something else."

"She likes him, Joan, I can tell," Geri said. "When do we get to meet him?"

"Geri," Annie said, "I'm hanging up now. I have a stack of manuscripts taller than I am. Oh, wait. Before I go, I do have one small question to ask you two—about the Date, not that it was one, exactly. It was just lunch. I don't know if I should e-mail him something, you know, something like 'Thanks.' He did pay for it, so I probably should. I don't know. What do you guys think?"

"Of course you should thank him," Annie's mother said. "Didn't I raise you better than that?"

"Raise me?"

Annie laughed. Geri laughed. And so did Annie's mother. Long ago, they'd come to terms with the missing mother years of Joan Hollerman Silver. It had taken a soul-rattling disaster to make it happen. But it had. When Annie's life fell apart, it was her mother who stepped in, gathered the broken pieces, and forced Annie to put herself together again.

"And here's what I think, if anyone's asking," Geri said. "Send him an e-mail while your mother and I go to Dillard's."

"Dillard's?" Annie said. "What does Dillard's have to do with anything, Geri?"

"Dillard's has the best dresses in Greensboro. I'm not showing up at your wedding in anything in my closet. And neither is your mother."

"Okay, ladies, it's time for me to say good-bye. Good-bye."

Annie's mother wedged one last thing into the conversation.

"E-mail him, Annie. It's only common courtesy. If I *had* raised you right, that's what you would do. Geri and I are going to the video store to rent a movie, talk to you tomorrow . . ."

Annie hung up the phone, walked to the computer, and typed out a short message. Before she had a chance to second-guess herself, she hit the send button to jdepaul@aol.com.

That's when the phone rang.

"I'm calling from the car. Did you send it?"

Annie smiled. "Yes, Mom, I did. You must've done something right with me. Now good-bye. Go to the video store. What're you going to rent, anyway?"

"*Mother of the Bride.*"

"Funny, Ma, but get it right. It's *Father of the Bride.*"

CHAPTER 13

Annie turned off the phone, to keep her mother at bay, and climbed into bed. Automatically she reached for a book from one of the stacks on the nightstand. One down, 4,998 to go. So many books. It made Annie think of Nandini Skyler, the literal-minded psychic.

For her last birthday, Laura had taken her to see Skyler, who, according to the neat hand-inked sign on the door of her Takoma Park apartment, specialized in readings and "lifescapes." It was the wackiest present Laura could think of, and Laura told Annie she needed wackiness "like orchids need rain."

"Work on your metaphors," is what Annie had told Laura as she hugged her and thanked her for the present.

They'd laughed, but Laura regarded her gift as more rescue mission than birthday present. The fearless, wow-great-hair girl she'd first met twenty years ago in Charlotte was making fewer and fewer appearances, like an aging diva on her farewell tour. In place of the original Annie—the one she used to call "the rainbow coalition" for her colorful clothes; the one who'd ridden a circus elephant down the busiest highway in Charlotte; the one who'd gone on drug buys with gang kids for the prize-winning series "Charlotte's Lost Generation"—was a guarded woman of careful tastes.

Annie seemed to be crushed down by her past. And her marriage. Trip was worth four or five tons at least. Laura told Annie she was compacting under the weight, that she had "osteoporosis of the soul."

"Better metaphor," Annie had said.

When Annie mentioned she'd bought a pair of Mephistos at the Comfort Shoe Store, Laura knew desperate measures were called for.

"You need to get some life back in your life," she said, handing Annie Nandini's calligraphed gift certificate. "You need a reason to reach back into your closet and pull out your Joan Crawford fuck-me pumps. Maybe Nandini can tell you where to look."

Laura then assumed her don't-cross-me stance, expecting Annie to say, "Forget it, I'm not going to any psychic." But to Laura's—and Annie's—surprise, she hugged her again and said, "How soon can we go?"

Nandini turned out to be a pretty, coffee-colored woman of some island ethnicity who called herself an "intuitive." She laid out tarot-like cards atop a faux Louis XIV desk with precise and graceful hand movements. She asked Annie general questions about what she liked—Laura, kibbitzing off to the side, answered half of them—then she made three pronouncements: "I see you surrounded by books, I see your life entwined with politics, and I see you making long journeys without leaving home."

Afterward, over dinner, Annie and Laura dissected their psychic adventure. They agreed that the first prediction was uncanny; that the second was uncannily ridiculous ("Yeah," said Annie, "every time the president leaves the White House, I get 'entwined' in all his traffic"); and that the third was baffling.

"Long journeys without leaving home," said Annie, mimicking Nandini's movements with her wineglass. "Hand me the remote, Laura, it must be time for the Travel Channel."

Every so often, like tonight, when Annie looked at the piles of books flanking her bed, she thought of Nandini.

"Surrounded by books." Such a literal-minded intuitive. It reminded Annie of that time another life ago when she'd done a story for the *Charlotte Commercial-Appeal* about autistic kids. A boy was pouring a glass of orange juice from a cardboard container and the teacher told him to "step on it" so they could make the bus. Next thing the teacher knew, the boy had his foot on the juice box.

"Surrounded by books," that was for sure. Piles at work and piles by her bedside. Any more and she'd be buried alive by them. Score one for Nandini. But only one. "A life entwined with politics"? Not this life. The only reason she went anywhere near the Capitol was to shop the Southern Market for the freshest sea bass in town. As for stationary journeys, she'd made a number of trips, but all of them involved airports and cars and places far from her home.

Annie opened the top book from the bedside pile. It was the latest Richie Philman tearjerker. She'd heard that Philman was thinking about switching agents and was considering Annie. If Annie had any hope of landing her—and her best-selling books—she'd need to know Philman's work.

To her surprise, Philman wasn't the hack she'd expected. This woman could plot. But Annie couldn't keep her mind on track. She tried to force herself not to think about the man in Baltimore. Ha. The more she didn't think about Jack, the more she thought about him. It was like going into the Firehook and not ordering a sticky bun. And when was the last time that happened?

So much for Philman's book. Her mind veered back to Baltimore. And to their lunch. And to her e-mail. She hadn't written him much; just a quick thank-you. Annie wondered if he'd read it yet. Then she rolled her eyes because she knew exactly where her mind would take her next: Wonder if he's written back yet?

"God, are you ever going to get on speaking terms with patience?" Annie grumbled as she walked over to her computer and hit the AOL icon.

When she'd sent Jack the message two hours ago, she'd promised herself she wouldn't check her mail until the next morning.

Ha again.

There were four new messages. None from Jack DePaul. Annie hadn't believed for a minute that she'd live up to her pact, but she didn't expect to feel this disappointed.

She signed off and returned to the leaning tower of books, thinking of John Brady, her tenth-grade heartthrob, and the sky blue Princess phone in her room that had never rung, even after she'd passed him a note in French class, even after she had sat by the phone for hours humming, "Let it please be him." Thirty years later, Annie thought, I'm still singing the same stupid song.

Annie reached for the She-Devil's new manuscript, *She-Power*. Some words of she-powerment might be helpful about now. Plus, she'd promised to read it by next week's signing of *Confessions of a She-Devil* so she could give Eda Royal, the She-Devil, her comments.

The first line of the introduction was, "Make a person-to-person phone call to the She-Devil inside you." Annie searched the ceiling for strength from a higher power, then she started thumbing through the pages, registering phrases here and there: "The She-Devil lives in every woman." "We have evolved far past the other sex." "Men—the storm troopers of history." "Be your own woman, and your own man." "Never depend on a man to pay your bills." "Never wait around for him to call."

The last sentence wasn't actually in the book; it was drifting through Annie's subconscious as she lay dozing, *She-Power* lying against her chest.

That night Annie slept fitfully, with dreams of single-breasted Amazons galloping through Rock Creek Park. She woke with the She-Devil's book on her bed and Jack DePaul on her mind.

CHAPTER 14

That morning, Annie made another deal with herself: brush your teeth, then check your e-mail. She slipped out of bed and into the bathroom and scrubbed until her gums tingled. She even flossed, thinking virtue might be rewarded.

But her mailbox had just one visitor, Briquianna, the wettest woman in the galaxy. So much for virtue.

Whether it was her fractured sleep or empty e-mail box, Annie headed to the office in a foul mood. Just to spite her, the sun beamed down brightly and the Starbucks guy gave her a vente latte when she'd only ordered a tall. By the time she dumped a satchelful of books on her desk she'd crossed-examined herself ruthlessly: What did you expect?/Why did you let yourself be vulnerable?/Why did you let him make you vulnerable?/Why are you such an idiot?/Why are you such an idiot?/Why are you such an idiot?/and WHEN ARE YOU GOING TO STRANGLE LAURA?

"Hey, Punkin." Annie's assistant, Fred Rassmussen, stuck his head in her office. "Don't forget to call the Ghoul today, he's already called twice."

As always, Fred radiated cheerfulness. It was his only mood, kind of like a car stuck in drive. Even before the first cup of coffee or after the fourth, even while opening the office in the morning or after a late-night dinner with an ungrateful writer.

Annie tried to scowl at the friendly face in her doorway, but it was like trying to be an iceberg in Honduras.

Fred was a former Lit professor from American University who had agreed to help out Annie temporarily when she first opened an office in D.C. That was twelve years ago. Since then, he had become her bulwark and, though he'd deny it, her surrogate father.

He was a big, round-faced man who wore a little square mustache and bow ties. He loved three things most in life: Shakespeare; his wife, Lillian; and Annie. Two of them were dead. He was seventy-four now but his enthusiasm for things was undimmed; he wrapped his arms around every day as if it were a grandchild.

"Well, Ghoul-boy is just going to have to wait," said Annie. "I have other things to do."

Fred didn't respond, but didn't move either. "I bet he's an asshole," said Annie, placing a stack of books on the left side of her desk, then picking them up and putting them on the right. "And he's practically illiterate. I don't know why anybody reads his stuff—rats chewing through people's faces . . ."

Fred remained in the half-open doorway, regarding Annie with mild benevolence, like a shepherd tending to his flock.

"The next time I suggest we even think about representing a thriller writer, just shoot me," said Annie, putting the stack of books back on her left.

Fred, still silent, folded his arms and settled comfortably against the doorjamb.

"Okay, okay, okay," said Annie as if she were finally confessing under torture. "I e-mailed that DePaul guy a thank-you after our date and he never wrote back, he never called."

"You told me it wasn't a date," said Fred. "It was only a lunch."

"Date, lunch, whatever. He didn't write."

"Let me just make certain I've got it right. You went out to lunch with him yesterday, wrote to him last night, then he failed to write back, despite the fact that you waited by your computer all evening and fell asleep slumped across the keyboard?"

"I wasn't slumped across the keyboard."

"Well, don't take it personally."

"Fred, everything is personal. You lived with Lillian for twenty-four years and you still don't get that? Everything with women is personal."

"I'm sure he had a good time, Annie. I'm sure he thinks you're wonderful. How could he not? I bet he got busy at work and then got home late. He'll write. Just give him time. 'How poor are they that have not patience.'"

"I guess that makes me destitute, then," Annie said. "Besides, give me a break: 'Busy'? 'Late'? 'Time'? Aren't those code words for 'inconsiderate swine'?"

"Annie, have you been reading the She-Devil again? You say nay to thriller writers, but I say nay-no-nyet-nein-never to anyone who calls herself a w-o-m-B-Y-N. As for men—that's M-E-N—let's just say we're more methodical than women would like. We tend to finish our work—clear the decks—and then move on to matters of the heart. And Annie, don't check your e-mail every fifteen minutes today. If he's any kind of a mensch, he won't just dash off something at work. He'll craft an elegant response tonight."

"Elegant response," Annie harrumphed. "You wouldn't have waited, would you, Fred?"

"No. But I'm old-fashioned. I don't like e-mail. I would have called."

Fred gave her a little salute and left. Before his cheerfulness even had time to dissipate, Annie was checking her e-mail. There was nothing but business messages and low airfare deals.

Annie had two choices. She could obsess or she could work.

"Men," she muttered. "'Clear the decks'? You're not the only ones who can clear the decks. I've got plenty of decks to clear."

She jutted out her chin and turned her attention to her desk. There was the stack of books she'd been arranging and rearranging just minutes before. And the stack of phone messages. And the stack of queries. And the stack of proposals. And the stack of mail. Stacks and stacks of stuff to be cleared.

Clear decks, that's what Annie was going for. Of the desk and of the mind.

She could have told Fred to handle the phones, but she knew who the first caller would be: Laura. And that was some deck-clearing she was looking forward to, reading Laura the I'm-fine-the-way-I-am-my-life-doesn't-need-fixing riot act.

Of course Laura called. After so many years of friendship they didn't even bother with the hi's or how-are-you's of normal telephone etiquette.

"So I guess things didn't exactly click yesterday, that's why your phone was off the hook last night, right?" was how Laura started the conversation.

"Wrong. And if you ever try to fix me up again I'll break into your house and snap the legs off of all those plastic horses you saved from your childhood."

"That bad, huh?"

"I didn't say that. What I said was, no more fix-ups. Ever. I'm too old for this. I'm becoming a lesbian, and don't worry, you're not my type."

"That's a relief, given what your type has been. Trip—need I say more? Besides, too old for what? What're you talking about? It was just lunch. What can two people possibly say over lettuce to get you this riled? I knew I should have called you yesterday. But this damn John Waters assignment. Some editor actually got me a part in Waters's new movie—a musical, of all things—and now that lunatic has me in the chorus dressed as a drag queen. A woman playing a man playing a woman. Anyway, back to Jack. Tell me everything."

Annie tapped her fingers against the sorrel wood of her desk, which she could do now thanks to deck-clearing.

"Lunch was fine."

Silence.

"And?" Laura said. "I hate it when you get this way. Stop pouting and just tell me what happened. Don't make me pull it out of you. You know I can and you know you'll end up telling me what's really eating you. Come on, this is me you're not talking to."

Annie laughed, though she didn't want to. Then she told her everything, as they both knew she would.

"So you sent him an e-mail and you haven't heard from him and you're ready to give up on men? You're worse off than I thought. Maybe he was busy; ever think of that?"

"That's what Fred said, but he's a man. I thought it was a solidarity kind of thing on his part."

"More like a stupidity kind of thing—on your part. You guys had a great time. You just told me so yourself. Tonight, I'll bet you my plastic horses, there's an e-mail waiting. And I bet it's long and meanderingly poetic. Besides, what do you mean I'm 'not your type'? What's your type anyway?"

"Quiet."

CHAPTER 15

By the time Annie left her office that day, it was nearly dark. Her main successes had been twofold: the reappearance of her desk's wood surface and the reestablishment of her self-respect. Yes, she'd checked her e-mail a couple more times that day—okay, three more times—but, she argued to an imaginary jury in her head, each time was for business. It had nothing to do with a certain editor at the *Baltimore Star-News*.

Annie shivered her way home that evening. It had been sixty-three degrees, sunny, and still when she'd walked the six blocks to work in the morning. But it was one of those late spring days when the sky changes clothes more times than a teenage girl before her first date. Now the sky was prison gray, the temperature had dropped fifteen degrees, and the hard wind made it seem thirty degrees colder.

As usual, Annie had dressed optimistically that morning— short sleeves, light slacks, no jacket. Fred had tried to give her his sweater to wear home, but she'd refused.

"Why don't you keep a spare something here for all the times you do this," he'd said to her before he left. "It looks like Antarctica out there."

"If I did that, then I'd be giving up on spring. Someone has to be her champion. I'll be fine, Fred, stop worrying," Annie said, and she thought she would be until she stepped outside on P Street.

By her fifth step, she was so cold that she ducked back into the Firehook Bakery for a cup of coffee to go. She added a sticky bun and made a dash for her apartment.

Six blocks later Annie was cursing herself for not taking Fred's sweater. "Let spring fend for her own damn self," she said to no one but the wind as she finally slipped into her apartment.

She'd never really wanted to live in a city. Given her druthers, she'd be living on a mesa overlooking magenta sunsets. But one thing had turned into another, and before she knew it she was borrowing $250,000 from Citibank for a two-bedroom apartment in Dupont Circle.

One thing turned into another. Isn't that always the case? One day you're furnishing your basement apartment with Salvation Army retreads and the next day you're filling your big suburban house with expensive antiques that look embarrassingly similar to the Salvation Army retreads.

Well, at least she wasn't living in Bethesda anymore. That house had been Trip's choice, because it had a porte cochere just like the "Big House" on Long Island, where he'd eaten meals prepared by Cook and been tended to by maids and housemen. The Big House was where his paternal grandparents had lived, where Trip's family spent every summer.

Annie had never liked Bethesda, Washington's toniest suburb. It was a gourmet ghetto where overpriced entrees came served on square plates. It had too many chic little stores that sold $750 hand-stamped linen dresses. And all the women looked casually perfect.

During the divorce, Trip had claimed the house was his because he'd bought it with his family money—despite the fact that Annie had paid half the mortgage. She didn't fight. All she wanted was her furniture, primitive pieces she'd found at auctions, garage sales, and antique stores. She liked their simple lines and the way the soft pine showed what they'd been through. She'd had to fight Trip on each purchase. His taste ran to the baronial: heavy mahogany and serious oak.

She threw her purse on an old blue cocoa crate that doubled as an entry table. In her bedroom she pulled a thick pair of sweatpants and a heavy fleece from her most prized possession—a battered white jelly cupboard from the 1850s.

"Ah, warmth," she said as she put on her fuzzy clothes.

Then she faced her computer. I do this every night, she thought. About this time every night. I am not checking to see if Jack has written back. This is not a John Brady, tenth-grade kind of thing. I have evolved far past that. This is a woman in her prime, in control—a Xena kind of thing.

And if Jack DePaul hasn't written back? I can handle it. Just because he seemed charming and smart at lunch doesn't mean he isn't an inconsiderate jackass jerk.

Annie sat down and signed on.

On the one hand, a remarkable number of messages appeared. Eda Royal wanted to send a new last chapter to her second She-Devil book; three young writers wanted her opinion on their manuscripts; there was a credit card offer, a lingerie offer, and something about online artworks; and there were seven messages she deleted without even opening.

On the other hand, there was no message from Jack DePaul.

Annie's shoulders sagged.

Yes, it may have been a John Brady kind of thing.

She stared at the screen for a few seconds. Finally, she answered the She-Devil and signed off. Then she went into the kitchen, grabbed the sticky bun, and ate her dinner.

CHAPTER 16

So. How did it go?" Matthew's question came out a little muffled, having had to dodge a mouthful of chips and salsa cruda.

About the time Annie was eating her sticky bun, Jack DePaul and his son, Matthew, were sitting in a booth at El Serape, a new Tex-Mex place just three blocks from Jack's apartment in the tren-difying Federal Hill neighborhood of Baltimore.

Jack pretended not to hear and responded with a question of his own. "How are things in the boneyard?"

Matthew was in his second year of graduate school, a budding archeologist, a fact that confounded his father and pleased him immeasurably. Right from the start, from the time of alphabet blocks and *Goodnight Moon*, Matthew had been a smart kid. Too smart for his own good, Jack often thought; everything came so easily to his son.

But by high school, Matthew had devolved. He exchanged soc-cer and swimming for hanging out. He drew cartoon space aliens. My son the artist. Jack tried out that phrase a few times; it never made sense. Neither he nor Elizabeth was the remotest bit artistic. Where did Matthew get it? And how did he go from rambunctious know-it-all to chubby little wiseacre with a lazy walk and dopey pals?

Then, in his sophomore year at college, Matthew took the low-level geology class—rocks for jocks. Suddenly he was hooked on strata. Next came classes in anthropology, ancient history, and chemistry. For the first time in his life, Jack couldn't talk to Matthew about his schoolwork. Eventually came graduate studies in archeology, something about pollen and prehistoric ecosystems in the American Southwest. Jack had gone through an archeology phase, too, but he was ten years old at the time and was only concerned about buried treasure. He definitely hadn't supplied Matthew with the science gene. That's why he was a journalist. Newspapers—last refuge of the data-dolt.

"Come on, Dad. 'Fess up. How did it go?" Matthew insisted.

"How did what go?" Jack said, his expression innocently blank.

"Your date."

"Oh, that. Okay." Jack dabbed a chip into the salsa cruda. "It wasn't really a date. Just a lunch."

"What was she like?"

"Nice."

"Nice?" Matthew grimaced. "Meaning fat and dumb as dirt?"

"No, no. She was really nice." Jack paused for a second. "Actually, she was great."

"Ah. Now we're getting somewhere." Matthew leaned forward, propping his elbows on either side of a salsa bowl, his chin resting atop linked fingers. He wasn't a bad-looking kid, Jack thought, with his field-research tan, scraggly goatee, and emerging sinews (the adolescent avoirdupois that had been the despair of his father was finally melting away).

"Start with the good stuff," Matthew said. "Is she cute?"

Jack pushed his glasses down his nose and gave him a schoolmaster's frown. "Son, I'm disappointed that you would be hung up on mere appearance. The important thing is that Miss Hollerman is a woman of no small accomplishment and intelligence and sophistication."

"She's a babe!" Matthew said with a lopsided grin not unlike the off-center smile that often graced his father's face.

Jack couldn't help but grin back. "Yeah. I gotta admit. She's kinduva babe."

"Who does she look like?"

"You mean like somebody we know?"

"No. Somebody famous. What movie star does she look like? If she looks like Gwyneth Paltrow, I'll introduce myself to her," said Matthew. "Let her meet the real stud of the DePaul family."

"You're a baboon," said Jack, with not completely mock anger. "Annie would only be attracted to higher life forms."

"Oh-ho. Suddenly she's 'Annie.' So, what does 'Annie' look like?"

Jack scrunched his eyes shut for a second. "Hepburn," he said.

"Hepburn!" said Matthew. "Dad, do you know anybody outside the Paleolithic era? How about Neve Campbell?"

"Who's that?"

"Never mind. Which Hepburn?"

"Both Hepburns. She has those strong Katharine bones, but Audrey's gamine charm."

"'Gamine charm'?" Matthew raised his hands in surprise. "Whoa, this is serious. What else?"

"Well, she's got the damndest head of red hair you've ever seen."

For the next fifteen minutes Matthew pumped his father. What did Annie do? How old was she? Was she funny? Smart? Clever? Sophisticated? Warm? What did you two talk about?

The more Jack described the lunch—no, no, it wasn't a date— the more it became something tangible; yes, maybe a date. It was as if the tastes, colors, and textures of lunch precipitated out of the telling. He spoke of Annie and she materialized.

"And right in the middle of pasta she started talking about a fla- menco dancer in Spain she wished she had seen. Imagine that— her most vivid travel memory was something that never happened. Isn't that sad? It made me want to . . ." Jack trailed off.

"Well. Anyway," he finished a little wistfully, "she's nice. I had a good time."

There was nothing wistful about Matthew's expression; he had a smile the size of Madrid. "Dad. I think you're back. 'Ding, dong, the witch is dead.'"

"Which old witch?" Jack answered in a little singsong voice. But he knew exactly which witch.

CHAPTER 17

Jack threw the mail on the couch and the *New Yorker* on the coffee table. He walked to the bedroom and, from four yards out, kicked his loafers into the closet. The apartment still reeked of Tuesday's dinner—popcorn. It occurred to him that if he were to invite someone over he'd better freshen up the place. He decided he'd bake some banana bread over the weekend, or at least keep the windows open for a day.

The eleven o'clock news was already over but Jack was too full to sleep. Another item for the life-lesson checklist: never eat Mexican food after 9 P.M. He put on sweats and a T-shirt and sat down at his old Mac.

Jack hadn't signed on to his home account for two days. Fourteen messages awaited him. Between BAMBI69 ("Hot Teens") and Zortman ("STOP SNORING NOW") was something from "ahollerman." It was entitled "lunch." He clicked on it.

"Jack,

"Thank you for lunch. You're charming in spite of yourself. I don't know about that tie, however.

"Annie"

A short message; only three sentences. If not exactly terse, certainly compact. Just a little eddy of electrons in the big river of bits

and bytes, but one that carried with it a question of great significance. Namely: What the hell do women mean?

The guy at the computer was not much better equipped to find
an answer than he had been in the days when he wore a letter-
man's jacket and clip-on ties. Does she like me? he wondered. She
called me "charming." That has to be good. But what about "in
spite of yourself"? Am I a jerk? A blowhard? Why did I tell her
about the grapefruit? Was I babbling like a street-corner guy wearing taped-up shoes? What about the length? Seventeen words. It's
very short. It's like the back of her hand. It's an insult. "I wouldn't
go out with you again if you were the last man on earth. See ya
'round, clown. Don't let the door hit your butt on the way out."
Cold. Stone cold.

But wait. What about the tie remark? It's friendly; it's funny. A
quip. A friendly tease. The tie sentence is good. The tie sentence
tips the balance. Although, what's wrong with my tie? I like that
tie. It's a Jerry Garcia tie. She doesn't like the Grateful Dead?
What? She listens to Jewel or Alanis Morissette? Whiners. Or the
Indigo Girls. She's a dyke! But she did grab my fingers. Did I have
pasta on the tie? Was I a slob? Did I have spinach in my teeth, a
booger hanging from my nose, earwax? My fly was open!

On the other hand, she did write "charming."

The squirrel cage of Jack's mind spun around for a few more
minutes. Eventually, it began to slow. When the calmer lobes of
his brain began to function again, he realized he had to write a response.

Jack called up a blank mail screen.

"Dear Annie," he wrote. No, he thought, too formal.

He began again. "Annie."

He stared at the screen for nearly three minutes.

Then he wrote: "Thank you for lunch. You were charming, too,
in spite of having me as your companion."

Jack pondered this opening. It sounded clever but didn't really
mean much. He made a sour face and deleted everything.

"Annie. I thought lunch was superb . . ." Too pompous.

"Annie. It's been a long time since I have . . ." Too needy.

"Annie. Appropriately, we were in an art museum . . ." Nerd.

"Annie. There was a moment during lunch when . . ." Windbag.

"Annie. I was wondering, does the hair on your head match the hair between your . . ." Just kidding.

"Annie. God, I think you're wonderful . . ." A little lacking in dignity.

Jack got up from his chair and windmilled his arms a couple of times. He inhaled deeply, held it, and let it slowly out. It was midnight. He sat down again and began writing. This time he wrote straight through without stopping.

CHAPTER 18

Thank God for small miracles: Joan Hollerman Silver had yet to master the Internet. She didn't even know Instant Messaging existed.

By 10:15 P.M. Thursday, she'd already called Annie twice—"No, Mom, I haven't heard back from him. I'm fine"—and when she called back at 10:30 the line was busy, as it was at 10:45 and 11.

Laura, on the other hand, was an IM junkie and knew that in times of stress Annie would take the telephone off the hook. Annie was the first buddy on her buddy list, and every time Annie signed on that evening, an Instant Message popped up on her screen.

"Well?"

"Nu?"

"Nothing yet?"

"I'll kill him tomorrow."

By 12:15 Annie's eyes were closing without her permission. In between checking her e-mail, she'd finally plowed through the She-Devil's new manuscript. It was worse than bad. It was obnoxious, overblown, and screechy. And it was sure to be a best-seller.

Eda Royal, the She-Devil, who'd formerly taught *Beowulf* to bored freshmen at Tompkins Cortland Community College in upstate New York, had tapped into something big when she dumped her husband, a nice but boring man who ran the local fish hatchery, and formed a support group for the newly divorced. She'd tapped into anger. Everyone in her group was really pissed off. Pissed off at themselves, their kids, their bosses, their lives, but mostly their husbands.

At one particularly rowdy meeting, a once-meek bookkeeper who'd married right out of high school said, "Lord almighty, what's gotten into us, the devil?"

"The she-devil!" someone shouted.

And so began Eda Royal's new career.

Before Annie brushed her teeth and headed to bed, she signed on to her computer. For the first time in twenty-four hours, it was not to see if Jack DePaul had written back. She wanted to write Laura, to tell her she'd been stupid to get so worked up, that it had been a fine lunch, but that was all it was, just a lunch, nothing else. And if Laura said *anything* to Jack DePaul the next day, that would be the end of their friendship, though she would continue to be Becky's godmother.

"You have mail," her computer announced.

"Fuck you," Annie said as she guided the cursor to the flag and clicked.

There was a message, from a "jdepaul." It was entitled "Lunch."

"Annie,

"Lunch was wonderful, wish we could have stayed longer. It was the perfect afternoon to idle away over coffee. Thinking back over it, I may have in fact been too brash. You were so easy to talk to I let my defenses down and was just myself. There may be some charm in that; there may be some boorishness. I hope the former outweighed the latter.

"However, even my brashness has its limits. Here's something I couldn't possibly have said to your face: You're quite lovely.

"Jack"

CHAPTER 19

Jack turned over the pillow to the cool side again, but it didn't help. His brain was feverish, not his brow. He stared at the clock: it was 1:40 A.M. Friday morning. Hopeless. He couldn't sleep. Farewell to sleep. Jack DePaul does murder sleep. Sleepless in Baltimore. Sleep has left the building.

Thoughts tumbled around inside his head like shirts in a dryer: What if I had actually read those college econ texts? What would I be like if I had gone to Vietnam? Could I have made the NBA if I'd been six foot four? But they were just diversions to keep the witch at bay. Despite what Matthew had said over dinner, she wasn't ding-dong dead. The nightmare bird was on the wing, soaring and circling, waiting, just waiting for a sleepless night like this.

Jack untangled himself from the covers and lay face up, hands behind his head. To ward off the raptor, he projected another image into the dark. This one was of Annie across a white tablecloth and pasta plates. He liked her face. It was complicated and angular; there were shadows of time and experience. The nose crooked slightly to the right; the mouth was animated. Everything about Annie was quick; he liked that, too. Answers, gestures, and questions darted out of her like hummingbirds. She laughed quickly and generously, she didn't hold back.

Nothing like Kathleen, the nightmare bird, the queen of hold-

ing back, the woman who measured out her emotions tryst by
tryst. After three years, Jack still didn't know if she was complex
and deep or just a good liar. "I can't do this anymore," she would
say. But she could and she did. She said she loved him; sometimes
he believed it. Every time he pressed her for commitment she said
she couldn't leave her husband. But she couldn't seem to leave
Jack, either. Once in a hotel bed, he had asked her why, and in a
moment of naked honesty she had said, "Because you try so hard."

He had tried hard—from the moment they kissed drunkenly in
a corridor of the Sheraton Hotel in New York three years ago.
Before then, they had been merely colleagues at the *Star-News*.
He had known her for a couple of years and found her ice queen
persona sexy, in an abstract sort of way. But that was before his
marriage began to fail and Matthew went off to college, before his
regrets began to outnumber his dreams.

By the time of the kiss, Jack's midlife had become a crisis. It
was a luxury, he knew—he had a car and a house and health;
he didn't live in Bosnia—but that didn't ease the ache or the
haunting questions. What had happened to the years? What
did he have to show for them? Matthew was the best thing he
had ever done. But his son wasn't something that he had
planned for or fought for, just a normal consequence of a mundane marriage at the usual time in the usual circumstances. He'd
had no grand struggle, no great passion. And now time was running away.

Then, at the last night of that conference in New York, after a
boisterous dinner with a dozen colleagues, when he found himself
by a hotel room door entwined with Kathleen, tongues deep in
each other's mouths, his hand between her legs, he knew he had
found that reason, that cause, that thing to plug the hole in his
heart.

Jack stared up at the ceiling. Funny how wrong you can be, he
thought.

He pushed Kathleen away again and pulled Annie Hollerman
back into his thoughts. He had told Matthew over dinner that
Annie was "effervescent," a word that had never been uttered in

the same sentence with Kathleen Faulkner. Not that Annie seemed like a bubblebrain; during their lunch he had noticed something muting her, like an open window letting a cool breeze into a warm room. Nothing sinister, just complex.

He thought again about Annie's story of her trip to Spain (what kind of a fool was her husband anyway?). It had been the best part of their lunch. When she had told him about the flamenco dancer she had never seen, he had felt a swooping, roller-coaster sensation in his chest. He had wanted to stand up, toss some bills down on the table, reach out his hand to her, and say, "Annie, get packed. There's a flight to Madrid, leaving at eight o'clock tonight."

It had made him feel, for the first time in months, like he was made of flesh and bone. Kathleen hadn't sucked him dry after all. And when he'd written to Annie earlier in the evening, he'd felt like an athlete stretching unused muscles. Back from the injured list, he thought, and in the game again.

E-mail was how he'd wooed Kathleen. She loved his words; she was greedy for them. Each time she said "never again," he'd entangle her in his net of verbs, his web of nouns, and haul her back. "Fuck me with stories," she'd say. And he would. Her husband, an executive in the local power company, never had a chance, and, as far as they knew, was oblivious to the drama being played out in his own marriage.

Jack pulled the covers aside and sat at the edge of the bed. He wondered, not for the first time, whether it was Kathleen he had been in love with or the writing to Kathleen.

From the widening perspective of separation, she now seemed more a fever than a relationship. After he and Kathleen spent that night together in New York, he had left Elizabeth. He couldn't live the lie. Kathleen was willing to live it every day. For Jack, the clandestine sex, so exciting at first, became increasingly mechanical. And afterward, drowsy and sheet-tossed, they seemed no more closely bound than before. He wanted a soul mate; she wanted a playmate.

Jack got up and put on a bathrobe. "Fuck you, and your white shirt," he said out loud to the bookshelves in his bedroom. He walked into the den and sat down at the computer.

Now there was Annie. "Oh well, you can't rewrite your past, can you?" she had said at lunch. Jack signed on and called up a blank message file.

"Dear Annie," he wrote.

"Where is it written that you can't rewrite your past?

"Do you remember that night in Jerez? That was the night we first met—the night we saw Renatta Vega-Marone. I remember, as if it were yesterday.

"I came to the central square around eleven and got a table just twenty feet away from the wooden stage, which was raised four steps up from the pavement. Behind it, like a huge Hollywood set, were the city's medieval stone walls.

"You appeared about midnight. By then the place was jammed. I watched you weave your way across the cobblestones searching for an empty chair. The night was warm, even for July. You wore a sleeveless blouse, a turquoise wraparound skirt, and sandals. I knew you were a tourist here, like me. You were squeezing between some crowded tables nearby when I caught your eye and waved. 'There's a place over here,' I said, removing my day-bag from the chair next to mine. 'Join me, please.'

"You smiled and sat down. We traded names and stories and ordered a bottle of sherry, because sherry is what people drink in Jerez after midnight. I liked you right off. I liked your smile; I liked that you were traveling alone and didn't care that you were traveling alone.

"Just as the sherry arrived an older woman in a red dress walked on stage accompanied by a young man carrying a guitar. The people around us applauded raucously. At the next table, an elderly man wearing a light straw hat told us the guitarist was only nineteen. The woman in the red dress was Renatta Vega-Marone, Spain's greatest flamenco dancer. She has gypsy blood, said the man in the hat. She had jet black hair and black eyes that swallowed you up. It was hard to tell how old she was. We guessed she was forty-five, maybe fifty. The old man made a point of telling us that Renatta was also famous for her lovers and that the boy—the guitarist—was one of them.

"But you had guessed it before he told us. Something in the way the boy held her hand as they walked on stage made you turn to me and say, 'Those two won't go to bed alone tonight.'

"The whole evening had been filled with dancing and music. Renatta and the boy were the last to appear. He sat on a small folding chair just to the left of center stage. His fingers blurred over the strings, but at first Renatta danced very slowly. She seemed stately, like a widow in a funeral procession. Then she moved faster and faster. Her heels hit the stage like antiaircraft fire. People began to leave their tables, to get closer. We got up and squeezed in behind the first row of spectators; the crowd pressed us together.

"She danced several numbers. She was mesmerizing, gut-wrenching. Magic. The harsh stage lights erased everything but the boldest shadows, colors, and shapes. It was like seeing a Picasso painting dance. For the final number, she began slowly again, then sped up like a locomotive. Even from where we were standing we could see her dripping with sweat. People around us were shouting 'Jaleo! Jaleo!' I realized that we were sweating, too. And then the most amazing thing. She began to slow down and down and down. The music tempo slowed, too. And then her steps were just: One . . . Two . . . Three/Four. One . . . Two . . . Three/Four. One . . . Two . . . And then she stopped. And the crowd went mad with joy. And you were crying."

"Jack"

CHAPTER 20

Well?"

Without turning her head, Annie said, "Good morning to you, too, Fred."

Annie had been standing in line at the Firehook Bakery, trying to decide between virtue and vice, when she'd heard Fred's voice.

"Well, was I right?"

She turned around and smiled.

"Exactly how right was I?" said Fred.

"He called me 'lovely.'"

"At least this one has eyes," Fred said.

Lovely. Such a simple, old-fashioned word. Like a lace doily. No one had ever called Annie Hollerman that before. When she'd read Jack's note about lunch, the word had taken her off guard. Now it was like a song that kept looping through her brain. Lovely. She liked the way the *l*'s wrapped around the velvet vowels, caressing her mouth each time she said it. Lovely. An old-time wooing word. Courtly, but so eloquently sexy.

"What'll it be this morning, Annie, the usual?" said Sarah, the young woman behind the counter.

Annie eyed the usual, an oozy pecan sticky bun.

Lovely. She heard its song again.

"Better make it the bran muffin—and a skim latte."

Fred, always the gentleman, pretended not to notice, even after Sarah laughed and said, "Whoever he is, he must be a hottie. How about you, Fred, the usual, or are you taking the high road, too?"

Fred's road never veered. It was the usual for him, double-shot espresso, twist of lemon, and a blueberry scone.

They walked upstairs to the office. Fred had a stack of queries to sift through. The good ones, or at least the ones with some promise, went to Annie; the rest were bounced back with a "thank-you-not-without-merit-but-not-for-us" rejection note attached.

The first thing Annie did was call Laura. "It's me," she said after the beep to record her message. "You were right. I was wrong. Don't gloat. He called me 'lovely.' Now I've got to lose five pounds fast."

Then she got down to work. Lynn McCain, the mystery writer who hated being called a mystery writer, needed serious attention. Not only had she burned out the publicists at Simon & Schuster, but her next book was coming up for negotiation and she wanted Annie to send it around to get an auction going. It would rain in Death Valley before that happened.

Though her books were still selling, she'd only made the best-seller list one time, and that had been five books before. Yesterday, McCain's editor had hinted to Annie that if the numbers kept going down, so would the advances.

Annie kept telling McCain that publishing is strictly what-have-you-done-for-me-today and how-will-your-books-sell-tomorrow? No one at Simon & Schuster gave two hoots about McCain's refrain that she was the next Reynolds Price. Most of them didn't even know who Reynolds Price was.

Now Annie had to call McCain and set her straight, not only about the auction that wasn't going to happen but about her behavior on her book tour.

She started to pick up the phone when Fred walked in.

"The Ghoul on line one. Shall I tell him to go back to the graveyard?"

"Nah, I better take it."

Annie pressed line one. "James, just the person I was reaching for my phone to call. How are you, and congratulations on the movie deal."

"A lucky break," James Gentile said. "Guess how many times it came close to falling through. This business we're in, it's enough to give you heartburn. In fact, I hear Bertelsmann just bought Merck so it can supply its employees with Mylanta and Prilosec."

Annie laughed. "I'm a Maalox girl myself."

While they chatted, Annie signed on to her computer. She was looking for the new last chapter of *She-Power* that Eda had promised to send.

". . . So what do you think about getting together?" James said.

The flag was up. She had mail, tons of mail. How could all that accumulate in less than twelve hours? As she talked to James, she scanned down the list of mail. It was the usual stuff, plus Eda's new chapter.

James continued to talk: ". . . there's a new chef at Café Atlantico who studied with Serge Sampo . . ."

Then, like a smell that hits you five seconds after you walk by it, she realized it wasn't just the usual stuff in her mailbox. Three messages below Eda's was another e-mail from jdepaul, this one entitled "Spain."

Annie started reading it. "Where is it written you can't rewrite your past? . . ."

". . . so Thursday night's good then? Seven-thirty?" James said.

"Oh, right," Annie said, not taking her eyes off the computer screen, reading about Jerez and Jack and Renatta.

"Annie? Thursday night?"

"Sorry, James. Alright then, Thursday night. Listen, something just came up. I've got to run."

What just came up was hope.

CHAPTER 21

By eleven that morning, Annie had already talked to Lynn McCain three times. She'd backed her off the auction notion, but getting her to be nice on her book tour was another matter.

"I don't care if Katie Couric is the second coming in a dress," McCain said. "She made me seem like an idiot. *'I can't remember when I've had so much fun figuring out who the murderer was.'* That's not what my book's about."

Actually, it was, Annie started to tell her. McCain's readers weren't academics who studied her works along with Faulkner and Welty. They were the mystery nuts, the women who wore cat T-shirts to the mystery conferences and spent their free time reading and posting on Dorothy-L, a listserv that gossips about mystery writers. They were the ones who had driven her first book to the *New York Times* best-seller list, and they were the ones she was losing with all her I'm-a-serious-Southern-writer talk.

McCain, as usual, refused to listen. "Look, Annie, those publicists at Simon & Schuster are eleven years old. They haven't even started menstruating yet. They can't do anything right. You've got to make sure the interviewers don't call me a mystery writer. I won't snap at anyone else if you can do that."

"Lynn, get real," Annie said. "I can't control what comes out of the interviewers' mouths any more than I can control what comes out of yours. Though, Lord knows, I'd like to. Just count to ten or something when you hear the M word. Sir Arthur Conan Doyle didn't go ballistic when he was called a mystery writer. You're only hurting yourself when you do this. So please, ease up. Okay?"

There was a pause. Finally McCain agreed. Sort of. "Well, I'll do the best I can. I may have to count to twenty."

At least Annie had accomplished something that morning. Jack, on the other hand, had accomplished nothing more than scanning the *Post* and the *Times* for stories he should have thought of first. He'd stayed up till 4 A.M. traveling to Spain and now he had a serious case of jet lag. Fortunately it was Friday; the weekend advance sections were already on the presses and Monday's centerpiece was over to the copy desk.

When the phone rang he answered sleepily, "DePaul."

"You must be color-blind. The skirt I wore that night in Jerez wasn't turquoise, it was purple. I think we need to test your eyes."

Annie's voice skyrocketed Jack's lethargy out the window. He grinned into the receiver. "Are you sure? I remember turquoise. And I'm a trained observer."

"Purple," said Annie firmly. "And you were wearing a light khaki shirt and blue jeans. And one of those silly berets the Basques wear. It seemed a little affected but I forgave you."

Any clever rejoinders that Jack might have said were derailed by his relief. His e-mail hadn't made her think he was a psycho, or, even worse, a nitwit.

"Well . . . I . . . did you . . ." he began.

"Jack."

"Yes?"

"I loved your e-mail."

Loved. It resonated like a temple bell. Something came out of Jack's mouth after that, but it was nearly lost in the reverberations. Finally, a few sentences later, he managed to ask Annie out for that weekend.

"I'm sorry, Jack. I'd love to, but this weekend's off. I'm taking Laura's daughter on a mother-daughter camping trip. Remember, Laura's got this thing about peeing outdoors and so it's up to me, the godmother." Annie paused for a second, then said, a sly note of conspiracy in her voice, "What about next Wednesday? Are you up for an adventure?"

"I'm all yours," Jack said.

CHAPTER 22

Y ou can do better than that!"

The She-Devil jammed a fist in the air.

"One more time. With all you've got. If you wanta be a She-Devil, you gotta shout! Okay? One . . . two . . . three: I'M A SHE-DEVIL!"

"I'M A SHE-DEVIL!" came the crowd's roar, followed by applause and laughter.

The meeting space on the second floor at the Bethesda Barnes & Noble was packed that Wednesday night. Women were sitting cross-legged in the aisles and standing back among the magazines. In the previous half hour, Jack had learned that he and his kind were responsible for crime, pornography, MTV, AIDS, SIDS, NATO, and holes in the ozone layer. He also learned that he must hand back the planet to women, who had previously run things in a long-lost golden age, known mythologically as the Garden of Eden, until, as the She-Devil put it, "men, with swords in their hands and swords between their legs, captured the human race."

Jack, who had nothing against NATO and kind of liked MTV, had tried to ride out the typhoon of rhetoric like a sailor, but instead of a mast, he clung to the sight of Annie sitting at the author's table. She was wearing loose, flowing pants and a matching blouse that managed to be pale and bright green at the same time.

Her hair tumbled down past her shoulders like a fallen halo. She looked cool and smart and Jack had the sudden thought that she was the most beautiful woman he had ever seen in his life. But just as quickly, he cautioned himself: maybe you're simply overreacting to the surrounding piercings and buzzcuts.

Jack had arrived just as the She-Devil began her talk, "She-Speaks." When he squeezed himself between the last row of folding chairs and the end of the New Age/Spirituality aisle, he discovered he was the only man in the crowd.

It was when the subject turned to cloning that he finally caught Annie's eye. The She-Devil, spotting the lone swordsman in the crowd, pointed to him and said, "In twenty years he'll be irrelevant." The crowd laughed and Jack looked for help from the author's table. Annie stuck out her tongue, smiled, flushed, and looked away, brushing aside an invisible strand of hair.

The She-Devil finished up her talk to rowdy applause. When she began signing copies of *Confessions of a She-Devil*, Annie walked over to Jack. "How'd you like it?" she asked him, radiating fake innocence.

"Not bad, for a castration," he said.

Annie gave him one of her quick laughs. "Would it hurt too much to walk over there?" she said, pointing to the café. "I'll just be five minutes and then you can buy me a cup of coffee. Oh, wait; first come meet the She-Devil. Don't worry, she won't hurt you. She even thinks you're cute—for an oppressor."

As if she'd known him forever, Annie took his hand and led him to the author's table.

"Eda, meet Jack, he's the man I told you about."

Eda Royal was a short dumpling of a woman, with a round pumpkin face. She squinted at him as if she were examining road-kill. Or at least that's how Jack felt under her gaze.

He was starting to stammer something about it being a pleasure to meet her, when she broke into a belly laugh. "Oh, for Christsakes, it's anything but a pleasure to meet me, after what I just put you through. You know I was only kidding, about the swords and all that stuff. It was just a locker-room pep talk, that's all. I got the idea from Monday

Night Football. Anyway, it is a pleasure to meet you. You're a brave—
or exceedingly stupid—man to come here tonight. Or"—she looked
over at Annie—"exceedingly smitten."

Annie and Jack were soon elbow to elbow at a little round coffee table in the Barnes & Noble café sharing lattes and biscotti.
This time there were no first-lunch jitters or first-impression
nerves. Jack didn't drop any food on himself; Annie stopped worrying that her voice was too bright or her expression too brittle.

"You know what was the best thing about your e-mail?" Annie
asked.

"The brilliant writing?"

"Yup," Annie said, "that, too. But the really brilliant part is,
now, when I think of Spain, I don't see Trip crouched over a
bunch of maps. I see the sweat dripping down Renatta's back. You
know how a tape recorder records over things? That's what your
words did. They wrote over my past."

They talked for more than two hours about everything: her job,
his job, body piercing in general, body piercing in specific (the silver stud in Sarah the Firehook Bakery girl's tongue that made her
lisp), where they'd be living if they could live anywhere (she
Colorado, he Arizona), her upcoming "bonding trip" with her
mother, his trip to Utah this summer with Matthew, and on and
on. When the bookstore closed at eleven, Jack, Annie, and a kid
with matted hair who looked like he'd just woken up were the last
out the door.

It was a warm night and the restaurants were still open; well-
dressed people, gazing at each other over flickering candles,
jammed the outdoor tables. Couples walked through the glow of
window displays showing the latest hand-stamped linen dresses.

"Where are you parked?" the two of them said at the same moment. They laughed, then paused, waiting for the other to finish.

"No. You first," said Jack.

"Over there," said Annie, pointing to the outdoor lot across the
street.

"I'm in the garage," said Jack. "Let me walk you to your car."

It wasn't until he stopped in front of Annie's Mustang that the significance of the moment struck him—struck him like a cartoon anvil shoved off a ten-story building. He was going to have to . . . he was going to try to . . . kiss Annie Hollerman good night.

At the prospect of this, something giggled up inside him so fast he had to turn away so she wouldn't see the silly grin on his face.

The question was how. It had to be a sophisticated approach, he knew, yet something manly. He decided to reach out for her hand then gently pull her to him. A dance move. Something suave. Something Fred Astaire. He turned back around, then hesitated.

It was Annie who moved first.

She put her hand gently at the back of Jack's head and made the inches between them disappear. She pressed her lips against his mouth. Softly at first. Then he furrowed a hand into her hair and pulled her body against him. She pressed hard at his lips and circled her arms around his neck. Then she wrapped her right leg around his left. A single tiptoe connected her to Earth.

Jack walked his fingers slowly down the ridges of her spine, down to the base of her curve. He pushed hard against her; he could feel the heat of her against his thigh. She could feel him against her hip.

Her mouth opened, she slid her tongue into him.

CHAPTER 23

Laura arched her left eyebrow as Annie sat down next to her at a window table upstairs at Teaism, a quirky café in Dupont Circle. "So? How was last night?"

Annie grinned and gave her the thumbs-up. "This guy could teach John Gilliam how to kiss."

"Way to go. I haven't seen that cocky grin on you in a million years. This is a good sign, a very good sign."

Then Laura started singing loud enough for people at the next table to turn around. "'Matchmaker, matchmaker, make me a match . . .' So I take it things are right on track with Jack?"

"You could say that," Annie said.

They were meeting in D.C. this morning because Laura had an afternoon interview with a lieutenant in the Russian mafia at an as of yet undisclosed location near the White House. Getting there was going to involve secret phone booth calls, passwords, and limousines.

Between bites of tea-cured salmon, Annie filled her in on last night's events. Laura sprayed her oolong-oolong when Annie told her about the She-Devil's meeting with Jack.

"And he stuck around after that? Impressive," Laura said between laughs.

"More than stuck around. We closed the place down," Annie said.

Laura arched an eyebrow again. "And?"

"And what?" said Anne. "And did I take him home with me? You can stop looking at me like that. The answer's no. No 'ands.' Jesus, Laura, I barely know his last name."

"It's DePaul. What else do you need to know? He's a great guy. He's got a great ass, I think. And by my count you haven't been to bed with a man for what, eight months? And that was with the energy geek, so it didn't really count."

"Nine, as long as you're counting," Annie said. "But that's why Kmart sells vibrators. That is where you bought me my last birthday present, isn't it?" Annie shook an accusatory finger at her friend. "If your mother only knew that her daughter shops the Blue Light Specials."

Laura rolled her eyes. "It'd be enough to put her in her grave, if cancer hadn't gotten there first." Then she stretched her hands across the table. "I miss her," she said.

Annie put her hands over Laura's. "Me too," she said.

Bunny Goodbread had died fourteen years before. Laura was far too young to lose a mother—as if you're ever old enough—and was so lonesome for a maternal presence that she had glommed herself onto Annie's family. Joan Hollerman Silver, the woman who never wanted to be a mother, found herself with a second daughter.

"Speaking of mothers," Annie said, "thanks to you, my mother's office has a little pool going on whether Jack's a keeper."

"I know. I put twenty dollars on yes."

Annie shook her head in disbelief. "Even for you, Laura, that's going too far. Besides, it's insider trading. I hope you lose every penny." She paused, then said, "Well, maybe I don't. I don't know what I want, Laura. The truth is, he seems great—we're going out again, on Saturday night. He's funny and smart and, okay, yes, he's sexy. But—"

Laura held up her hand, stopping Annie's words. "I know, sweetie. Believe it or not, I thought about it a lot before I told Jack about you. He's a journalist. You were a journalist. Very past-tense. You are an agent now. It's time to bury that past once and for all. For Christsakes, Annie, what's the worst thing that could happen?"

CHAPTER 24

The conference table was too big for the room. It had nearly historic dimensions, as if designed for the signing of a peace treaty. The seven *Star-News* features editors who gathered around it each morning invariably clustered at one corner so they wouldn't have to bellow across its shiny, laminate bulk.

This Thursday morning the corner was strewn with the usual meeting flotsam: newspapers, printouts, photographs, coffee cups, coffee mugs, and a box of Krispy Kremes. The strewing had been done by the usual participants: Jack DePaul, Features editor; Mike Gray, Arts editor; Melissa Pendragon, from the design desk; Kathy Turnbow, editor of the Sunday magazine; Jerod Council, the features photo chief; Lisa Petrillo, who ran the home and family sections; and everybody's boss, Steve Proctor, the features managing editor.

"Did you guys see Kurtz's column in the *Post* this morning?" Turnbow asked as she stood over the Krispy Kremes wrestling with temptation. She was a resolute woman in her late forties with a health club figure and pretensions of youthfulness. "He had an item about a weird plagiarism case at the Pittsburgh paper. A writer there—a rising young hotshot, by all accounts—took a prize-winning story from the eighties and copied the exact form of it, paragraph by paragraph, just filling in new information."

"What do you mean?" asked Proctor.

"The guy was pretty clever," said Turnbow. "Both his story and the original—it won a Penney-Missouri Award—had to do with a new medical procedure on a child. The Penn-Mizzo piece had a complicated structure; it went back and forth between the surgeons in the operating room, the family waiting for the result, and the science behind the procedure. The Pittsburgh guy did the exact same thing, he just had a new procedure, new surgeons, and a new family."

"I've never heard of structural plagiarism before," said Petrillo. "Is that so bad? Doesn't every Ravens game story have the same structure?"

"Yeah," said Council, "is it a theft or an *'homage'*?"

Jack wiped Krispy Kreme crumbs from his mouth and jumped into the conversation with both loafers.

"*'Homage'* my ass, Jerod. You telling me it would be okay if one of your photographers copied a *National Geographic* spread picture for picture, but he just shot them a year later and at different times of day with different lenses?"

All the editors at the table smiled. Jack was starting to speak in italics. "Oh boy, here we go," said Council, who was expecting just such a response. Jack had the same role in the morning meetings as coffee: to awaken and agitate. He loved fomenting debate and challenge. It wasn't universally appreciated, but the features group depended on Jack to shake things up. That morning, his opening comment had the desired effect. Everybody piled on, talking at once. After a couple of minutes, Turnbow regained the floor.

"It wasn't just structure," she said. "This guy also borrowed phrases and descriptions. Apparently, that's what tipped off some Pittsburgh editor. Turns out he'd been a Penney-Missouri finalist the same year the original story won. What are the chances of that?"

"What happened to the guy?" asked Proctor.

"Suspended. Six months unpaid leave," said Turnbow.

"That's bullshit," Jack exclaimed. "How about: Fired. Six months' hard labor."

This remark generated another round of hubbub, during which Jack asked, "How did Pittsburgh justify this, Kathy? What did they say: 'Dear readers, we've decided that credibility isn't important anymore so we're keeping our plagiarist on the payroll'? I don't get it. I don't get the people who do it or the papers that allow it. If newspapers don't have some basic integrity, we might as well turn 'em all into Web sites."

"Jesus, Jack, did you just fly in from the planet Black-and-White? These things are never that simple," said Gray. "There are gradations and circumstances."

"Bullshit," said Jack, folding his arms against his chest, as if this were some kind of final ruling. Of course, it wasn't. The meeting sidetracked into everyone's favorite gradation. The name Janet Cooke came up; so did Stephen Glass, Patricia Smith, and Mike Barnicle. ("Barnicle," Jack snorted in disgust. "Now he's got a fucking TV show.") Somebody remembered that Michael Bolton had plagiarized a song from the Isley Brothers; somebody mentioned Martin Luther King's Ph.D. dissertation.

Finally, Proctor, glancing at his watch, said, "Look, guys, if we're generating this much talk, there's gotta be a story here. What is it?"

"For me it's 'Why?'" said Jack. "Why do they do it?"

"Why don't you ask the Pittsburgh guy, Jack," said Council.

"That's it," Jack said, pointing a finger at him, "let's ask the Pittsburgh guy. That's the story. We find out who this guy is, what drove him to it, what he was thinking when he did it, and everything."

"Yeah, but do readers care?" Petrillo asked. "Isn't plagiarism just an issue for journalists?"

"It's not about plagiarism," Jack said, his enthusiasm growing the more he talked about it. "It's about everybody. It's about inspiration and failure. It's about the difference between 'homage' and theft. It's about the pressure to perform. It's about . . . it's about . . . the hubris of human ambition."

"Oh no, not another Hubris of Human Ambition story," said Gray, pounding his head in mock despair.

Everybody laughed, Jack included. "It'll be great," he said. "We'll call it 'Thief of Words.' Proc, do you think we can get Gammerman to do it? She'd be great."

"I'll ask Metro. What about some other cases? I can't believe that Isley Brothers thing. Somebody should do a Nexis search on all the plagiarizing hotshots of the past who fell to earth. Let's track them down and do a where-are-they-now story."

"Brilliant, Proc," said Jack. "Steinberg should be finished with the Camden Yards story in a week or two—he's only been working on it since the nineteen-forties. He can start the where-are-they-now part after that."

CHAPTER 25

The three o'clock coffee run had come and gone. The main feature stories for the next day had been sent to the copy desk. The little imps of panic that live in every newspaper office slipped back into their hiding places—at least in the Features department; over on the news side they still had hours of vigilance.

Jack stopped fretting over Laura's Russian mafioso interview and the USDA's denial in the biogenetic corn story. He felt fairly confident about his Solomon-like decision on the Sisqo quotes. He'd left in one "bitch" and one "nigger" but cut out everything that even hinted at "motherfucker."

He leaned back and put his feet up on his desk. He spread yesterday's *Times* across his lap, but ignored it. It was time to consider more pleasurable things. Like Annie Hollerman, for example. Musing about Annie was becoming a treat for Jack, like wrapping his hands around a cup of hot chocolate on a February afternoon.

He liked her presence. He tried to put the right word to it. Maybe "alacrity." She had a kind of cheerful readiness. Alacrity Hollerman. He liked how she had kissed him first, and strongly, too. He could feel again her thigh pressed hard against him, hard between his legs. "Bold" and "sexy" were good words, too. And she had a spray of freckles down each arm.

But there was something else. Ever since Matthew had made it safely out of adolescence, Jack seemed to have fallen back in. He was feeling insecure and incompetent; he moped. He wanted to feel safe with someone. Safe to reveal the deepest truths about himself, even if the deepest truth was that Jack DePaul wasn't nearly as deep as he had always assumed. After just two conversations and one kiss, he was beginning to feel safe with Annie. He was sure this feeling didn't come from desperation or Kathleen rebound. Nothing about Jack and Annie felt forced or fake. Their banter was barbless. He could make her laugh. She banished mopiness. There was nothing fraught about their times together. And everything concerning Kathleen Faulkner had been fraught.

It was in this mood of happy melancholy that Jack wrote Annie the following e-mail.

"Annie,

"During our lunch and after the She-Devil, I tried to regale you and make you laugh. But my jollity wasn't completely true. The truth is, I've been feeling dried up and hollow lately. Not myself. Not the self of years past. Now the wind blows right through me sometimes.

"After all these years, I come to work some days and feel like a stranger. I want to ask for directions. For most of my life I was confident to bursting. I felt that 'life piled on life were all too little,' as Tennyson had Ulysses say.

"Now, on bad days, I'm a stranger to myself. And yet, I can close my eyes and still be the man I knew. Hurtling down a summer road at night, clouds turning the moon to tatters overhead, porch lights shooting by like comets, drugstore signs glowing like Orion's belt, devil wind blowing through the windows, a hand on my jeans. Someone saying yes.

"I'm sorry you didn't get to meet that Jack. But then there is you. There is your life and your confidence and your yes. And maybe all is not lost. And this strange new sadness may be no more permanent than a thundercloud.

"See you Saturday night.

"Jack"

He read the message over. It was too earnest. He read it again.

It was overwrought and even worse, purple. He cut a few phrases—though not as many as if he were working on a reporter's story—and pressed the send button. He waited for the rush of remorse, but it never came. After all, it was the truth. And it felt good to be telling it.

The clock over the door of Proctor's office told him it was time for the daily afternoon news meeting with the other section editors. He gathered up the story budget for the next day and, with a cheerful readiness to his step, headed to the conference room.

When he returned forty minutes later, the phone was ringing, as it inevitably did at Jack DePaul's desk.

"DePaul," he said brusquely.

"Hollerman," Annie replied with a fake abruptness that made Jack laugh.

"I'm calling with bad news, I'm afraid," said Annie. "But first: I got your e-mail. Just so you know, you're not the only one who feels the wind blow right through them. But you're a wonderful writer, Jack. I think you should quit your day job and start writing. I know just the agent who could make you a star."

"Thanks, Annie. That's sweet. But I don't think so, I'm just a guy working—"

"I know," Annie interrupted, and then said in a melodramatic voice, "you're just a guy working in the comma factory."

That made Jack laugh again. "What's the bad news?"

"Lynn's melting down in Virginia Beach. You think you've got crybabies? She refuses to speak and she's the keynote speaker. Now it's up to me to get her in front of that podium Saturday night. It's that or let her self-destruct. Then, remember, I'm off to North Carolina to go to that writers' conference and see my mother."

Jack knew all about Lynn McCain's tantrums and Annie's odd bond to her. Annie had told him about it over coffee the previous night. How she'd found McCain's manuscript in the slush pile at the Leeland agency, where she first worked when she moved to Washington. Greg Leeland had made his name and money selling nonfiction books by the heavy-hitting Washington journalists. He had no interest in an assistant librarian from Lexington, Virginia, with a mystery set in the Shenandoah backcountry. Greg Leeland's idea of the Shenandoah was an evening at the uber-posh Inn at Little Washington. Annie had to beg Leeland to let her try to sell McCain's book.

To everyone's surprise but Annie's, *Don't Come Knocking* wound up in a bidding war, with Simon & Schuster finally paying $300,000 for a two-book deal. A year later, Annie started her own agency and McCain, whose first book made the *New York Times* list, came with her, along with all her problems. Because she was Annie's first client, Annie felt obligated to step in after McCain alienated all the publicists.

"Well, how about tonight? I could come down to D.C. right after work. Maybe dinner?"

"Great, let me just check my calendar." There was a pause and Jack heard the rustle of papers. "Oh, damn," said Annie. "I can't. I'm meeting an author. What about tomorrow night?"

"No. Shit, I can't. I'm going to the opera. I promised the music critic. It's part of his plan to make me cultured—symphony, chamber music, opera. I once tried to convince him that Bo Diddley singing 'Who Do You Love' was one of the masterpieces of Western music. So he made me go with him to see *Turandot*. It sounds like some kind of bland fish. Whatever it is, I hate opera."

"That's too bad," Annie said. "I was looking forward to seeing you. We'll have to postpone it until I get back from North Carolina. A week in the Tar Heel state, first bonding with my mother, then having my carcass picked dry by a bunch of needy writers. Want to come?"

North Carolina with Annie. Jack liked the thought. But North Carolina with Annie and her mother *and* a hundred J. R. Thelmans? "Another time," Jack said and meant it more than Annie could guess.

"Coward," Annie said. "I don't know why I ever agreed to this writers' conference. Too late for regrets now. Oh well, if you can't come with me physically, you'll have to come with me cybernetically. I'm taking my laptop. I'll write. Write me back, okay?"

Chapter 26

To jdepaul@aol.com
From ahollerman@aol.com
Subject: The Jewish Canon
Jack,

Drum roll, please. . . . Yesterday I cajoled (euphemism for threatened) Lynn McCain into giving her speech. She was terrific, and as far as I know, offended no one. Maybe I have a future as an editor. Isn't that what you guys do, bully people?

I know this runs counter to Philip Roth and the Jewish Mother canon, but my mother and I are having a blast. It's like we're old girlfriends, talking about everything. *Everything.* Tonight, I forced her and her best friend, Geri, to go to a part of Greensboro they'd never been so I could have barbecue.

She and Geri talked about all the men they'd had in their lives—two and one, respectively. When it was my turn, I just said, "You guys were born too early. You missed the Seventies." At that point my mother started talking about the new Piggly Wiggly that'd just opened. Some numbers are better left unmentioned.

Off we go to Asheville tomorrow to visit my

Buddhist/horse trailer salesman friend. I met him years
ago when I was desperate for clients and took on
anyone, and I mean anyone. Including "Mary, The Story
of an Unhappy Ewe"—390 excruciating pages of New Age
channelings from an English sheep who'd learned the key
to happiness. I'm not making this up.

Only desperation could explain trying to sell a book
about horse trailering. But the book sold easily. You
wouldn't believe how many little girls in America
(including Laura's) have pressed their parents into buying
first the horse, then the trailer. And Tom made a bundle,
for a horse-trailering book.

The truth is, I didn't just take him on because I was
desperate. I took Tom's book because he called me one
day with his pitch, and the next thing I knew we'd been
on the phone for an hour talking about cosmic truths I
hadn't thought of since I'd read "Siddhartha" in high
school.

So guess where Tom's taking us? To his Buddha-man's
meditation meeting, where you're supposed to find that
quiet place inside (I'm still looking) and be one with it
while your legs are pretzeled into yogi-like contortions,
your back is soldier-straight, and you pretend to ignore
the spasms pumping at the base of your spine and
screaming upwards. It's worked for him. He's the
calmest human being I know. And Lord knows, I could
use a little of that myself. Not to mention my mother,
who makes Pee-Wee Herman seem tranquil.

Then it'll be on to dinner where my mother and I will
rest our weary backs and have a long night of soulful
discussion.

Oh, by the way, there was one of those soft blue-velvet
skies this evening. I thought about you.
Annie

CHAPTER 27

That yoga thing was payback, admit it."

"I'm admitting nothing," Annie said. "Except how centered I feel—and you should feel. When's the last time you sat still for forty-five minutes?"

Joan Hollerman Silver clicked her Peach Iced fingernails against the plastic wood-grain corner table at Mr. C's Sea House. "Never," she said, examining the back of her left hand. She blew on her fingers and watched the gold whirligig on her ring twirl around.

Annie looked at her mother's nails. They were perfect, just like the rest of her. Ever since Annie could remember, her mother turned heads, even those of her high school boyfriends. ("Your mom's a fox," Joe Montone said to Annie in eleventh grade.) With her night-train hair, olive skin, and prominent cheekbones, Joan Hollerman Silver looked like a Middle Eastern Ava Gardner. Even at seventy-one, men watched as she walked by.

Her mother always looked pulled together, carefully riding the fashion trends. In the late sixties, Annie was wearing Indian print granny gowns and trying to wrestle her unruly hair straight by sleeping with it wrapped around orange juice cans. Meanwhile, Joan Hollerman Silver transformed the funky Carnaby Street look to elegance with her tailored miniskirts, tastefully patterned panty hose, ribbed Poor Boys, and sleek dark hair that curved obediently under her chin.

Annie's mother liked to look good; in fact, dressing up was her biggest hobby, next to playing video poker in the casinos. So when she gave birth to a daughter forty-four years ago, she was delighted that she'd have a little girl to follow in her Bruno Magli footsteps. Except the little girl was Annie, who, in five minutes, tore, stained, or crumpled all her perfect little outfits.

"I can't believe I let you talk me into going there. Couldn't we just have bonded at the beach?"

"Mom, now we're moving into payback territory. All those years in Atlantic City, with me blistering in the sand while you browned like a Thanksgiving turkey. That makes two things you didn't pass along to me, your dark skin and your . . ."

Annie pointed across the table to her mother's chest.

Joan Hollerman Silver was stacked. Built, as Annie's high school boyfriends used to whisper, like a brick shithouse. Annie's chest was constructed more like a wooden fence.

"I wasn't the only one responsible for your genes."

"Yeah," Annie said, "there's that. You could have at least chosen someone taller."

They laughed. It had taken them a long time to be able to laugh about Milt Hollerman, husband and father. He'd been a stocky, handsome man; some said he resembled the actor Victor Mature. On a Monday morning in May, when Annie was ten and Joan was thirty-seven, Annie woke up to find her father gone. No note, no good-bye, just an empty space in his closet—and in Annie's heart. He didn't come back for three years, and when he did, it was with a new wife and baby.

Fifteen years later, also on a Monday—but in November this time—he drove his sky blue Chrysler into a highway embankment near Newark. The weather had been clear; as far as investigators could determine from the wreckage, there had been nothing wrong with the car. New Jersey state troopers called the accident "suspicious" and closed the books. Nope, not a lot of chuckles there.

When the waiter came, Annie ordered broiled salmon, her mother a steak.

"Stop looking at me like that. I'm the mother, you're the daughter."

"Then start acting like it. *Steak?* Do I have to remind you how high your cholesterol is? I specifically brought you to a fish place. Omega-three fatty acids and all that stuff. If you don't start listening to me, I swear I'll bury you next to Milt."

"Such a mouth on you, Annie Beth Hollerman. You've been the most headstrong child since you were born—two months early. You couldn't even wait for your own due date."

They were heading into family legend territory. Annie and Joan had a set of stories they tossed back and forth, the way a father and son might toss a football.

"I know, I know," said Annie, "and you spent twenty-five dollars on a brown satin dress from Lord & Taylor that I cut to shreds."

"It was thirty-five dollars," Joan said, "and that was a lot of money forty years ago. A lot of money for a four-year-old pischer to throw away because she didn't like the drape of the bodice."

"It wasn't the drape," Annie said. "How many times do I have to tell you? It was the elastic. It was too tight around my waist and I was trying to cut it out. Much like the surgeons will be trying to cut out the plaque in your arteries."

Joan Hollerman Silver assessed her daughter carefully. Willful from the day she was born.

"So, you were telling me about Jack," she said.

"No I wasn't," said Annie, "I was telling you about your high cholesterol and clogged arteries."

"Funny, I could've sworn you said Jack. By the way, Laura called. She's already gotten her dress. And Becky's all set to be the flower girl. Maybe we can find a brown satin dress for her to wear—you could alter it first."

Annie threw her hands up in the air. "Okay," she said with a stagy sigh, "I'll stop about the steak. But no cigarettes while we're eating. It's disgusting."

Annie was going to add, "And Becky's too old to be a flower girl," but stopped. The sudden moment of stillness caught them both by surprise, and in that moment, like a freeze frame in a movie, mother and daughter just looked at each other.

For the 197th time since Annie had arrived in North Carolina yesterday, Joan Hollerman Silver had raised the name of Jack DePaul. Annie hadn't been able to bring herself to say what she was starting to feel about him. But now, to her own surprise, she was about to.

"You know, Mom, he's pretty terrific. But I guess Laura already told you that."

After all these years, her mother had finally learned when to be quiet. She just nodded.

"I mean, it's not like I know him all that well. But it seems like I do. I don't know, maybe it's wishful thinking, maybe I'm just trying to obliterate my years with Trip, but when I think about Jack, it's almost like Trip never happened."

Annie told her mother about the Spain e-mail; how, now, it seemed as if she had gone to Spain with Jack, not Trip.

"Too bad," Annie said, "I can't get him to write me a new *Charlotte Commercial-Appeal* chapter."

Annie's mother stiffened. She hated thinking about that time even more than she hated thinking about her first husband leaving or her second husband dying. The pain of watching her only child go through that kind of hell was bad enough; what made it worse was that she blamed herself.

Annie saw the look in her mother's eyes. "You know I've told you this before, but I want to say it again—I couldn't have made it through without you."

Her mother looked away for a second and gathered herself. "It would have never happened if I'd been a different kind of mother. If I'd been more—"

Annie grabbed her mother's hand. "Stop. We've been over this before. *I* made the choice. *I* made the mistake. It was *me*, not you, who lifted someone else's words. I was on deadline, pressed for time. I was scared that I'd lost it. That I wasn't Annie Wondergirl anymore. I panicked and made a bad decision. Maybe the world's worst decision. But that's it. It had nothing to do with you or your canasta games. So what if you never read me Dr. Seuss? And, so what if you wanted me to be more like Joan Cherry and run for class president and look like her in those dorky little Villager outfits? *That's* not why I plagiarized."

Plagiarized. What an ugly, plundering word. It sounded like a disease, which it was to Annie. Something akin to leprosy. And she'd been a leper all these years. In fact, that had been central to the unwritten contract between her and Trip. He was the good boy, she was the fuckup.

"Plagiarized," Annie said. "It's not the easiest word for me to say. But Jesus Christ, Mom, it's been almost twenty years. I've left Trip, my career's going gangbusters, and I'm dating a journalist, of all things. Don't you think it's time I should be able to say that word without it getting stuck in my throat?"

Annie took a swig of water and made a throat-clearing noise. "Care to join me?" she said. Then, to the tune of the Toreador Song from *Carmen*, she sang, "Play-ger-her-ii-iized, play-ger-her-ized, play-ger-herized oh play-ger-herized . . ."

To the waiter at Mr. C's Sea House, the two women at table 17 were cheap dates: one glass of wine and they were so tipsy, they were mangling *Carmen*.

Annie's mother raised her wineglass and said, "Finally."

They were about to toast when they realized the glasses were empty. Joan motioned to the waiter for two more glasses of wine. He nodded, turned, and rolled his eyes.

"So, are you going to tell him?" Joan said.

"Huh?" Annie said.

"Tell Jack. About what happened in Charlotte."

Annie ran her finger around the rim of the empty glass. "One step at a time, Mom."

Both women knew there were many steps between singing an aria to plagiarism and revealing your deepest shame to someone you cared about. She'd done it with Andrew, and he'd left her.

She'd done it with Trip, and he'd used it against her. The thought of doing it again made her queasy.

Joan reached her hand across the table and placed it on top of the wineglass, on top of Annie's hand. "I hope that step comes soon. Then you can be free of it once and for all."

Annie watched as her mother turned away, pretending to look for the waiter. "Did he go to France to get the wine?" Joan said. But Annie saw the tears in her mother's eyes.

"Finally," Joan said again—this time meaning the waiter, who was arriving with two glasses of wine and their meals. He put a shriveled piece of dry salmon in front of Annie and a big, oozing slab of meat in front of Joan.

Joan eyed Annie's meal. "Looks like something I cooked," she said.

"I didn't think that was possible, but you're right," Annie said. "So much for omega-three fatty acids."

"Hold on," Joan said. She took the serrated knife by her plate, cut her steak in half, and put it on the bread plate. "Here. Live a little."

CHAPTER 28

As soon as Annie and her mother returned to their hotel room, Annie checked her e-mail. She'd been thinking about last night's message to Jack on and off all day. Maybe she shouldn't have said the thing about the sky. Men like mystery. There was little mystery in "Oh, by the way, there was one of those soft blue-velvet skies this evening. I thought about you."

Annie wished she were the kind of person who could hold back. "I thought about you"—not much held back there. She wished she could be like Sofia, the Lebanese bombshell wife of her old boss, Greg Leeland. Once, when Annie was standing with some friends at a cocktail party, Sofia walked up. One of the men said, "Hey, Sofia. I haven't seen you in a while." Sofia speared him with a dangerous look and in her heavily accented English purred, "Eeet eees gooodt to be rrrare."

Annie felt about as rrrare as ragweed.

"I thought about you." Those words had nagged at her all day like a whiny three-year-old. Earlier at the Buddhist Learning Center, when she was supposed to be meditating on stillness, she was thinking about those four words and everything they might mean: she was starting to care about Jack in a way she hadn't cared about a man for years. Somehow Jack DePaul had found the dopamine floodgates in her brain and opened them wide. She was scared and excited at the same time; it felt like her blood was carbonated.

She'd spent the next forty-five minutes sitting cross-legged on a forest green carpet with her eyes closed, trying as hard as she could to chase away conscious thought. Every time she wiped her mind clear, those four words bounced back.

"I thought about you."

Well, Annie thought, I did think about you. Why not say it? And if that scares you away, Jack DePaul, so be it.

Annie clicked on the mail flag. There was a message from Jack, entitled "I thought about you, too."

Maybe Sofia was wrong. Maybe eet wass goodt to be forthrrrright.

To ahollerman@aol.com
From jdepaul@aol.com
Subject: I thought about you, too
Annie,

There was a soft blue-velvet sky here, too. Not in Baltimore—has there ever been a soft blue-velvet sky over Baltimore?—but one in my memory, from an August day years ago. Your words—"soft," "velvet"—made me think of it. And I wondered: how can I explain that particular sky, that particular day, to Annie? How it turned maroon then navy as the sun dropped away. How bright the night was, how warm. How a young boy crossed the street from his house and entered a moon-licked orchard full of ripening apricots and furrows of black water.

How he ran through that orchard, from furrow top to furrow top; ran from tree row to tree row, in and out of moonlight as bright as a neon sign. How the leaves were like wrought iron against the sky. How the boy ran from black to white to black to white, more moonchild than manchild. How the aurora of a county fair flickered on the northern horizon and how, muffled by the summer-swollen leaves, the calliope jangle of the midway sounded no louder than the ghostly twitter of bats.

I wondered about all of that. And I thought about you.
Jack

Annie slumped against the padded headboard on her bed, the laptop resting on her thighs. She'd been holding her breath and didn't even know it. "Whew," she said.

"You okay?" her mother said through a mouthful of toothpaste. Ostensibly, she'd been brushing her teeth at the sink, but thanks to a well-placed mirror she'd been watching Annie since her daughter had plopped down on the bed and plugged in her computer.

"Yikes," said Annie as she fanned her face with her hand.

"How's Jack?" her mother asked.

"How'd you know?"

"Annie, what am I, an idiot? You rush in the room like there's a fire in the hall and grab your computer before you even take your shoes off. I'm not halfway inside and you're already checking your e-mail. There's only one thing that gets someone to move that fast, and it's not business. So, what'd he say?"

"Mom, he wrote me the sweetest letter. It was kind of old-fashioned. It made me feel like someone from a Jane Austen novel."

Joan Hollerman Silver smiled, a toothpaste crescent moon on her face. "Courting through cyberspace. How modern. Annie, I don't suppose you'd like me to read what he wrote. I could help you write a reply and—"

Annie held up her hand. "Forget it, Ma. If I let you read this, I might as well print it out and post it in your office. I've got it handled. I know exactly what I'm going to write back."

To jdepaul@aol.com
From ahollerman@aol.com
Subject: Don't Stop
Jack,

I could almost hear your calliope. Don't stop. Send me more. And next time, take me with you. Take me to places I've never been. Give me a new past to remember.
Annie

CHAPTER 29

And so it started. For that week, Jack's and Annie's nights belonged to e-mail, and, message by message, memory by memory, the story of their history began to unfold.

Each evening, Annie returned to her hotel room, plugged in her computer, hit the little red flag, and found, awaiting her, chapters of a life she never knew she had. She visited jungles, rocky coasts, and deserts and never left her hotel room.

Each evening, Jack would sit in front of his outdated Mac and force inspiration to come his way. It was slow going at first. He even started to feel some sympathy for his reporters. Maybe they aren't just whiners, Jack thought. Maybe there's something to their bellyaching; he'd forgotten how hard it was to be creative on command.

Some nights he'd work far into the next morning, fueled by microwave pizza, calcium-fortified grapefruit juice, and Annie's return e-mails. By the third night, the words were flying so fast from his fingers, he decided he was right the first time—reporters are whiners.

Her request, "Take me to places I've never been," was lighter fluid to his imagination. He was starting to feel young again—energized, alive, swelling with possibility. The idea of rewriting—creating—Annie's past was powerful and powerfully attractive. At first he wasn't sure why, but later, looking past the pixels, he could see that maybe, if he could write her another life, he could write himself one, too.

Annie wasn't the only one who'd missed the dance. For maybe the thousandth time in the past twenty years, Jack cringed at the memory of a five-minute phone call to the Peace Corps, turning down the Togo teaching assignment for a managerial position at the *San Diego Tribune*.

These new chapters he was writing would have everything his old ones lacked: adventure, passion, and laughter. And this time, he'd be with the right person. He wondered if Annie was the one. And he decided, as he often did, to ask Pablo Neruda.

CHAPTER 30

To ahollerman@aol.com
From jdepaul@aol.com
Subject: Annie's Trip to Chile
Annie,

Pablo Neruda was trouble. I knew that. Of course, I knew that. I don't know why I introduced you. I must have been crazy. He was an aging, balding man with a big round nose who looked like a chubby Picasso, but women gravitated to him like apples to Newton's head. And he gravitated back.

He liked redheads in particular. Loved them, really. Matilde Urrutia was a redhead; he married her twice and wrote her books of poetry. And still I. . . .

But you know the story as well as I. You were there.

You met Pablo at that fancy party in Valparaiso. Remember the house—it belonged to a foreign minister—and the huge double staircase? I can still picture you in that coppery silk dress, stunning against a backdrop of tuxedos.

We had joined a circle of people surrounding Pablo, who was talking about whales, of all things. He was very funny, going on about blowholes and volcanoes, his slightly bulging eyes glinting mischievously. When I introduced you to him, he looked you over and said to me, "Well, Pablito"—he always called me "Pablito," meaning "little Paul"—"maybe I've underestimated you."

He was about to say something clever—I could see in his eyes that he was making poetic calculations—when a waiter passed by with a tray of champagne glasses. Someone took a glass from the tray and, turning back, spilled its entire contents over the front of your dress. You cried out. The whole party stopped dead in its tracks and stared at the beautiful woman with the huge dark stain across her chest.

Naturally, Pablo came to the rescue. "My dear," he said, "we can't let this accident spoil your night. Here, let me take away the sting of it." And he took a glass from the waiter's tray and splashed the front of his tuxedo jacket with the contents. There was a collective gasp. What a gesture. "Now," he said, "you're not alone."

People applauded. Everybody in our group took a glass and toasted to "spilled champagne." Of course, you thanked him; of course, the two of you chatted; of course, one thing led to another, as it always does with Pablo Neruda, and three nights later we were heading to his house for dinner.

From Valparaiso, it took us more than an hour to drive to his house, Isla Negra (that's what he called his place, "Black Island"). It sat on a cliff overlooking the ocean. The air smelled of seaweed and earth. On the horizon, the setting sun turned the undersides of the clouds a dusky orange.

Pablo came out to greet us. He shook our hands and, making an offhand gesture to the clouds, he said to you, "How delightful, they're turning the color of your hair." Big deal, I thought, I could have said that.

He opened the front door for us. "Welcome to Isla Negra," he said. The room was filled with fantastical things. The mermaid prow of a ship jutted from a staircase. The window ledges were lined with crazy bottles of every color. Devil figurines hung from the ceiling; a collection of beetles hung on a wall. Grinning African masks surrounded a fireplace. There were telescopes, astrolabes, signs for eyeglasses, signs for a grocery, a collection of costume hats. It was like stepping into a poet's mind and finding the place where all the images are stored.

"Pablo, it's wonderful," you said. "Where did it all come from?"

I looked at you. Where did this "Pablo" come from? What happened to "Senor Neruda"?

Pablo shrugged. "Here and there, I travel so much. These are my toys, I find them everywhere. As I got older I discovered I couldn't live without them. The child who doesn't play with toys isn't a child. But the man who doesn't play has lost forever the child who lived within him. So I built Isla Negra like a toy house. I can play here all day long."

You laughed and clapped your hands, and spun round like a little girl.

"Yeah, it's terrific," I said. "Whaddya got to drink?"

Pablo thumped his forehead lightly with the heel of a hand. "You're right. Forgive me. Let's go to the dining room."

He led us through more rooms, each one filled with stuff. Butterflies, canes, carved frogs, crystal vases, a huge paper mache horse, desks made from doors. It took us forty-five minutes to get to our destination. You had questions about everything and he had a story about everything.

The dining room was extravagant, too. In the center was a heavy oak farm table that seated twelve. At one corner were three place settings, each different from the other. There was a Dutch door at the far end of the room leading to the kitchen; an ornately carved sideboard held wines and liquor bottles. The left wall of the room was filled with paintings, including a portrait of his wife

Matilde signed by Diego Rivera; the right wall sprouted twenty little shelves, each one displaying an antique pistol.

Pablo took three glass tumblers from the sideboard and poured a cola-colored liqueur into them. "What's this?" I asked, holding it up to the light of a chandelier made from colored beads.

"An elixir from the Orient," said Pablo, looking impish. He raised his drink and we again toasted to spilled champagne. The liqueur was bittersweet and had an aftertaste of walnuts. He filled the tumblers again. This time we toasted old friends and new acquaintances. We toasted many things that night.

You and I were the sole dinner guests. The only other person in Isla Negra besides Pablo was a cook who, from time to time, popped open the top of the Dutch door to deliver another dish.

The food was not ornate. One course consisted simply of fresh tomatoes with coarse salt; another was a plate of marinated mushrooms. We ate grilled sea bass sprinkled with herbs, small red potatoes roasted with garlic, a crusty bread. The flavors exploded in my mouth. At least, that's how I remember it, thinking back through the haze of years and alcohol. One thing is certain: we had a lot to drink that night. Liqueurs, wines, and—for old time's sake—champagne.

The food and drink and hours flowed on and Pablo did, too. In his measured, sleepy voice, he told us tales of his youth, his diplomatic years in Asia, his love for the people and mountains and rocks and trees of Chile. Everything Pablo did was an adventure; every famous person his friend; everything was poetry. He was a raconteurial tidal wave.

But you weren't intimidated at all. You were bold and brazen and uninhibited. You also were more than slightly drunk. You matched him story for story. He told us about winning the Nobel Prize, you told him about winning your fourth-gade poster contest. He talked about Che Guevara and his rebels; you talked about the She-Devil and her rebels.

It must have been almost 2 a.m. when it happened. You had started to tell him about our night with Renatta Vega-Marone, when Pablo looked up to the ceiling and slapped his hands against his chest. "Ah, Rennie," he said, "what a woman."

"You knew her?" we exclaimed together.

"Oh, yes," Pablo replied. "We met, maybe twenty years ago. It was in a little hill town behind Cordoba. She and her gypsy friends kept me captive for two days."

"Captive?" I said.

"Perhaps I exaggerate a little. It was complicated. Anyway, she said she would dance for me if I would write her poetry." He put out his hands, palms up. "What could I do? I said, 'Yes.' She danced. I wrote."

"How many poems did you write her?" you asked him.

"Many, many. I don't remember. In the end, I exchanged the poems for my freedom." He said all this with such a sly expression that I wondered if any of it was true.

Pablo must have seen the look on my face, for he said, "I see you doubt this story, Pablito. Do not doubt it." And abruptly he stood up.

Moving with inebriated care, Pablo climbed onto his chair and, from there, stepped to the top of the big table. Tiptoeing deftly past the glasses and plates, he reached the middle of the room. Turning to face us, he slowly arched his back and dramatically raised his arms above his head. He began dancing, deliberately at first. A clap of the hands above his head, a stomp of the boot heel against the tabletop. Clap. Stomp. Clap. Stomp. Then faster. Clamp/stomp, clamp/stomp, clamp/stomp. And faster, making the plates and glasses rattle to the rhythm. Then, with a wild yodeling sound, he stomped to a halt.

We cheered like he'd just scored a game-winning touchdown. You put two fingers in your mouth and whistled like a stevedore.

Pablo bowed, grinning broadly. "You see, Pablito?" he said. "I was a captive." Then he motioned to you. "Come, red-haired Annie. Be my Renatta. Dance with me."

Before I could blink, you were on the table facing Pablo, hands over your head, matching him clap for clap, stomp for stomp. I don't remember how long it went on—the dancing, the laughter, the tipsy bodies entwined—but when the two of you nearly fell off the table following a particular flourish, I said, "Okay, you two. Let's call it a night. Come on, Annie, we should go."

"Ah, Pablito," he said, "the night is still dark. Stay. Learn. Learn to live a little."

"I don't think so," I said. "It's time for us to go." I reached up a hand to help you down.

"No, Pablito. I won't let you take her. She's my captive," he said, and stepped down onto one of the chairs, braced himself against a wall, took a pistol from one of the shelves, and pointed it at me.

Things happened very quickly after that—though I can still see each moment clearly, as if in a sequential series of photographs.

You grabbed a wine bottle from the table. "Don't do it, Pablo!" you shouted. And you threw the bottle at him. The bottle hit Pablo a glancing blow on the head. I ducked. The gun fired.

Well, the gun didn't exactly fire. Pablo pulled the trigger and a little flag, with the word "BANG" on it, came out the end of the barrel.

Pablo collapsed on the chair. We rushed over to him, but he was okay. In fact, he was laughing. Laughing so hard he couldn't speak.

Oh, yes. Pablo was trouble. And I wouldn't have had it any other way.

Jack

CHAPTER 31

That night, instead of reading the day's writing samples from the students of the ninth annual Tar Heel Writers' Conference, Annie was staring into space. Or more accurately, time.

The fact that it was a time that never existed was irrelevant. Now a copper silk dress with a champagne stain down the front hung in her memory as clearly as the white shorts she'd worn to Friday night services at Camp Reeta. And Pablo Neruda would forever be just Pablo to her.

Annie replayed the scenes at Isla Negra—dancing on the table was her favorite, but the grin on Pablo's face as the "BANG" flag popped out was unforgettable. Such mischief in one pair of lips.

She knew she should be writing comments on the stack of papers in front of her. Instead, she hit the reply button on Jack's e-mail.

To jdepaul@aol.com
From ahollerman@aol.com
Subject: Dancing Devils
Pablito,
   Pablo called last night. To tell me I was doing God's work: encouraging would-be writers, even if they have no more talent than a termite. And after today's session at the conference, termites aren't looking very talented.

If only it were true, that Pablo Neruda could call me. I could use some sage words from the master about now. He'd have known what to tell the man who wrote "Glock Speaks," a first-person mystery from the gun's point of view. And he'd have known how to answer your e-mail, how to match you word for exquisite word.

Instead you'll have to do with my words. Two to start with: Thank you.

I loved our trip to Chile.

Though I'd forgotten about the devils hanging from the ceiling. Did I ever tell you I dreamt about them? That night in my drunken stupor? Remember when we got back to our hotel room, I'd cocked my fingers into a gun, pointed at you, and said, "Bang, bang." We fell on the bed laughing. Then I passed out—way too much elixir—and the next thing I saw were Pablo's devils, dancing around me.

At first they were laughing. Then they started dancing closer and closer—they definitely weren't laughing anymore. I tried to run away, but one of them grabbed my foot. I should have been scared, but I was mad.

When I was eleven there was a bogeyman who waited for me in my dreams nearly every night. He looked like Jethro from the Beverly Hillbillies except he was mean and hairy and half his teeth were missing. He'd always chase me, getting so close I'd wake up in a panic. Then one night, just as he was about to pounce, I got tired of being scared. I yelled at him as loud as I could, "Get out of here!" The bogeyman froze, looked at me in surprise, and melted just like the Wicked Witch of the West.

The night after our dinner with Pablo, I did the same thing with the devils. But instead of melting, they sulked away, a silly bunch of red-faced demons dragging their tails between their legs. The next thing I remembered was waking up with a very bad headache, snuggled in your arms.

Annie

CHAPTER 32

Snuggled in your arms." A sweet phrase, Jack thought. Sweet as a Krispy Kreme. (His stock of similes was low: it was 9:15 in the morning and the coffee hadn't kicked in.)

Jack would have preferred to meditate on the last four words of Annie's most recent e-mail but he had to postpone the luxury. First thing on the morning's agenda: Arthur Steinberg.

Steinberg's desk was at the far end of the Features department. Jack worked his way there circuitously, as if he were sneaking up on a wild mustang. First he popped in on the managing editor, next he talked to the family editor about a Father's Day story, then he tried to convince the classical music critic that the Persuasions coming in behind Phoebe Snow on "San Francisco Bay Blues" was a sublime moment in musical history (a discussion that only got him committed to the next concert by Baltimore's Handel Society), and then he chatted with a Features reporter about a story on the Chesapeake Bay's crab patrol. Only after all that did he finally approach Steinberg himself.

"How's it going, Arthur?" he asked.

Steinberg flinched like a rabbit that's just felt the raptor's shadow. "Fine," he said with a wary smile. "Fine."

Jack leaned on Steinberg's computer terminal. The desk below him was piled with files and clippings, as well as crumpled tissues, wrappers, and mummified bits of food. Steinberg was a dour pack rat with frizzy hair and wire-rim glasses; he had a pack rat's irritating diligence and personal hygiene. If he weren't such a smart and elegant writer, the paper and the city fire marshal would have evicted him years before.

Jack smiled down; Steinberg tensed. He knew what was coming next.

"What's the status of the Camden Yards story?"

"Almost done, Jack. Maybe another week."

"Arthur, I know this will come as a shock to you, but the *Star-News* has decided to publish daily, not monthly."

"You were the one who wanted Camden Yards to be a big Sunday blowout, Jack. It takes time."

"Yeah, yeah, Arthur, but in between Camden interviews I want you to start on this 'Thief of Words' thing that I told you about. At least get the library going on a Nexis search for other newspaper plagiarists."

"I did that already," Steinberg said in a voice full of righteousness. "And the Camden interviews are done. I'm starting to write."

Jack was about to say something snide about taking a week to write the Camden Yards story, but decided Steinberg's eggshell ego couldn't take it. Instead, he updated him on Ellen Gammerman's part of "Thief." It seems that the *Pittsburgh Press* plagiarist had only reluctantly agreed to an interview; he wasn't going to give them much. Gammerman had decided to broaden the story with experts and other cases.

Jack headed back to his desk, this time in a straight line. After he attended the morning editors' meeting and gave the lobbyist story a final read-through, it was nearly noon. So he grabbed his gym bag and headed out to the Athletic Club. He would pedal the stationary bike for forty-five minutes, watch the lunchtime basketball players, and think about Jack-and-Annie e-mail.

"Snuggled in your arms." A brilliant phrase, he decided, better than anything Arthur Steinberg ever had written or ever would write. Jack sat down in front of a locker and opened up his bag.

"Snuggled," he said aloud, drawing a puzzled frown from a hairy-backed guy toweling himself off.

Jack poked his once-flat stomach and squeezed his soft left biceps. "Snuggled in your arms." *I need to start lifting weights again,* he thought.

Later that night, arms sore from three sets of fifty-pound curls, he wrote the following:

To ahollerman@aol.com
From jdepaul@aol.com
Subject: Annie, the snake slayer
Annie,

I remember the Jethro nightmare. You told me about it the day we biked to McIntyre's ranch. That was before you lived in New Jersey, when you lived in Hemet, California, a little town just a mountain away from the desert. You and your mother lived at 317 W. Tremont St. It was a completely ordinary house except for two things: it sat across from an apricot orchard and was three doors down from me.

We knew each other from first to sixth grade. It was at the beginning of junior high, just when we began to see each other with completely different eyes, that you moved East.

We were best pals. You were Dorothy, I was the Tin Man; you were Guinevere, I was Lancelot. We did everything together. We biked all over, from the Ramona Bowl to the Soboba Hot Springs, to the hole in the mountain they said was an old uranium mine. You told me I would glow at night afterwards—and I believed you. I even checked in the bathroom mirror one night. We read a million books and swung for hours on the swings in your backyard. We named the clouds.

One Sunday in April, when we were both eleven, your mother packed a big lunch, put an old tablecloth in the trunk of her white Impala, and drove us over the mountain and down toward the desert for a picnic.

It was cool driving up to the pines but warm as a muffin on the other side. About halfway to the desert floor we pulled off to an overlook. Below us stretched range after range of dry hills and wide valleys. It seemed like we could see clear to Arizona; it seemed like we could see the curve of the earth.

The mountainside, brown and lifeless in the summer, now sparkled with spring. A short jump down from the overlook was a meadow dotted with color. Your mother thought it might be a good picnic spot, so she scrambled down the rocks to investigate and we came climbing after.

In the meadow, every cactus blossom was a different shade of yellow or magenta. There were flame-tipped ocotillo, tiny golden daisies, greenish-white jimson trumpets and the deepest purple wild indigo. We ran all over. We chased a blue-striped lizard. We popped the hollow brown pods of a strange bush covered with white flowers. You told me they were from the planet Mars and the pod dust could defeat our enemies.

After we had spent hours in the meadow, or maybe it was only 20 minutes, your mother decided it was too rocky for picnicking. She told us to go back to the car and we'd continue on. You climbed up first; I followed a few yards behind. When you made it to the top, I was just below you on a flat granite boulder. I was looking for the best route up when I heard a loud cht-cht-cht-cht-cht. My heart froze. Not six feet away was a rattlesnake, coiled, head raised. Its rattle vibrating like a blender. "Jump, Jack!" yelled your mother. But I was too scared.

Everything disappeared—the meadow, the road, the great blue bowl of the sky—everything but the rattlesnake. I remember thinking, in the middle of my fear, how beautiful it was, with its shining diamond skin.

"Don't move!" you yelled. This was better advice, since I couldn't make myself move anyway. And suddenly,

CRASH, a rock the size of a pony smashed down by the snake and careened into the meadow.

I looked up at you and back at the snake. It had disappeared; gone, like a conjuring trick. Had you knocked it off, or had it just slithered away? We never knew. "Are you okay?" you asked. "I'm fine," I said. "It's gone."

I climbed up to you. "Thanks," I said, "thanks, Guinevere." "No problem, Lance," you replied, and we slapped our palms together.

That memory is still vivid, not because it was traumatic—I never had nightmares about it—but because it was our first grand adventure together.

We continued to the desert valley and had our picnic by a wash lined with creosote bushes and mesquite trees. We spent the rest of the day driving along county roads and exploring a desert gone crazy with flowers.

In late afternoon we stopped by a stretch of sand dunes. You and I jumped out and ran up the nearest one. "Look out for snakes!" your mother yelled. The sand was very soft, for every two steps up, we sunk one step back. But eventually we reached the summit.

Before us, the ridges of the dune field coiled across the valley floor like great serpents. To the southwest was the mountain, its eastern slopes a melancholy blue. Overhead, wisps of cloud began to glow pink and salmon in the fading sky. Behind, your mother watched us from the hood of the car.

On top of the world, we stood. And then you reached out for me and I reached out for you. And, holding hands, we hurtled down the face of the dune, rolling, tumbling, somersaulting until the sky was the sand and the sand was the clouds and the clouds were the dunes and the dunes were the mountains and the mountains were the road and the road was the flowers. And everything was everything.

Jack

CHAPTER 33

Annie had come armed to the Rhododendron Room of the Asheville Hilton. A stack of books sat between her and the twenty-three hungry faces staring at her. She'd been talking so long that the sound of her own voice was beginning to irritate her. Yet still they listened with an almost preternatural concentration, some furiously taking notes, others nodding in earnest agreement, as if hidden in her words was the secret that could ward off all the rejection notes of the future.

". . . And these," Annie said, pointing to the stack of novels, "are your best friends. If you want to be a writer, read. And I'm not talking about how-to books. I'm talking about learning from those who do. Gabriel García Márquez for the fabulous, John Steinbeck for simplicity, Daphne du Maurier for tension, Kazuo Ishiguro for control—which we all could use more of—Barbara Kingsolver for heart, and never forget Vladimir Nabokov. His love affair with words should be a lesson to us all. Words. That's what I'm talking about."

Annie's voice grew louder; her index finger jabbed at a ragged, marked-up copy of *Lolita*.

"Words," she said. "Beautiful, evocative, scary, cold, bitter, harsh, sweet, silly words. Words. That's why we got into this business, right? Because we love them; we love how they make us see and feel and hear. How they take us to places we've never been; how they shape our mind, our memory; how they can show us anything and everything, where everything is everything . . ."

Annie had gotten so worked up that she'd closed her eyes, and before she realized it, Jack's latest e-mail had invaded her mind.

When she opened them again, she saw three hands raised in the air.

"Yes, Abbi?" she said to the dark-haired woman with the star and moon earrings who'd written a novel about gypsies.

"When you say, 'Everything is everything,' do you mean that whatever we write, we should make sure that all the words are equally important and—"

Annie waved her hand. "Good try, Abbi. The truth is, I was just blathering. Let's get back to the real issue—how to get published."

For the next hour, Annie explained how to beat the odds in the publishing business, even though she knew how long those odds were. The day's session ended with critiques with would-be authors.

In the afternoon, Annie and her mother took a sightseeing drive. Then they ate dinner at a vegan restaurant that Abbi the gypsy writer had recommended. To Annie's surprise, her mother actually liked the tofu gyro and wanted to order the tofu crème soufflé for dessert. But Annie made her order the raw sweet potato pie to go instead. The soufflé would take an extra twenty minutes and she was anxious to get back to the hotel room to write to Jack.

To jdepaul@aol.com
From ahollerman@aol.com
Subject: Everything
Jack,

I'm still dizzy from our tumble. Rolling down hills has always been one of my favorite things to do, and now I remember why.

Annie Hollerman of Hemet, Ca.—I like that. I like the way it feels. I particularly like the idea of my mother packing a picnic lunch (her idea of cooking was defrosting) and scrambling down a rock, except I don't know if Donna Karan makes hiking boots.

And I would have slayed that snake for you.

After my talk, where I warped out into the power of words (and quoted you, by the way), I met with five writers whose works I had critiqued. There wasn't a talking gun in the bunch, thank God. Though three had written mysteries. Talk about glut. There's a mystery sub-genre for every niche you could imagine: food, dogs, cats, horses, boats, suffragettes, priests, nuns, rabbis, psychics, Buddhists, nihilists. And that's not including the disabilities: quadriplegics, paraplegics, agoraphobics, the hearing impaired, the sight impaired, not to mention the sleuth with Tourette's syndrome.

Mercifully, the mystery writers I talked to today didn't dabble in medical oddities. One of them was actually pretty good. His book was about a garbage man, of all things. I think he's actually discovered a new sub-genre: trash.

In the late afternoon, my mother and I took a spin around the mountains here. I'd love to show you Asheville. It's beautiful. They call it the Sedona of the East, because it's got a ton of weird quartz configurations they call vortexes, just like the ones in Arizona. Supposedly, the vortexes provide the perfect spiritual vibrational pull, kind of like a DSL line to God.

Say what you will about the new age mumbo jumbo of the magnetic pull in the world's oldest mountains, but when the deep lavender mist hangs low in the Smokies and creates an echo of peaks and valleys, it's a stirring sight that can churn up spiritual rumblings in the most skeptical of souls.

Even my mother, who's about as spiritual as Judge Judy, was awed by the beauty of these mountains. We were driving up and down the blacktopped curves of a road so shiny and new it was like floating on a black satin ribbon. Just as we got to the bottom of a little valley, we passed a waterfall.

Waterfalls aren't unusual in the Smokies, but there was something startling in the perfection of this one. Maybe it was the way the rocks aligned and caught the sun, or the innocent clarity of the water, or the green of the surrounding forest, or maybe it was that my mother and I had finally found the way to love each other for who we are, as opposed to who we're not. Whatever it was, it took us both by surprise.

I pulled the car to the shoulder and stopped. We were silent for a few moments as we watched the water tumble over the rocks. "It's like it's holy," my mother said. I could barely hear her; she said it so softly.

We sat there for about ten minutes and when I drove away, she said, "I felt like organ music was going to start any second. I've never seen anything so beautiful."

I thought about writing you there with me, as you've been writing me places with you. But then I realized it would change the memory, as your writings have changed my memories. And this memory, this shared moment with my mother, is one to keep.

There must be something to this vortex thing. After the waterfall trip, I've been feeling a strange desire to eat brown rice, throw the I Ching coins and denounce my earthly possessions. So the next time we meet—how about dinner at my place Saturday night?—I'll be the one dressed in orange and magenta with my head shaved smooth.

Annie, the snake slayer

CHAPTER 34

Laura Goodbread walked up to the mezzanine conference room near the national desk. She was a few minutes early for the meeting; only Kathleen Faulkner was there, sitting at the conference table. Kathleen glanced up at Laura, then resumed checking things off on that day's story budget for the Metro section.

There had been a daily 4 P.M. news meeting at the *Star-News* since Gutenberg was a paperboy. It had been pushed ahead to 4:15 in the early nineties, but out of habit or tradition everybody still called it "the four o'clock." (The name stayed the same even during the Gulf War, when it had been held at 3:30 to accommodate breaking military news.)

The four o'clock was usually wall-to-wall editors—one from each department—but on this day, Laura Goodbread had been deputized to represent Features because Jack was busy and the other Feature bigwigs were unavailable. Laura didn't mind; she secretly enjoyed the four o'clock, its unvarying routine reinforced all her prejudices that editors were rigid, soul-sucking pod people. And, in Laura's opinion, Kathleen Faulkner was the queen soul-sucker.

Laura sat down on the opposite side of the table and looked her over. Could her Jack DePaul hunch be true? Would he be attracted to her? Kathleen was cool and tightly wound; Jack was warm and loose as old sweat socks. Still, she had a patrician beauty and Jack was a competitive little bastard. Laura could see him chasing her just for the pure challenge of it.

Next through the conference-room door came Cleo Brown, a wire editor, and Thurman Descanso from Business. Cleo and Laura had arrived at the *Star-News* around the same time and had roomed together for a few months. Cleo slapped her budget down on the table and squeezed her considerable bulk into a chair.

"How's the DePaul project going?" she asked Laura.

"Great, just call me Yenta, the matchmaker," Laura said.

"What's the DePaul project?" Descanso asked.

"A few weeks ago I fixed Jack up with a friend of mine from D.C., a literary agent," said Laura. She noticed that Kathleen had glanced up from her papers, so she looked at her directly when she added, "I think they're in love. DePaul's writing her e-mail poetry."

Kathleen looked down quickly but stopped writing, her pencil remaining frozen above the papers.

"DePaul? Poetry? Jesus, what's the newsroom coming to?" Descanso said.

"Don't be an animal, Thurm," said Laura. "Unlike the Business department, we have sensitive souls in Features."

Descanso, a tidy man who wore tailored suits and got a haircut every two weeks, grinned broadly; he liked being called an animal. "Does this literary agent have a name? Maybe she'd like to meet a real man."

"Annie Hollerman," said Laura. "But you're too late, Thurm, she's taken."

More editors came into the room, beginning the usual hubbub. Laura noticed that Kathleen's pencil still hadn't moved.

Thirty minutes later, the meeting ended with tomorrow's page one stories mapped out.

Laura headed back to the Features department, followed by Kathleen, who passed her on the way to Jack's desk.

"We missed you at the four o'clock," Kathleen said to Jack, who was pretending to be on the phone. "It's just not the same without you."

Jack had also pretended not to notice her approach. But an image, like a flashback from a fevered opium dream, had arrived in advance of her: naked Kathleen, back arched, legs spread, sweat. Jack looked up at the demure version in front of him and wondered if there was such a thing as the devil.

"I'm sure the four o'clock will survive without me," he said. "What's up?"

"Nothing much. Just wanted to check with you about the conference. Proctor and I are both taking the nine-seventeen Metroliner to New York. If you do, too, then we can all get a cab together to the hotel."

"I don't know yet when I'm going."

"You should book now," said Kathleen. "The train was filling up when I called last week."

"Yeah. I've been procrastinating. I did book a room, however."

A miniature smile shaped Kathleen's mouth. "I know," she said. "I'm three doors down."

"What a coincidence." Jack said it as sarcastically as he could, but felt a tiny jolt of excitement surge across his chest anyway.

"Yes, isn't it?" she said and walked away.

Jack stared daggers at her. Bitch, he thought, you think you can play me like a trout. Well, we'll see who's hooked and who's not. But the aftershocks of that jolt vibrated on, and, to his shame, he could feel a little glow of triumph deep inside: she had come crawling back.

Jack rubbed his face in his hands. Okay, he thought, the devil may exist, but now I have the exorcist—Annie Hollerman.

CHAPTER 35

That night the exorcism rites were held at the base of Jack's old Mac. He considered her previous e-mail, the one inviting him to dinner. At her place.

At her place. That could only mean one thing.

She's just upped the ante—again, Jack thought. Now it's my turn. Okay, Annie Hollerman, fasten your seat belt.

To ahollerman@aol.com
From jdepaul@aol.com
Subject: The Tiger
Dear Annie,

Saturday sounds great. But how about here, in Baltimore? I promised to loan my car to Matthew for the weekend, so I can't drive down to D.C. Shall I make dinner reservations? I know just the place. The food isn't great (this is Baltimore after all), but the view is. Say 7:30. Come to my apartment, and we'll drive to Remmy's.

Before I see you in person, I have another story to tell you. It begins in Nepal.

Annie is there. Jack has taken her. It comes to her like a dream—her memories of that thin jungle, where the

newborn Ganges braids and unbraids the Himalayas.
They are there to see a tiger. They are there to find each
other.

Annie didn't know the place existed, this place of
rattan and teak, with a porch exactly as high as the back
of an elephant. She didn't know that lantern light turns
the walls to honey; that iridescent moths call out the
night and drum against the window screens to awaken
the stars.

She didn't know, until Jack brought her there. Brought
her to a room full of shadows, a room with a bed, a
chair, a rattan chest, a bed stand, a ceramic basin, and
a pitcher of water.

Over the bed a ceiling fan slowly moves the heat
around. Across the bed lies a cover full of colors. It was
stitched together by old women who have forgotten love
and only remember how things end. Its pattern is as old
as the river.

Annie sits on the bed barefoot, arms around her
knees, and watches Jack turn the lantern down to an
ember and take off his traveler's things. She watches the
shadows slip around his body, naked as the moon,
touching him everywhere. She rises and pours water into
the basin. She dampens a hand towel and wipes the long
dusty day from Jack's skin.

And then she is a shadow, too, touching him, kissing
him, her tongue fluttering, flying all over him. Then her
sighs mix with the sounds of the forest. The hoo, hoo,
hoo of monkeys. The barking of miniature deer. The
brrrrrr of insects.

Slowly, the shadows shadow each other. Slowly, until
there is a sound, a deep cough, outside somewhere in
the forest. Then the shadows stop and the cicadas stop
and the infinite forest rustlings are swallowed up. And in
the silence, Annie's sighs echo back to her. Jack picks
her up and carries her from the bed, out to the railing at

the far edge of the lantern glow. He holds her with his body. She is filled with him and filled with the night. They look down into the darkness.

There is another cough. It's off to the left, not far. It is a tiger, at the edge of the forest, come to see them. For a moment the forest holds its breath. Every foot is frozen above dry leaves. Annie has never heard a stillness so loud. Then a star skitters down the Milky Way. The forest sighs and begins to speak again. Frogs start a rhythmic churrrt, churrrt. Crickets pick up the gossip.

The tiger has gone, but he will never leave them. For now, Jack and Annie cannot help but know that there's something there. And it's powerful and it's beautiful and it's real.

Jack

CHAPTER 36

Annie scrolled back to the top of Jack's e-mail. She began to reread it, then stopped and looked over at the other bed. Her mother lay on her back, making soft snoring noises, like a miniature choo-choo train. Satisfied that her mother was asleep, Annie returned to the laptop screen and scrunched down deep into the pillows and even deeper into the forests of Nepal.

When she came back, she lay against the pillows in the darkened hotel room, her face fluoresced by the glowing green portal to another world and time. After a few minutes she straightened up, smiled at the screen propped against her legs, and started tapping the keyboard, thankful that her mother had always been a heavy sleeper.

To jdepaul@aol.com
From ahollerman@aol.com
Subject: Cat's-eye Green
Dear Jack,
   Dinner in Baltimore sounds great. I can't wait. We can talk about tigers and jungle and other steamy things that now are embedded in my memory.
   I'm becoming like Lynn McCain—you know, my reluctant mystery writer. She also confuses what's real with what's written. Her books are very autobiographical;

the characters are based on her family members and the sleuth is basically her. Though she makes up some of the stories, many come from her life. She once told me she can't remember anymore which ones are real and which ones are fiction. I used to think she was exaggerating, just getting carried away with her Appalachian storytelling schtick.

But after traveling the world in your e-mails, I know what she's talking about. Words can etch into your mind and change your memories.

Who'd have thought memory to be so malleable? You grow up believing what you remember is true, that memory is like steel: stiff, unbending, impervious. But age changes certainty, doesn't it? Instead of steel, memory seems more like lead, soft and yielding, or maybe even mercury, the liquid metal in constant change. Liquid memory, doesn't that sound like something Jim Morrison would have sung about?

A while back I read an article in Scientific American about memory experiments on mice. The researchers concluded that memory wasn't reliable, not in mice and even less so in humans. Apparently we mix and match bits and pieces of our lives to form what we think are real memories, like some kind of crazy quilt of experience. Not only that, but our mood determines what memories we choose to store. Isn't that amazing? So if you're depressed, you're more likely to ferret away unhappy events.

And if you're happy—as I am now reading your wonderful e-mails—you'll make the happy times your memory.

Jack, you've given me happy times. And happy new memories. Now it's my turn to give you one, though I'm sure you remember it already. It was after we left Nepal, we traveled slowly south and west to Tangier . . .

You're standing in the ancient market. You close your eyes; breathe deeply; smell the dust on the narrow streets. A thin, sharp line of color races to your brain. Just beyond that, something fuller, slower, more abundant. You let yourself sink into the smell. You see it. Green. You smell green, cat's-eye green, lover's-eye green, the green of the hidden pond you found one afternoon, the pond you made love by, the green of her eyes.

You inhale deeper and see the rest of it. Green and billowy. You look closer. You see more colors. Little edges of copper, saffron, and crimson move in and off. You stand there breathing deeply. Trying to remember that memory. What is it? If you believed in past lives, you'd say it was an ancient memory, a smell from another time, another culture.

"It's some kind of spice," the woman next to you says.

You look at her. Today her eyes are green. The green of your hidden pond, where you made love to the first woman who left your life when all you wanted was for her to stay.

You look at the woman standing next to you. The sun is against her back, its golden light washing over her. She leans over and skims the back of her fingers across your face into your hair. She looks into your eyes. What does she see? Lost loves? Her hidden ponds or yours?

She sees a man so like herself she wonders if this isn't some cosmic joke. If once again, the mischievous gods who play her pieces aren't bored, want to shake things up a bit, want to see what she'll do. Will she be stupid again?

"Breathe," she says to you, as her lips press against your eyelids. "Smell it? You know what it is?"

She moves her lips down your face to your mouth, where she whispers a kiss, so lightly you wonder if you haven't made this all up. If you open your eyes, she, the smell, the memory of the hidden pond, your broken heart, will all be gone.

She presses against you. You feel her chest expand, her ribs opening, to take in the air.

"It's the smell of hope."

Annie

CHAPTER 37

Corset? Garter belt? Negligee?

Thong? No, not anymore, Annie thought. Well, really, not ever.

She walked through the Victoria's Secret on Connecticut Avenue. Now she had a reason to replace her tattered underwear: her date with Jack that night.

She wound slowly around the display tables, running her fingers across the silky fabrics, running her mind across Jack's last e-mail and their first kiss in the Bethesda parking lot.

She'd been surprised at how deep his chest had felt when she'd wrapped her arms around him, how solid he'd felt against her, a little bear of a man. He'd pulled her hard against him. Once again, she could feel his warmth; his fingers entwined deep in her hair, as if he were hanging on to a runaway horse. She remembered the first touch of her lips on his, the jolt, the rush, the hot glittery feeling that started in her abdomen and glissaded down like glowing fireworks.

Annie grabbed a table of push-up bras for support. A saleswoman came swooping down and she pretended to examine a puffy gray one.

"We're having a special sale—buy one of our Angel bras and get a coordinating panty for half price," said the saleswoman, a thirtyish blonde with too much lip liner. "I'll bring you the matching panty. Iced pewter?"

Annie dropped the washed-out bra in her hand. She'd never owned anything that drab in her life. "No thanks, I'm just looking." Annie tried to put enough edge in her voice so the saleswoman would retreat for good.

She walked to a rack of silky nightgowns in deep jewel tones. She held the sapphire one to her body and looked in the mirror. Good color, delicate cut, sexy straps. Definitely eye-popping material. Get real, Annie thought, like you're going to have time tonight to stop in the middle of things to slip into something sexy. Go for taking something off.

A fancy bra? No, too architectural with all those underwires and hooks and strategic pads. A camisole? They're soft and inviting, they skim your breasts with lace or satin and innocently drape down to your waist. She imagined Jack's fingers tracing her outlines across the smooth fabric. A camisole, definitely.

Annie piled an assortment over her arm. On her way to the fitting room, she spotted a rack of matching tap pants. Bingo. Tap pants. Perfect. Men love them because they're slinky and loose; women love them even more because they hide flaws.

The lip-liner lady led Annie to one of the cubicles. Everything inside was pink, except the little white hearts on the pink wallpaper. "Let me know if you need a different size or anything," she said.

Annie stripped to her bikinis and stood before the mirror. What had happened to all those miles on the treadmill and the cross-trainer, all those lunges and squats, all those leg lifts? Then again, there were all those sticky buns and ice-cream cones. What'd she expect, Cameron Diaz? Things could be worse; her arms were good (all those push-ups), her waist hourglassed (thanks for the genes, Mom), and her calves were shapely.

She slipped a lilac camisole over her head and felt it glide over her breasts. She rewound Jack's tiger e-mail and began to play it slowly out. He stood on the balcony before her; jungle noises all around. He reached out; she felt his fingers brush the base of her throat and slowly travel the path of her breastbone. They left off somewhere far below, but almost immediately she felt them again, two hands this time, tracing her clavicles.

Then, turning his palms away from her, he slid the backs of his hands down her chest, down over her breasts, down and down until they turned around and she felt fingers gripping her hips. She felt herself pulled toward him, until she could feel his breath feather her face. But the kiss never came; instead he stopped just short.

Through half-closed eyes she saw him briefly study her face, then slowly he began to kneel. As he descended before her, she could feel his lips brush the same pathway that his fingers had just traveled.

Down he went, his hands slipping around back to her bottom. Then he was on his knees looking up. There was a hand at the band of her underwear . . .

"How's everything going in there?" It was the saleslady.

"Fine, fine, everything's fine," Annie said, trying to hide the gasp in her voice. "I'll call you if I need you."

Annie waited until she heard the woman walk away, then crumpled down on the pink plaid chintz stool. Jack was gone; the jungle noises were replaced by a Muzak version of "Michelle." It was just her, face flushed, dressed in a purple camisole. She zipped through the rest of the lingerie she'd brought into the fitting room.

"Do you have any plain bags?" Annie said to the saleslady, who'd just slipped her purchases into a pink-and-white-striped bag with big white block letters announcing "Victoria's Secret."

She was going to her office to meet Fred this morning, to go over what happened last week when she was away. If she walked in carrying that bag, she might as well just announce to Fred—and herself—that when she drove to Baltimore tonight, she wasn't planning on coming back till tomorrow morning.

"Sorry, this is all we have."

CHAPTER 38

Jack went outside to tell Annie there would be a fifteen-minute wait for a waterfront table. He found her leaning against a railing, her back to the harbor and the sun. She wore a sleeveless brown silk dress with a delicate bamboo print. The early-evening light, refracting through the masts of anchored boats, created a nimbus of her hair and made amber of her skin.

As he walked toward her, Jack took stock of things. His fifty years were resting lightly that evening. Unless he was forced to sprint to the National Aquarium and back, he could fool himself into thinking he was thirty, maybe thirty-five. Courtship was rejuvenating, like an illegal serum made of monkey gonads. He breathed in deeply. A sea smell spiced the air.

"You seem happy," Annie said as he joined her.

"I am happy. I feel positively . . . positive," Jack said.

"Me too," she said. "I've been looking forward to this night for a long time. Since we tumbled down the hill together in California."

Jack paused.

Just as Annie started to silently berate herself (Trip was right, I scare people away with my big mouth), Jack took her hand and said, "You can't know how long I've been waiting for this night.

You look beautiful framed in the sunset. I've never dated a woman who glowed before."

Annie laughed. (Trip was wrong, so what else was new?) "Must be the irradiated papaya I ate this morning."

"Baltimore becomes you. Baltimore doesn't do that for many people."

Annie turned to face the water. From Remmy's she could see the entire sweep of Baltimore's Inner Harbor. "But it's beautiful."

"This is just a necklace on the skunk."

"Jack, you want everyone to think you're a curmudgeon. But I know better. Don't forget, Pablito, you send me e-mails."

Over dinner, the conversation turned to writing. Annie told Jack stories about manuscripts from hell, by way of the transom, and she complimented him again. "You've got to write," she said. "You're better than most people who get published."

When Jack turned the compliment around ("You're better than anybody on my staff"), Annie said, "I admit that all this e-mail has got me wanting to write again."

"Again?" asked Jack.

He didn't know it, but he had just invited Annie's newspaper years to the table. Should she tell him? She teetered on the brink of truth. But at the last moment she backed away. It was too early for that reality. Instead she waved her hand dismissively and said, "Oh, I used to write in college and all. Nothing serious."

Night fell and Baltimore's necklace began to shine. The big pink neon Domino Sugars sign dominated the northern skyline. The lights of Planet Hollywood, the National Aquarium, and other tourist attractions made luminous nets in the harbor's wavelets. A light touch of humidity softened the air. On such a night you could believe that romance conquers all and, for the first time in history, Baltimore and Paris could be compared.

As dinner wound down, Jack pointed across the water to a wooded park on top of Federal Hill, directly across the Inner Harbor. "My place is right behind those trees," he said. "That's where you drove up this evening. Let's go and I'll show you the view from there."

Twenty minutes later, they'd driven back to Jack's apartment and walked across the street to Federal Hill Park, a block-square patch of green overlooking the city. From this vantage point, Federal troops had once trained cannon on the city and its Confederate sympathizers. Now the soldiers and cannons were frozen in bronze.

As they approached the park's northern edge, Annie took Jack's arm. If any other strollers noticed, it would have seemed an innocent move. But it was a new stage in the evolution of their romance; they had left the primordial ooze and stepped onto land. Jack liked feeling Annie's arm linked in his. He leaned slightly up against her.

The view of the city and harbor was panoramic. Jack began pointing out landmarks.

"Want to make fifty dollars?" he said. "Here's a bet: How tall is the dot over the *I* in the Domino sign?"

"What if I lose?" Annie said. "I don't have that kind of cash on me."

"You can work it off," he said, cocking an eyebrow.

Annie examined the big sign, holding her fingers in front of her face in a perspective square. "I know this is a trick question, but here goes. Six feet."

Jack did a double take and reached for his wallet. "Good Lord, Annie, how the hell did you know that one?"

"Just a lucky guess. Put your wallet away. You paid for dinner, let's call it even."

Jack turned and pointed in the other direction. "See those lights? That's Camden Yards. Listen, you can hear the crowd cheer."

He continued the city tour for a few more minutes, then turned to go back.

"Not yet," said Annie. "First, kiss me."

Jack cupped her face in his hands and brought her lips to his as tenderly as he knew how.

The soundtrack for this scene should have been lush strings and a tasteful choir. But instead, Jack and Annie heard giggling and a mocking voice saying, "Awwww, ain't that sweet?"

They turned to discover that they had been putting on a show for a posse of neighborhood teens gathered under a maple tree. They couldn't help but laugh, too. "Come on," said Jack, "let's really give them a show."

This time they performed a softcore clinch to the sounds of hooting and an approving, "You go!"

They walked back through the park, buzzing with the voltage they'd just created. Jack had his arm around Annie's waist. They kissed again at the entrance to the apartment complex; they kissed in the elevator; they kissed by Jack's apartment door.

CHAPTER 39

They kissed before he closed the door.

They kissed as he led her to his living room.

They kissed as they stood before the old wooden icebox filled with CDs and the CD player.

"What would you like to hear?" Jack whispered.

"Surprise me," Annie whispered in his ear and, before he could pull away, slipped her tongue into it.

They kissed again in silence.

"I thought you were going to surprise me," Annie said into his mouth, and pushed her body against his.

Jack grabbed her and pressed her even harder against him. "There isn't enough blood left in my brain," he said into her mouth.

Annie squirmed away and smiled. "Maybe you should put your head between your legs."

"Maybe I should put my head between your legs," he said and pulled her back into a kiss.

"I think you should, but only to music," Annie said as she put her lips to his ear again.

Then she pushed him away and turned him toward the icebox. "Choose fast."

There wasn't much choosing involved. Jack had already put a

pile of CDs on top of the icebox, imagining a slow seduction of sultry music, wine, and words. But if he wasn't mistaken, within two minutes of arriving, Annie had told him to go down on her. Fast. Where have you been all my life, Annie Hollerman? He snatched the top three CDs and began pushing buttons.

While Jack loaded the CD player, Annie reached behind her and unzipped her dress. As he finished, she tapped him on the back. "Take my dress off."

Jack turned and slipped the straps down her arms. The dress fell to her feet. She stood before him in a lilac camisole and white lace tap pants.

He reached out; his fingers brushed the base of her throat and traveled down her breastbone, stopping at the purple silk.

"It's beautiful," Jack said.

"I bought it for tonight," Annie said and closed her eyes, remembering his imagined touch on her in the Victoria's Secret dressing room.

Amazingly, his hands were now following the same path. He traced the lines of her clavicles and then, turning his palms away from her, he softly slid the backs of his hands down her chest, down over her breasts, down and down until they turned around and she felt his fingers gripping her hips.

She saw him briefly study her face, then he slowly began to kneel. She felt his lips brush the same pathway that his fingers had just traveled. His hands slipped from her hips to her bottom. He pressed his mouth against her panties, breathing hot air into the hair caught behind the white lace. He hooked his fingers around the elastic and slid the panties off her body as Miles Davis began a slow imagining of Rodrigo's Spain.

Annie dug her fingers into Jack's hair and pressed him against her as she took a step back and onto the sofa. For a while—Annie could not have said how long—Jack knelt before her. Finally, she pulled his wet mouth up to hers and the monthlong journey, which began with, "What you need, Annie Hollerman, is a man with a good ass," reached, what now seemed to them, its extraordinary and natural destination. Annie opened her legs and Jack found himself inside her.

It was some time later—neither Jack nor Annie could have said how long—and they were dancing to Jennifer Warnes's hypnotic soprano. *"Way down . . . way way down deep,"* she sang, reminding them of the place they had visited together that night.

They turned through the music, arms enmeshed, bare bellies pressed together, damp thighs lapping against thighs. Jack brushed his lips across Annie's face and found her mouth again; he drew wet fingers up her back.

Around the room they danced, naked feet sliding slowly across the carpet, naked backs illuminated by dim light drifting in from an open window and the digital glow of the CD system, naked legs brushing up against the couch, where they had become naked together for the first time. *"Way down . . . way way down. . . ."*

CHAPTER 40

Annie opened her eyes. In front of her was a wicker nightstand and an oriental lamp she'd never seen before. A bed sheet of an unfamiliar blue was twisted between her legs. Something warm pressed against her.

She turned around to see what it was. Jack DePaul's bare leg, then all of a bare, sleeping Jack DePaul came into view. He was facing her, splayed out in the Mighty Mouse position: on his stomach, left leg straight, right leg and right arm bent ninety degrees.

She couldn't remember when they'd fallen asleep. One thing was certain, she hadn't wanted it to stop. Not the naked dancing, or his chest rubbing against her breasts, or her legs wrapped around his hips, or his mouth all over her. She'd felt strong as a werewolf in the midnight of his apartment. But finally Jack had guided her to his bed—this bed—had spooned up against her, said a jumble of sweet things that ended with, "No more, you're going to kill me," and fled from consciousness.

She looked at him. He wasn't moving. For a horrifying second she thought: What if I *have* killed him? He is fifty, after all. How old was Nelson Rockefeller? But, no, she saw his chest rising and falling against the mattress. She lay on her side, propped two pillows under her head, and examined her exhausted lover.

This was the first time she'd seen his face without glasses, in the light. His nose had a crook and bump that she hadn't noticed before. It added a craggy note: Richard Dreyfuss aging into Spencer Tracy. His beard swirled in and out of colors—brown, white, gray, brown. The sheet covered half of his rounded butt. If only you knew how right you were, Laura Goodbread. His chest looked deeper than she had remembered. She put out her left hand against it to measure. He shifted and she quickly pulled her hand back.

The movement stirred the air between them and Annie was suddenly engulfed by a new sensation. She put her fingers to her face and breathed in the musky, sweaty smell of sex. She breathed in again. A primal perfume of lust and pubic hair. She closed her eyes. It was a smell that made her want to say dirty words and buy crotchless panties.

Annie looked again at her sleepy hero splayed out in his heroic cartoon posture. She leaned over him and sang, "Here I come to save the day."

He jerked awake and slowly focused on her face. "Hi, angel," he said, and then, after a moment, "what happened?"

"I think you passed out." Annie moved to within kissing distance of his mouth. She felt like one of Rubens's women, made for sex, acutely aware of her curves. She felt the air trace the outlines of her body; every cell in her skin was saying, "Touch me."

Jack pulled her to him. They kissed long and hard. When they came up for air, Jack looked over at the nightstand clock. "Jesus, it's ten o'clock. Should we get up?"

Annie smiled, the taste of sex on her lips, the smell of it in her nose. "Not yet, Mighty Mouse."

CHAPTER 41

Come on, he won't notice," Jack said. "He's a guy."

Annie scrunched the left side of her face in a get-real look. "You don't think a long silk, spaghetti-strapped dress and Joan Crawford fuck-me shoes are a *little* dressy for a coffee shop? You think he won't notice *that?*"

Jack looked Annie up and down. "Hmmm, nice," he said. "You're right. He'll know you didn't just drive up this morning. But he knows that anyway. I told him we had a date last night and, with any luck, you'd be joining us for lunch. He's a grown-up, Annie; he can handle the fact that his father's not a virgin. Come on, he's dying to meet you."

"He'll think I'm a trollop," Annie said.

"Yeah, so?"

In deference to Annie's spike heels, they drove the four blocks to One World Café, Jack's favorite breakfast hangout. As usual, the mismatched tables were jammed with latte drinkers and Sunday *New York Times* readers. Luckily, a trio in running shorts got up just as Jack and Annie walked in.

Annie claimed the table as Jack waited in line. She'd wanted to wait for Matthew, but Jack said he was always late. "Plus, I don't know about you, but I'm starving. I worked hard last night."

By the time Matthew arrived—twenty minutes after the agreed

noon meeting—Jack and Annie had finished two sticky buns and were starting on a spinach-feta omelet. Their table was turned away from the door and they didn't see the brown-haired young man, who looked like a memory of Jack, standing in line, watching them.

Matthew looked at his father talking and waving his fork around like a little baton. The woman, holding a coffee cup that never quite reached her lips, was laughing. Laughing, Matthew was certain, at something his father had said, because he recognized the triumphant grin on his father's face.

Their body language surprised him. They were looser—younger—than he expected. The woman touched his father's hand and he squeezed hers in return. Their familiarity gave him an unexpected pang—she wasn't his mother—but his father had needed someone for a long while, and, judging by his smile, he might have found her.

Matthew thought about saying something snappy like, "Hi, I'm the younger, better DePaul," but he knew this meeting was important to his father. When they'd arranged to meet for lunch, Jack had told Matthew at least three times that Annie might join them.

So with all the dignity a twenty-two-year-old can muster, he walked over, reached out his hand to the woman in the long silk dress, and said, "Hello, I'm Matthew."

Then, because he was only twenty-two, he smiled at his father and said, "Nice dress, Annie."

For an hour, the three of them sat knee to knee at the small table, drinking coffee and talking. Matthew regaled Annie with Anasazi research and how the PC spin on them was all wrong. "Gentle natives?" he said, making the same sweep of hand that Jack did when he got excited. "Peacefully grinding corn in *matates*? How about roasting skulls by the fire? They were cannibals."

Jack had already heard the details of Matthew's work, but he encouraged his son on, saying, "No way," or "Amazing," or "That's incredible," at the key—and infrequent—moments that Matthew was silent. Jack smiled; his son was taken with Annie, too. Matthew's discussions with Jack about his research had been far drier.

And Annie? Jack watched as she listened to Matthew. She seemed more interested in the Anasazi than could be humanly possible. With each question she asked, Matthew seemed to swell bigger and bigger as he dug deeper and deeper into the arcana of paleobiology. When Annie suggested he consider writing a book, Jack thought Matthew might float to the ceiling like a giant Bullwinkle in the Macy's Thanksgiving Day Parade.

It would be easy to think Annie was just being nice; she was, after all, meeting the son of the man she thought she was falling in love with. But the truth was, Annie found Matthew charming. Annie remembered that Jack had once written of the man he used to be, before he felt the wind blow through him. Watching Matthew, she could see who that man had been.

It was nearly 1:30 when Annie stood up and told the DePaul boys she had to go back to Washington. "I'm still trying to catch up with work since my North Carolina trip," she said. Then she reached over the table and gave Matthew a hug.

"You're everything your father says you are—and more," she said.

At another time in her life, Annie would have stayed the afternoon—and the night. But if she'd learned anything in her forty-four years, it's that men need time to process. Jack was looking a little frayed, plus she knew he wanted time alone with his son.

Jack walked Annie to her car. Before she got in, they kissed and held each other, hands on waists, like two swing dancers.

"Thanks, Jack, I had a great time," Annie said. Then she rolled her eyes, groaned, and said, "God, could I get any more inane? Let me try again . . . You were wonderful . . . I mean . . . it, we—"

Jack kissed her in midsentence, then said, "You were wonderful, too, Annie. Really wonderful. I know there's a better way to say it, but right now I can't think how—except to say I think we should see each other again, as soon as possible. Tomorrow night?"

"Can't. I'm meeting an author."

"Then Tuesday night?"

"Your conference, remember?"

"Oh, shit," said Jack, "I forgot about the stupid conference. Well, I'll be back Saturday afternoon. What about Saturday night? What if I came down to D.C.? What if I brought my sleeping bag?"

"I don't think a sleeping bag will be necessary, do you?"

With the subject of sleeping together reintroduced, they looked at each other silently for a second, both reviewing images from the past night.

Finally, Jack broke the spell. "I'll e-mail you tonight, okay?"

"You better," said Annie, "or I'll chop your hands off. Worse: I'll sic Laura on you."

When Jack returned to One World, Matthew was finishing up his omelet and the leftovers on Jack's plate, too.

Before Jack could ask the obvious question, Matthew answered it. "She's awesome, Dad."

Jack nodded. "I think so, too. But could you try to be a little more specific?"

"What can I say? She's smart and funny. She's got great hair. She's hot. I can't figure out what she's doing with an old fossil like you."

"I can't either," said Jack. "It must be the e-mails."

"Yeah," said Matthew. "This rewriting the past thing is powerful voodoo. Remember Jennifer? The girl I was with at One World a couple of weeks ago? She's a total babe. I'm going to have to try it on her."

"You're missing the point, Matthew. Jennifer is what, twenty? First you have to have a past in order to rewrite it."

Matthew shook a forkful of feta at his father. "The point is, Dad, you better not screw up this time. Annie's a keeper. She's real. You can tell. She shouldn't be another stop on your midlife crisis tour."

Jack wondered just when it had happened that his twenty-two-year-old son became the dad and started giving him advice on life. He looked at Matthew for a second; his heart was flooded by one of those tsunamis of love that parents feel. *If I never do anything else in my life, at least I've done this. I wish it had been different* between your mother and me, he thought, trying to telepath his regret to Matthew's brain. I wish I'd never told you about Kathleen Faulkner.

But if Matthew was tuned to his father's emotional bandwidth, he didn't show it. Instead, he stuck the piece of feta in his mouth and said, with a smirk too cocky by half, "Of course, if you blow it, I could be next in line. Just call me the Graduate."

"Watch it, pal," said his father, "or I'll rewrite you right out of existence."

CHAPTER 42

Would she want a small wedding the second time around? Should they have klezmer music? Annie pictured Jack dancing the hora. (Trip had refused.) Maybe they should just skip the wedding and live together. Somewhere halfway between Baltimore and Washington? Yuck, that's Columbia. But Ellicott City would work. They could find a funky cottage; her primitive stuff would look great with his sturdy mission furniture.

They were sitting on their sunny veranda eating tomatoes, basil, and mozzarella drizzled in aged olive oil and a touch of balsamic—she was wearing an orange batik wraparound skirt and a gauzy white shirt that caught the breeze and brushed her nipples—when a ugly green sign announcing the Beltway suddenly came into view.

Annie blinked and read the white letters again. "Holy shit, how'd I get here?"

Then she realized where she was: in her car, on I-95 South. Her hands were on the wheel; she was driving.

The Beltway already? What had happened to Columbia, Laurel, Scaggsville, Burtonsville, and all the other towns between Baltimore and Washington? She didn't remember passing any of them.

Somewhere after getting on Baltimore's Key Highway, Annie

had left her body in charge of driving and her mind in charge of replaying last night. Once again she had dinner at Remmy's, walked in Federal Hill Park, explored Jack's body and had hers explored. Then, most likely around Laurel, her thoughts had catapulted forward—to the hora and a summer dinner of tomatoes and basil on a big white veranda.

After coming to at the Beltway, Annie tried to stay focused. But no sooner would she force herself to concentrate on the lines in the road or the upcoming exit signs than she'd hear Jennifer Warnes and find herself dancing in the moonlight with Jack.

Somehow, she managed to reach her Dupont Circle apartment.

The light on her phone was blinking. Five new messages. The first four were from her mother (why had she told her about the upcoming date with Jack?), the last was from Laura, who had called at 8:30 that morning to see if Annie had spent the night at home. "Just making sure you did the right thing. Was I right about his butt? I expect a full report."

After a long shower, she thought about a nap. She should be tired, shouldn't she? But the endorphins were still carbonating Annie's blood, so she threw on some clothes and headed for the office to finish up the pile of paperwork that had spread over her desk like kudzu while she'd been in North Carolina.

It was the brightest day of spring. The tufts of clouds merely accented the light blue sky; summer's humidity was still in hibernation. Red, purple, and blue pansies tumbled out of clay pots and window boxes on P Street.

Annie found herself humming, "I'm walking on sunshine . . ." and smiling at passersby. Everywhere she looked, there were couples. They were talking intently in the cafés and holding hands on the sidewalks; men and women, men and men, blacks and whites, browns and browns, Democrats and Republicans. With all this love around, Annie thought, this could be Paris. Why hadn't she noticed it before?

Could she be in love? The sensible-shoe side of her brain said, "No, it's way too early." Okay, if not love, then serious like? "All right," said sensible shoes, "but call off the wedding and cancel the caterers. You've been planning weddings after every first date since Eli Weintraub in eighth grade."

Annie unlocked the heavy, brass-trimmed doors of her building and stepped inside. For a moment it was last night, and she was stepping back into Jack's apartment. This was a very serious like.

It wasn't simply her body celebrating the end of loneliness. She was sure she wasn't just trying to convince herself of that. When she had first met Jack it was like being reacquainted with an old best friend. Then the e-mails came. Just the past week she'd read another article, this one in *Newsweek*, about breakthroughs in the study of memory. Good memories can cover over bad ones, it had said. Ever since Jack had taken her to the night of flamenco, her past had become a better place. He was making love to her and healing her at the same time.

Annie walked into the office thinking she owed Laura big time—at least a dozen sticky buns.

"Hey, Punkin. What are you doing here?" It was Fred, feet up on his desk, several manuscripts on his lap.

"I could ask you the same question. You were here yesterday," said Annie. "My excuse is I'm nowhere close to catching up from the trip. What's yours?"

Fred swung his long legs down to the floor. Annie noticed that he was wearing his usual work outfit: slacks, white shirt, bow tie.

"I needed to keep my mind busy today. I couldn't do it at home. Alone."

Annie frowned. What was so special about today? She looked over at the wall calendar. And she knew. It was May 19, Fred and Lillian's anniversary. It would have been their twenty-seventh.

"Oh. I'm sorry, Fred."

Fred made a wry face. "No need to be. It's not your fault she's no longer with us. I'm glad you got to know her."

"Me too," Annie said. "I love that story about how you met. Tell me again. Fireworks, right?"

Fred smiled and put his feet back up on his desk.

"Fireworks, indeed," he said. "I met her on a rooftop in Georgetown. It was the Fourth of July. Some friends had invited me to a fireworks-watching party. There were twenty or so people. Lillian and I had both been divorced for a few years at the time and we were the only singles. It didn't dawn on me until after we were married that the hosts had fixed it up that way.

"I first saw her up there on the roof. She was holding a glass of champagne and eating a hotdog. She was wearing a straw hat and a blue-and-green madras sundress. Men don't usually remember details like that, but I remember it exactly. The way she stood, lanky and loose-limbed like a teenage girl, how tanned she was. 'Who ever loved that loved not at first sight?'"

"Shakespeare?"

"Shakespeare stealing from Christopher Marlowe."

"What happened?" Annie sat down on a chair next to Fred's desk and put her feet up, too.

"I did every charming thing I could think of. I regaled her, I poured her wine, I juggled nectarines. It started sprinkling during the fireworks show so I held an umbrella for us both and wise-cracked about the shapes and colors of the explosions. In other words, I was an utter idiot."

Annie laughed. "But something worked. She fell in love with you."

"Not really. Not at first. I think she felt sorry for me. And she appreciated the effort. 'You were very game,' she used to say. Eventually, you're right, something worked. We were married nearly a year later, on her birthday."

"Oh. Today."

"Today."

Annie felt her heart drop, but Fred leaned forward and gave one of the feet propped on his desk a squeeze. "Let's don't get too melancholy. Lillian would hate that. It's also a day of celebration. A celebration of the twenty-seven great years we had."

"You're lucky, you have no regrets," Annie said, thinking of the twelve regretful years she spent with Trip.

"No regrets? Rubbish. I have a thousand regrets. We always wanted to go to Sicily and never did. There's an artist in town, Linda Pepper; we both liked her work. I kept saying I was going to buy Lillian one of her paintings. It got to be a joke between us, the gift she never got. I never took her to Café Atlantico."

"But Café Atlantico wasn't even open when Lillian died," said Annie.

"I know, Annie. I know."

The two of them sat silently for a moment, feet up. Then Fred said, "I think your man has the right idea about regrets."

"My man?" said Annie, a flush creeping up into her face. "Who's that?"

"You know very well who I mean: the estimable Mr. DePaul. At least I presume he's estimable. I like how he's writing away your regrets with his messages. I thought about that this morning over coffee. I was thinking that I wished I had done that for Lillian. Then I thought, maybe it's not too late. Maybe I should write a memory of Lillian and me on a date at Café Atlantico. She would have loved the tuna tartare on tablespoons."

Fred got up and stretched his big hands toward the ceiling. "It's too beautiful a day to be inside any longer," he said. "I'm going for a walk. There's a double-shot espresso somewhere nearby with my name on it. Don't work too long, Punkin." Then he gave her a sly smile and added, "Or you'll regret it."

CHAPTER 43

Mom says I get to be flower girl. But I'm almost thirteen, you know, so couldn't I be like a junior bridesmaid or something?"

On another day, Annie would have teased Becky about the apple not falling far from the tree. But how could she? A few hours before, she'd been playing the same fantasy.

"Becky, hasn't your mother given you the Gloria Steinem lecture yet? 'You can be anything you want to be'?" Annie said. "Go get her for me, okay, sweetie? And tell her I owe her a dozen sticky buns."

Annie looked into the little black holes on the telephone receiver as she waited for Laura to pick up. She thought about Fred's farewell and tumbled the word "regret" around for a while. It was a squat, ugly troll of a word that perched like a succubus over the sleeping past. Its silent cry of self-pity echoed forever.

Just a few weeks ago, Annie would have ridden such morbid thoughts to the most painful moments of her life. Once again, *Charlotte Commercial-Appeal* city editor Mark Snowridge would stand by her desk, nervously jangling the change in his pocket, and say, "Molitor's piece is bullshit, Hollerman. I refuse to run one more column about cutesy license plates. How's your Metro column coming? We really need it for tomorrow. But it's gotta be into the desk in the next half hour." Inevitably, she would answer, "No problem. It'll be there." And he would reply, as he always did, "You're the aces, H. You always come through." And, as always, she would feel the rising panic and see herself look at the clock, look back at her blank computer screen, and again reach for a folder filled with clippings of columns she'd gathered over the years.

But today she avoided the tour route from hell. Instead, thoughts of echoes and pasts took her to Nepal, where she and Jack had heard the sounds of a tiger and where she had been wrapped up by the shadows of Jack DePaul's body.

She might have stayed in that rattan room for hours if Laura's voice hadn't come through the little black holes Annie was staring at so blankly.

"Annie? You there?"

Annie put the phone to her ear and said hello.

"A dozen sticky buns?" Laura said. "Jeez-louise, this is better than I'd hoped for. Okay, Hollerman, time to talk. Was I right?"

For the next twenty minutes, Annie gave Laura a blow-by-blow description of her night with Jack. "He's terrific . . . he's . . . he's . . . terrific. Did I say he was terrific yet?"

In response, Laura had only one word to say: "Wow."

"Yeah," Annie said, "wow is right. But it ended all wrong. When we said good-bye, I was so tongue-tied I sounded like an idiot. I really need to write him something, but I'm not sure what. I can't decide between honest mush or jaunty irony."

"Hmmm," Laura said. "I've been out of the game so long it's like asking Bob Hope to host the MTV Awards. What about honest irony? Forget it, that's an oxymoron. Jaunty mush?"

Fred's conversation came back to Annie. "Laura, you're a genius! Jaunty mush. I've got it. Four words. How about, 'Great night. No regrets'?"

"Perfect. He'll think you're a genius. Men don't believe in morning-after regrets."

CHAPTER 44

That night, Jack caught a couple of innings of the O's game on TV, then sat down at the Mac. As he signed on he considered the threesome at lunch. "She's real," Matthew had said. Well, he hadn't raised a fool: Annie's real, all right. Is she getting someone just as real in return? Do I want her to? Am I afraid to?

The string of question marks would have stretched on longer if his message list hadn't contained something from ahollerman.

Jack clicked on and read Annie's four words. "Great night, no regrets."

He stared at the screen for a while, thinking about how past deceits seem to drag around behind you like Marley's chains. Oh, fuck it, he said to himself, just write her what you feel. And he did.

To ahollerman@aol.com
From jdepaul@aol.com
Subject: Regrets
Annie,

I came back from One World about two this afternoon. (Matthew says you're awesome. I agree.) I started to straighten up the living room and while I was putting the pillows back on the couch I found a pair of women's underwear, a small hair clip, and a little tangle of wavy red hair. It made me laugh out loud. It's been a long, long time since I had a couch in such disarray and strewn with a woman's things. I closed my eyes and immediately it was last night, Jennifer Warnes singing, and you were in my mouth. I close my eyes right now and you are in my mouth.

You say 'no regrets.' We both know that's not true. Of course you have regrets. And you wonder: Is he really what he seemed? Is there less or more there than meets the eye? Does he mean any of it? Was I a fool? How will it be when we meet again?

But it may be, and I hope it is, that the regrets are small and time will erase them. And after all, no matter what, we had the night. Electric, pulsating night. And I have the memory of your beautiful vibrating body.

I can't wait till we're together again.

Jack

CHAPTER 45

Before Jack could take a second sip of coffee on Monday morning, Laura Goodbread was standing by his desk. All five feet ten inches of her loomed over him as he sat with the *Post* propped in his lap.

He slid his glasses down his nose with his index finger and looked up.

"Yes, Ms. Goodbread, is there something I can do for you? By the way, fine job on City That Reads."

Laura sat down on the edge of his desk and leaned over to Jack. "We've got to leave employee-employer land for a moment, okay?"

Jack nodded. We're going to Annie-land, he thought. No matter, he'd been there all morning himself.

"About Annie."

Jack nodded again. For an instant, he saw a small redhead in purple silk and white lace. "What about Annie? She's fabulous. Everything you said. I owe you for this. In fact, it's going to show up in your evaluation under 'Works well with editors.' That'll be a first."

"Very funny," Laura said. "But I'm serious. Don't do anything stupid. She's had enough hurt in her life."

Jack pushed his glasses back up and focused on Laura for a second. "I don't know what'll happen. Who does? But I have no intention of hurting her. Why would I? Even a slime-sucking editor like myself can recognize a good thing when he sees it."

Laura stood and smoothed down her skirt. "Good," she said. "Now that that's settled, what's the word on Houston? Did you get them to spring for the trip? Remember, you owe me."

"That's against the rules, Goodbread. You can't mix personal and professional favors. I'll keep trying, but I wouldn't be packing my bags if I were you. 'Profits are off, the budget's tight,' is what I'm getting from the top."

Laura scowled. "Christ, Jack, that's total bullshit. We both know it. They've got enough money to send an army of editors to that circle-jerk management conference this week, but they can't come up with four hundred bucks for me to go to Houston? You tell me which the readers would prefer: more smooth-talking editors or a story about a dying girl's last chance?"

It wouldn't have been smooth for Jack to tell Laura the truth: that the only thing he'd ever found interesting about the conferences were his nights with Kathleen and that Laura's dying-girl story was compelling. She'd found a seven-year-old Towson girl with inoperable brain cancer. Her parents had taken out a second mortgage to pay for a trip to Houston so she could be treated by an alternative doctor specializing in pediatric brain cancer. Laura had planned to follow the family, report on the first treatment, investigate the doctor and the patients he'd saved (and lost), then later track the girl's progress.

"It's got everything. It could win us a Pulitzer," Jack had told the editor when he'd tried to get money for the trip.

Not this year, the editor had said. We don't have it in the budget.

"If it were my paper," Jack said to Laura, whose face was turning a visible red, "I'd send you. It's a great story. That's not the issue. I don't control the money. I wish I did."

"Yeah, well maybe you can take that up at your conference," Laura said.

Jack watched her stride away, a printout fluttering to the floor in her angry wake. He knew he was facing a three-day pout, at least. He took the delayed second sip of coffee. It helped. Newspaper people didn't bleed printer's ink, they bled caffeine.

He had just turned back to the *Post* when a new shape loomed over his desk. This time it was Arthur Steinberg's squat five feet seven inches.

"Arthur. My, isn't this is a pleasant surprise?" Jack's voice oozed false jollity.

"Not really," said the ever-dour Steinberg, who had arrived even more rumpled than usual. His tweed jacket lacked a button and his shirtfront was seeded with shreds from a chewed cigar.

"What can I do for you, Arthur?" asked Jack, this time without sarcasm. Arthur never understood newsroom banter anyway. He took it so personally that Jack thought one day a pointed remark would drive him to the top of the Bromo Building with a rifle.

"I'm having trouble with this 'Thief of Words' story," he said. "I haven't found the names of very many plagiarists."

"Damn. How many do you have so far?"

"Only fourteen."

"Fourteen! Jesus, Arthur, that's plenty. That's more than enough. Stop already."

"You sure?"

"Arthur, you're brilliant as always," said Jack. "Start calling these guys. If we get only five or six to respond, we're fine. Look, I'll be at a conference in New York tomorrow through Saturday. As soon as I'm back in the office next Monday, let's sit down and go over what you've got. Gammerman's in Pittsburgh right now doing the *Press* interviews. We should be able to wrap things up pretty quickly."

"Okay," said Steinberg and slouched away as if he'd just been reprimanded.

Jack watched his disheveled idiot savant head back to his pod. At least that was one story he didn't have to worry about while he was in New York.

Chapter 46

So that's where her underwear had been. She was still chuckling about it Monday morning as she walked into her office with a vente latte in one hand and a bran muffin in the other.

Tucked between the cushions of Jack's striped sofa. She pictured his face as he fished them out. She couldn't find them yesterday morning, but she hadn't searched his apartment very hard; she liked leaving a piece of herself there. Plus, after a night like that, she liked feeling uncovered, unwrapped, and naughty. So she'd gone home underwearless, a dangerous woman on the loose.

Looking at it from the perspective of a mundane Monday morning, she was embarrassed about her "no regrets" e-mail. Jack had seen right through the macho bluster; he'd been right about every concern. Of course she had regrets. Of course she worried that she had been foolish.

His answer, by contrast, had been sweet and smart (and grew sweeter and smarter the more she compared the two). "It made me laugh out loud. It's been a long, long time since I had a couch in such disarray and strewn with a woman's things."

How long? she wondered. And whose? The pyrotechnic woman? He'd talked about her at their first lunch, but gave no details other than that he should have known enough to stay away.

And when Annie had asked him about her on Saturday night, he'd waved his hand and said, "Ancient history."

Yesterday, after concocting their four-word opus, Laura had filled her in on what she knew, but it was only speculation. Some turbo-bitch editor in the newsroom named Kathleen Faulkner, who looks like Sigourney Weaver and is married to a guy who works for the power company.

"Like a lineman?" Annie had said.

"Get real," Laura said. "Like a flack."

"She works in the newsroom? He sees her every day?" Annie said. "Is this something I should worry about?"

"Annie, Jack asked me to fix him up with someone, remember? That's got to mean something. But who can tell how men's minds work? Don't worry, I'll find out."

Annie cursed herself for bringing it up. "No, absolutely not," she said. "Swear to me you won't say anything to Jack."

"Right," Laura said. But neither believed she meant it.

Annie put the latte and muffin down on her desk and began tackling the morning's voicemail when she was interrupted by the sound of a familiar gruff and cheery voice.

"And what is so rare as a day in May?" said Fred, poking his head into her office.

"I thought it was 'a day in June,'" said Annie.

"It is, but James Lowell never lived in the swamps of Washington, D.C."

"I'm glad to see you looking so happy this morning. I was a little worried. You know, the anniversary and all. I even called you last night, but no answer. Did you go out?"

"Yes," Fred said. "In a manner of speaking. Lillian and I went to Café Atlantico. The tuna tartare in tablespoons were her favorite, as I thought they would be. She was so charmed by the presentation, she insisted we go into the kitchen and tell the chef. Over dinner we planned a trip to Sicily. For my benefit, she pretended to be excited about seeing the Roman ruins at Syracuse.

"Annie, it was miraculous. I was up until . . . I don't know when. I'm sorry if I ignored your call. I got lost in the writing. It was as if she were there. By the end, the night at Café Atlantico was nearly as real as the night on the roof in Georgetown. I got to tell her I loved her, all over again—"

Fred's voice caught for a moment. He stopped talking and loudly cleared his throat. Annie didn't know what to do; she'd never seen Fred other than buoyant. She took a sip of latte to disguise her confusion. But before she put the cup back down on the desktop, Fred was merrily back on course.

"The anniversary is over, but I'm going to continue writing. I'm taking Lillian to the Cy Twombly sculpture exhibit at the National Gallery. I went there yesterday afternoon after I left you. It was extraordinary—a monument to the death of culture. He makes piles of plaster that look like something left behind by an elephant. 'Classical forms resonate in the transformation of Twombly's found objects.' I've never heard such twaddle. The triumph of pseudo-intellectual art babble. Lillian and I are going to laugh our way around his so-called sculptures.

"Then I'm going to put her into my first honeymoon. She'd get a kick out of taking Yvonne's place. We went on a train trip from Paris to Venice to Rome. I imagined Cary Grant and Eva Marie Saint in *North by Northwest*. The trouble was, Yvonne's idea of travel involved lying on the beach and swimming up to a bar for piña coladas. Lillian was adventurous and gay. Yvonne was more like . . . well, no offense, Punkin, she was more like your mother."

"Oh no, not that bad," said Annie through her laughter.

"Maybe worse. Anyway, please thank your Mr. DePaul for me. He's really stumbled onto something."

Fred left Annie with thoughts of trains and regrets and an overwhelming desire to hear Jack's voice. It was 9:10. He'd probably just gotten into the newsroom and was drinking his first cup of coffee. Would she seem too eager if she called first thing? She considered Saturday night. "Take off my dress." She decided it was too late to be demure and picked up the phone.

"Features, DePaul," said the now-familiar voice.

"Books, Hollerman," she answered.

"Oh, hello," said Jack, who then added, in a rush, "thanks for your e-mail Sunday. Thanks for Saturday night. Thanks for liking me. Thanks for being you."

"Wow," said Annie. "That's pretty good for a Monday morning. Thank you, too. Your e-mail was better than mine."

"Well. It's not a contest, Annie," said Jack. "Just for the record, though? Yeah, it was better."

She smiled into the receiver. "Okay, Mr. Show-off. Since you're so good, I've got an assignment for you."

Annie told Jack about how he'd inspired Fred and about Fred's rewriting moments with Lillian, including a new first honeymoon.

"You know, Fred isn't the only one who's had a bad train ride. I always thought it would be so romantic. For years I pestered Trip to book one. I dreamed of riding through Russia or on the Orient Express. Trip didn't want to have anything to do with conductors speaking in foreign tongues. He finally relented enough to go on a cross-Canada trip. He'd taken some French in college so I guess he figured he could handle the Montreal part.

"It was horrible. Every minute. The food was bad, the toilet overflowed, it was so overcast we never saw the mountains. Trip was grumpy the whole way. One day he accused a porter of stealing his voice-activated tape recorder. It turned out he'd left it at home.

"Jack, you promised to write me something from the conference. Take me on a train. I need to erase that Canada trip. Take me someplace exotic."

CHAPTER 47

To: ahollerman@aol.com
From jdepaul@aol.com
Subject: Night train

The Singapore railway station is sweltering. It must be 100 degrees on the platforms. The place smells of ripening fruit and over-ripe people.

You're sitting on a bench under the Track 4 sign reading a paperback by Alice Hoffman when I return with the tickets. You don't see me, so I stop a moment to study you.

We've been traveling for two months. Australia, Bali, and Jakarta are behind us. We've ridden ferryboats and buses and hitched a half-dozen times; once we were picked up by a limousine. We've gotten caught in thunderstorms and slept in hammocks. At the harvest festival in Denpasar, a toothless old man chased us out of his shop. He thought we were stealing a shirt we'd already bought.

You've pulled your hair up; weeks of sun have coppered your shoulders. You're wearing a thin wraparound skirt you bought in Darwin. It's patterned with stylized Aboriginal birds. Your legs drape over the backpacks. I look at you and think to myself, how did I get so lucky?

"I got the tickets," I say when I approach.

You smile and shade your eyes with a hand. "Good. I'm glad to leave. Singapore is too . . . too. Too modern, too crowded, too expensive. When do we leave?"

"We've got a couple of hours," I say, sitting down beside you.

"What train are we taking?"

"Did you know that a train called the 'Eastern & Oriental Express' runs from here to Bangkok? It's pure luxury. Waiters, air-conditioned compartments, fancy chef, ironed napkins in the dining car, Spiegelau crystal. They told me it has a piano bar and teak furnishings."

"Wow!"

"Well . . . we're not going on that train. It takes three days and costs $1,500 each. Ours is something called the 'Keretapi Tanah Melayu Berhad.' It's one-tenth the price. But we do have a sleeper and the train's a 'Special Express' so we'll be in Bangkok by tomorrow night."

"Does it have air conditioning?"

"Um. I'm not sure."

The sun's a dusty red ball on the western horizon when we leave the station around 6:00 that evening. The Keretapi Tanah Melayu Berhad is jammed and there's nothing made from teak. Signs in four languages, including English, warn: "Please guard your possessions." But it seems clean and efficient and there are fans in the sleeping cars, if not air-conditioning units.

We dump the backpacks on the tiny bunk beds in our compartment and, as the train lurches its way along, we walk to the outdoor observation platform at the end of the last car. The white cityscape of Singapore falls behind us as we head north, crossing the causeway to Malaysia. Soon we're gliding through a green steam bath of fields and jungle. The air hums with flying insects and insect-eating bats.

After about an hour the train approaches a tin-roofed shantytown and slows to a stop. A crowd of hawkers appears, and in a babble of voices they offer to sell fruit, colas, gum, and various gimcracks to passengers at the windows. The merchants who gather around the observation platform are insistent even though we wave them off. When the train begins to crawl forward again, they walk away reluctantly, but a herd of coffee-colored children run alongside laughing and shouting, hands outstretched toward us.

"I think they want us to throw them some coins," you say. "Do you have any?"

I fish in my pockets. "Only some Singapore subway tokens."

"Throw them those, we don't need them."

I toss the tokens to the kids, causing a wild scramble. But it doesn't last long and, hooting and hollering, the gang takes up its pursuit again. Soon they're just a few yards behind us. But this time, instead of begging, they start throwing the tokens back at us, laughing.

We duck inside until the train reaches the edge of town and begins to speed up. When we return to our perch our little assailants, standing far down the track, wave goodbye to us.

We stand by the observation railing until, with tropic suddenness, evening turns to night. As the countryside, outlined by cooking fires and solitary light bulbs, recedes into the darkness, we wrap ourselves in each other, only thin cotton separating our bodies. After a moment you pull back, your mouth just an inch from mine, and say, "Let's go to the compartment." This seems like a very sensible plan to me and we start back, my hands on your waist as you lead me along the narrow corridors to our car and sleeper No. 23.

Inside I pull you to me and we trade kisses until we can't ignore the fact that we're turning the compartment, which was warm to begin with, into a sauna.

"God, it's hot," you say. You pull the little chain on the overhead fan, which begins to turn about the speed of a merry-go-round. "Try the window, Jack."

It only opens partway, but it's enough. We kneel on the padded bench that extends below the window and stick our heads out into the breeze. Then I take off my shirt, soaked with sweat, and let the air cool my body. You unbutton your top and let it billow around your small pale breasts.

After a while we feel raindrops, and hear them tap-tapping on the metal roof of the compartment. I turn off the lights and sit down on the padded bench, lean back against the wall, my legs stretched out. You sit between them and lean up against me, your back against my chest.

Your head, moving slightly to the train's metallic beat, rests against my shoulder; my arms encircle your waist; the breeze cools us; occasional raindrops come through the half-open window spattering our arms and faces; the darkness itself seems palpable.

"Jack, do you think we've met before?"

"What do you mean? Like 20 years ago?"

"More like 120 years ago," you say. "We fit so well, it seems like a memory. Just before on the platform when I was in your arms, everything was so familiar. Like I'd been in the tropics with you before."

"Like reincarnation?"

You nod and say, "Maybe. It sounds silly though."

"Rossetti didn't think it was silly, he wrote a poem about it:

I have been here before,
But when or how I cannot tell:

I know the grass beyond the door,
The sweet keen smell,
The sighing sound, the lights around the shore.
You have been mine before,—
How long ago I may not know:
But just when at that swallow's soar
Your neck turned so,
Some veil did fall,—I knew it all of yore.

"He could paint *and* write?" you say. "Doesn't seem fair. Know any more poems?"

As the miles click-click along, I repeat for you every sweet and melancholy line I know, from Thomas Wyatt to Robert Frost, from Charles Lamb to W. B. Yeats to our friend Pablo. And you hear them in my voice and feel them through my chest as the train carries us into the night.

When at last I run dry of verse, I bend down and kiss your neck. We lie there a time in silence, my hand moving against your thin cotton skirt to the vibrations of the car. After a while, you take my hand away and move something, then you put my hand back. You've unwrapped your skirt and now my fingers rest on bare skin.

"Touch me," you say.

Later, with the smell of you mixing with the dark green smells outside, we rock along in the rain and the heat. I look out into the darkness and hope the journey never ends.

Jack

"Your mail has been sent," announced the little black letters on the screen. Jack stood up, stretched, and closed the lid on his laptop. Annie had asked for something exotic on a train. A ride through Malaysia was about as exotic as it gets. It gave him a wicked sense of triumph. Stick that in your voice-activated tape recorder, Thomas Harrington Boxer III.

While some of the details of the train e-mail had come from Jack's own experience (or from *National Geographic* specials), most had been made up out of thin air. But in a way, all of it was true. Jack believed this is how he and Annie could have been and could still be. It made him restless to think of it, itchy to travel, itchy to change. Worse, it made him play with the fifty-year-old's most hopeless of fantasies: that he was twenty-five years old again.

He walked to the window. It was nearly midnight, nearly Wednesday morning. Below him, pedestrians still clogged the sidewalks of 59th Street and the southern edge of Central Park. The management conference had never been held at the Plaza before. Jack had ducked into the hotel several times during past trips, just to gawk at the Palm Court's rococo decorations and use the bathrooms, but this was his first stay.

He wasn't tired, though he'd been up since 5:45. He'd taken an early Metroliner, to avoid sharing the three-hour ride with the other *Star-News* editors. He wasn't just avoiding Kathleen; he liked traveling alone and wanted some extra time in the city before the afternoon's opening session. He'd spent the morning walking around the Garment District. He enjoyed the hurly-burly of the streets and being buffeted by the young and the purposeful.

Looking down from his room, Jack watched a cop on horseback point out something to a couple in fancy clothes, who then walked hurriedly toward Fifth Avenue. He had the sudden urge to join them, and five minutes later he was on the Plaza's front steps, breathing in the May evening.

As he headed east, beckoned by the bright windows of FAO Schwarz, he passed two Central Park carriages, parked side by side. The drivers were having a tabloid conversation. Jack overheard one say, "I think he did it. Hell, I'd of cut her up, too."

He'd always wanted to ride in one of the horse-drawn carriages. Two years before, he'd broached the idea to Kathleen, but she wanted no part of it. She'd worried that a fellow conferencee might see the two of them together. "Besides, it's so hokey," she'd said. "It smacks of prom night—or middle-aged affair."

It was odd being here in the evening without her. Jack's usual conference routine was to go to dinner, separately, with colleagues; beg off late-evening drinks, pleading fatigue; return to the hotel, shower; and sneak to her room, not to emerge again until early the next morning.

"You know, they had to tear up all that work on the Sixty-fifth Street bridge," one of the carriage drivers was saying. "Yeah," the other answered with a long-suffering sigh, "this city . . ."

Annie would want to go on a carriage ride, Jack thought. She'd love the combination of kitsch and romance. Maybe tomorrow night I'll write her a carriage ride e-mail. He started to plot out a little adventure but it was washed away by a sudden wave of loneliness. The joy of traveling alone didn't extend much past five in the afternoon. And a laptop screen was a poor substitute for a real redhead.

It was only when Jack reached Fifth Avenue that he awoke to the obvious. Why am I fretting about e-mail? Annie and I are both single and free; we like each other; we want each other. On the first possible weekend, we'll come up to New York together, pay a driver, and go on a damn carriage ride for real.

He walked down the avenue as midnight came and went and didn't feel at all a day older.

CHAPTER 48

Annie now knew how it felt to be a sixteen-year-old boy. Since Saturday night, her brain had slipped below her belt. While she could occasionally think of things other than sex—say, work—her thoughts quickly bounced back to the subject of pleasure. She was so acutely aware of her body, that if she turned a certain way she could feel her blouse rubbing against her chest and her underwear pressing into her. Since Saturday night, she'd been turning that certain way a lot. Even going to the bathroom was an erotic experience.

"I don't get it," Annie said to Laura. It was their nightly phone call. "If God could come up with the lock-and-key theory of enzymes, why couldn't he do a better job with the human race?"

"Annie, nothing comes more lock-and-key than us. Penis. Vagina. I don't know about you, but it seems like a pretty good fit to me."

"You're being too literal. So the body parts fit. Big deal. Wouldn't it be better if the psyche parts fit, too? Boys turn into walking dicks when they become teenagers. It's not until they hit their forties that they can start thinking about anything else than sex. But bam, we hit our forties and get hit upside the head with the estrogen hammer. Now the only thing we can think about is what they were thinking about when they were sixteen. I feel like a Georgia O'Keefe painting with arms and legs and wet under-wear."

"Yeah, you're right," Laura said. "Strategic error on the Creator's part. Steve says I'm going to kill him if I don't calm down. It's good to see you so stirred up—finally. I was worried you were going to waste your forties on electronics. I assume Jack DePaul has something to do with your biological rant?"

"Yuuup," Annie said. "He's coming here Saturday night. I don't know if I can make it till then."

"Annie, just get in your car and drive to his house now. Attack him the second he opens the door. Men love that sort of thing."

"I would, but he's in New York."

"Right, I forgot. The circle-jerk conference the paper could find money for even though we're supposed to be 'tightening our belts.' But I have to hand it to Jack. I'm going to Houston after all to do that story I told you about. The dying girl. He finally weaseled the money out of them. I'm leaving Friday morning and I'll be back Sunday night."

"It's a hell of a story, Laura. I wish I were doing it."

"I know, but let's don't get maudlin. Don't you have sex to think about? Surely in that tower of books by your bed there's something steamy. That should keep you occupied till Saturday."

"I've got something better," Annie said. "Jack's e-mail, when it comes tonight. He's taking me on a train ride. Tunnels. Trains. Locks. Keys. I've got Mr. Giggles plugged in and ready to go. I'll read and you-know-what at the same time."

"God Annie, just don't electrocute yourself. Remember, the *Post* runs cause of death in its obituaries."

An hour later, Annie lay in bed with her laptop on her thighs. She'd tried to read, but a computer game of Hearts was the only thing her mind could track. Sort of. She'd eaten the queen of spades four times in a row.

She'd cleared her mailbox so she could watch the little red flag pop up with each new message. The first two were trash. The third was from Jack. It was called "Night Train."

By the time Jack had Annie rocking to the train's metallic beat, the tap-tapping of the rain on the roof of their compartment was mixed with the buzz-buzzing of the Conair Touch 'N Tone in Annie's hand.

You've unwrapped your skirt and now my fingers rest on bare skin. "*Touch me,*" *you say.*

Annie mouthed the words "Touch me." Suddenly, before she could read Jack's next line, the little white Instant Message box popped up. Someone called Plot-Twister had invaded the upper right corner of her computer screen:

"HI, IS THIS ANNIE HOLLERMAN, THE BOOK AGENT?"

The vibrator dropped from her hand and buzzed on the sheet like a dying moth. "Jeeesuz . . ." Annie cried out and looked around, half expecting to find someone watching her.

"Damn Big Brother Instant Messaging," she said as she clicked the X on Plot-Twister's message and sent him tumbling back through cyberspace. This wasn't the first time a would-be author had found her e-mail address and Instant Messaged her. But it was easily the most inopportune. If it hadn't been past midnight, she'd have called Laura to tell her about it.

Instead, she scrolled back to the top of Jack's e-mail. *The Singapore railway station is sweltering . . .*

And so was Annie.

CHAPTER 49

For the next two nights, Jack and Annie's e-mails criss-crossed the wires between New York City and the nation's capital. On Wednesday night, Jack took Annie to his kibbutz, where he rewrote both their pasts. This time, he was single. This time, a new volunteer with long red hair arrived on a scorching summer day.

"At first we didn't recognize each other, it had been 15 years," Jack wrote. "But there was something about your hair and eyes, the way they matched each other, that seemed so familiar. Then when you said, 'Hi, I'm Annie,' I realized you were my snake slayer."

That night, after picking grapefruit, she and Jack sat before a campfire and sang songs with all the other volunteers. During "Parsley, Sage, Rosemary and Thyme," they slipped away. As a crescent moon fell below Mt. Carmel, they made love for the first time.

Then on Thursday night, Annie found herself in the Marais district of Paris. She and Jack were lying on a bed in a room so small they could reach out from the side and touch the walls. In front of them was a loaf of ten-grain bread, dark purple grapes the size of Ping-Pong balls, two buttons of goat cheese wrapped in oak leaves, and a bottle of red wine. After dinner, they made love on top of the breadcrumbs. Two hours later, they walked arm in arm down the four flights of stairs of their pension that two hundred years before had been a Carmelite nunnery. At a sweaty subterranean nightclub they danced to bad French rock and roll.

In return, Annie told Jack about her summers in Atlantic City, about the gallant Mr. Peanut, who looked so elegant in his top hat and cane, and how Singing Sam the Ice-Cream Man would sell her a chunk of dry ice for a nickel.

"Then I'd drop it in a pail of seawater," Annie wrote, "and a big cloud of smoke would rush around my face. I'd close my eyes and pretend I was up in the sky. You make me feel like I'm up in the sky again. Do you think we're moving too fast?"

Jack read this message at 12:50 on Friday morning. He'd been so wired after writing her the Paris e-mail that he had gone out for another late-night stroll in New York. When he got back he'd signed on just in the hope of a return message from Annie.

He quickly wrote back two sentences. "Hell, Annie, at our age, we've got to move fast. Hang on tight, my love, it's going to be a great ride."

Annie read those sentences Friday morning at work. They made her feel like she'd had wine for breakfast. By 4:30 that afternoon the buzz was still there. She tried to concentrate on the task at hand—a cover letter for a promising new collection of short stories—but all she could think about was the e-mail she'd be getting from Jack later that night.

She was thumbing through the thesaurus for a more intriguing word than "promising" ("Auspicious"? Too baronial. "Inviting"? Too Southern. "Tempting"? Too salacious.) when she heard Fred's voice beyond the glass partition. He was speaking to a squat man with frizzy brown hair. Fred left him by the front door and poked his head into Annie's office.

"There's a guy here from the *Baltimore Star-News*," he said. "He doesn't have an appointment but says he needs to talk to you."

"What's he want?" Annie said.

"He wouldn't say, only that it has something to do with a story he's writing."

"What's his name?" Annie said.

"Arthur Steinberg."

CHAPTER 50

The man walking into Annie's office wore a frayed green-checked sport coat and gray suit pants. His tie was too wide, his shirt wrinkled. He could have been a homeless man trying to keep up his dignity with a professional look, but he lacked the shopping cart and the painful air of failure. He stuck out his hand.

"Hi. I'm Arthur Steinberg with the *Baltimore Star-News*. Sorry to drop in like this, unannounced, but I had another interview in D.C. this afternoon, so I thought I'd stop by here on my way back to Baltimore."

"What can I do for you?" Annie asked with a bland smile, though there were alarm bells going off in her head. Something was wrong about this. She knew very well that reporters don't just "drop in" unless they have particularly unpleasant questions to ask and don't want to tip their hand by calling first. She learned back in her college newspaper days that it's easier for someone to hang up on you than close the door in your face.

"Well, I don't know if you read it, but a few weeks ago there was a story in the news about a reporter at the *Pittsburgh Press* and a case of plagiarism."

She'd steeled herself for something unpleasant, but not this. It was like a wild punch to the head. Her ears rang, her body went numb, the bland smile froze on her face. The careful life she'd built for the past twenty years, brick by brick, to close off her past, lay around her like so much straw. Everything that happened afterward in her office seemed unreal, removed. Arthur continued with his explanation. His overly concerned voice was full of the same tired euphemisms that Annie herself had once used when she'd been a reporter trying to get unwilling people to talk. But it was as if she were seeing him through binoculars and hearing his voice down a well.

"We're doing a piece on him—why he did it and how he's dealing with the aftermath. He's been incredibly cooperative. He told me it's cathartic to talk about it and hopes his story will help other journalists.

"Anyway, along with the *Pittsburgh Press* story, we're doing a sidebar on other reporters who've faced similar traumas in their lives. I've talked to a number of others and wanted to talk to you. I'd like to know how it affected you, what you think about it after all these years, and how you've made peace with that part of your life."

Annie had no idea what to say. Had there ever been peace, or had it been just an uneasy cease-fire? Finally, she stammered out, "How did you find out about me?"

"The same as all the others I've interviewed. You know, a Nexis search, and I also talked to some experts. There's a guy at Poynter who specializes in plagiarism cases. The *Commercial-Appeal* printed an apology on the Metro cover. It didn't mention your name but the local alternative weekly did a big story on you and the whole incident. I'm sure you remember."

She remembered. *Creative Loafing's* media watchdog, Jerome Klein, had written a column about her and the *Commercial-Appeal's* reaction. Andrew Binder had been mentioned; so had the term "A-Squared." The headline had read, "Shooting star shoots herself in the foot." And then she remembered something else: Jack.

"I don't need much of your time, Ms. Hollerman," Arthur was saying. "A quick comment is all. People like to know that you can overcome mistakes and move on to a successful life. You're a perfect example of that. Besides, it's not that big of a deal, it's a small sidebar, just a few quotes, that's it."

"No," Annie said. She wanted to shout it, scream it, but it came out a kind of low rasp. She cleared her throat. "No, I have nothing to say about that." Then she hesitated. "Wait. Do you know Jack DePaul?"

Arthur looked at her with a quizzical expression. "Sure," he said. "He's my editor."

CHAPTER 51

Fred approached the door tentatively and peered in. Annie was standing by her porthole window.

"What was that about? Are you okay?"

She turned and said, "No, not at all."

Fred walked into her office and sat down in the chair by her desk, the same one that minutes before had held Arthur Steinberg.

Annie turned back to the window.

"Want to talk about it?"

"No . . . Yes . . . I should have talked about this a long time ago," Annie said, still facing the window.

Fred waited for Annie to speak. She stood by the window for a long time, then walked to her desk and sat down.

She fiddled with a pencil, rolling it between her fingers. Then she looked up and said, "He's doing a what-ever-happened-to story."

She paused, then finished: "And his what-ever-happened-to subjects are plagiarists. In other words, me."

Fred shook his head as if to clear a blurry image. "Plagiarist? You? What're you talking about, Annie?"

So she told him, the whole story, the chapters of her past that no one in her present knew but Laura and her mother: how she beat out the Cliffies and Princeton grads for her job at the *Charlotte Commercial-Appeal*, her meteoric rise to golden girl, her life with Andrew Binder, and that morning when her editor had called her "the aces."

"I knew there wasn't a chance in hell that I'd have a column ready in a half hour," Annie said. "But I didn't have the guts to tell him. And maybe even more than that, I didn't want anyone else to be 'the aces.' I'd kept an idea file, filled with clips from other papers. Something to springboard me into my own story. After he left, I panicked and reached for that file. I found the most obscure column in it, something from a paper in Indiana about the lunacy of high-density public housing.

"Scattered-site housing was a big deal then. Some townhouses for poor people were being built in southeast Charlotte, and all the rich white people who lived nearby were furious and putting pressure on the city council. So I took that man's column—Jim Morrill, I'll never forget his name—and put my name on top. I changed a few words here and there, but it was his column, not mine."

Annie stopped and Fred sat there, his head bowed, his face resting in his cupped hands.

"Annie the plagiarist, that's me. When I sent that story to the Metro editor, I knew my life would change one way or the other. Till this day I ask myself if I hadn't been caught, could I have learned to live with that lie? And here's the most repulsive part— yeah, probably so."

Fred raised his head from his hands. "This isn't the Annie Hollerman I know."

"Maybe not," said Annie, "but this is the Annie Hollerman I've been running away from my whole life. Deceit came easy to me. It's how we negotiated our way through trouble. I'm not saying this to excuse what I did, there's no excuse for that. It's merely an explanation.

"In my family, it was always easier to lie than to face unpleasant realities—like maybe I wasn't 'the aces,' after all. It starts with little lies, like telling the librarian you've already returned that overdue book when you've really lost it. Or 'helpful lies,' like my grandmother lying to my grandfather about how bad his cancer was. Or my mother telling me my father was away on business, when he was really starting a new family in another state. Harmless lies—as if that's possible. You don't mean any harm, but soon lying becomes second nature.

"It seemed harmless when I told the editor at my college paper that I'd worked at my high school newspaper. The truth was, I'd worked for my junior high school paper. No big deal. Just another harmless lie. But then one day, you find yourself in a panic and you slide into a lie and it's no longer harmless."

Fred thought about Annie's words for a moment, then he said, "That was a long time ago, Annie. People change. I've known you for twelve years and I've never seen that side of you."

"But I can never erase it," Annie said. "It'll always be with me, even if I have changed. And now this reporter's doing that story, it's all going to come out again. Jack DePaul hates people like me; he's spent thirty years in the business. Truth is in his blood. If he doesn't already know about me, he'll know soon enough."

"You're running from a ghost, Annie. If Jack is any kind of man, he'll know the truth: that people change and that he'd be a fool to let you go for something that happened twenty years ago. But you know, you have to call him right away. He has to hear this from you, not from one of his reporters. Call him now, Annie."

"I can't. He's at a conference in New York. He won't be back till later tonight. I'll call him then. I promise."

CHAPTER 52

After Friday's conference sessions, Jack and his boss, Steve Proctor, had gone to dinner at a new fusion place in SoHo with the managing editor of the *Orlando Sentinel*, a sports guy from the *Kansas City Star* and two features types from the *L.A. Times*. They'd bitched about reporters, bitched about the pernicious effect of profit margins, bitched about the decline of newspaper readers. All in all, an enjoyable evening.

On returning to the Plaza around nine, they'd met a handful of other attendees, also back from dinner, and the whole contingent decided to head to the Oak Room for drinks and more rounds of bitching. But Jack begged off; it was e-mail time with Annie.

Up in his room, he took off his shoes and socks and propped up the pillows against the bed's headboard. He put the laptop across his legs and signed on. He was about to check his e-mail when there was a light knock at the door. He frowned, wondering if he should answer it. It was Proctor, he was sure, trying to get him to join the crowd at the bar. There was another knock; he put the laptop aside and got up to answer it.

"Hello, Jack." She stood in the doorway, her dark hair pulled up, a thin gold chain around her slender neck. She wore black jeans and a white shirt—a man's white shirt. The sleeves were rolled up partway and the top two buttons were undone.

"Kathleen."

"Can I come in?"

Jack remained at the doorway. "What are you doing here?" He stared at her without expression. Kathleen looked away.

"Well, you didn't come to my room," she said softly, "so I thought I'd come to yours."

"Why would I want to go to your room?" Jack asked. He kept his voice as even as he could. The calmer he was, the deeper the words would cut.

"Don't do this, Jack, please," Kathleen said. "I just want to talk. After all that we've meant to each other, you have to talk to me."

What had they meant to each other? After nearly four years, Jack still didn't know and wasn't sure he wanted to know. He'd kept his distance at the conference. Their paths had crossed, of course. They'd even talked politely between the "Jump-Starting the Staff" and the "How I Stopped Hating the Budget and Learned to Live within My Means" seminars. But the urgency for her, the exciting deception, the yearning for the nights, had all been replaced with a mild numbness. His heart had stayed calm; his body had been quiescent. Was he surprised that she had come to his door? Probably not. But he hadn't wanted it and he hadn't waited for the knock.

Jack noticed that she was wearing the dangly coral-and-jade earrings he'd bought for one of her birthdays. She'd kept them in the box for a few months and then told her husband she'd bought them at the Baltimore Craft Fair. The white shirt, the coral-and-jade earrings—Jack didn't know whether to laugh or bury his face in his hands.

He moved aside. "Okay. Let's talk." Kathleen stepped past him.

The room had only one king-size bed. Kathleen hesitated a moment and then climbed up on it and sat with her back against the pillows, her arms around her legs like a little girl. Jack went over to a desk by the window, pulled out the chair, and turned it toward her.

"Do you have to be so far away?" she said. "Why don't you sit over here?"

"I can hear you fine from here," Jack said.

"Don't be cruel. Come sit on the bed. Please. I promise I won't touch you."

Jack moved to the bed and lay on his side at the foot, facing her. "I don't think we have much to talk about," he said.

"We have everything to talk about," said Kathleen.

For a half hour, Kathleen pleaded her case. She didn't move much, she kept her arms around her legs, her chin on her knees, but her voice quavered with emotion. She said many things that he had been hungry to hear for a long time. He felt some guilt that they affected him so little. But on the other hand, he'd heard many of them before: I love you. You said you loved me. You said I was your destiny. I miss you. I miss your touch and your words. I think about you every day. I've never felt this way about my husband. For years I thought I needed you both, now I'm not sure. I can't get you out of my mind. Give me another chance. You complete me. I need you. I want you.

Jack contributed only a few "ums" and "uh-huhs" to this long confession. Finally Kathleen unwrapped herself and came over to him at the end of the bed. "Please say something, Jack," she said, on her knees, looking down at him. "I know you still feel something for me."

Jack studied her face. Some curls of hair had gotten loose and hung at her neck. She was swallowing hard and holding back tears.

"Does this mean you're leaving your husband?"

"Do you want me to?" she asked.

CHAPTER 53

Oh, sorry, I must have the wrong room," Annie said and was about to hang up the phone.

"Who are you calling?" said the female voice at the other end of the line.

"Jack DePaul. The operator must've rung the wrong number," Annie said.

"This is Jack DePaul's room," said the woman.

There was a pause. Then Annie said, "May I speak to Jack?"

"He can't come to the phone right now; he's in the shower. Who's calling?"

"Annie Hollerman. Who's this?"

"Kathleen Faulkner. Jack told me about you. You're the book agent in Washington, right?"

"That's right."

"Oh, you're the one he's been writing all those e-mails to. He told me about that. He used to write me every day, too. He's quite good with words, isn't he? Did he write you about the moonchild in the apricot orchards? Were you his snake slayer, too?"

"I . . ." Annie couldn't catch her breath. It felt like her lungs had collapsed and sealed shut tighter than a vacuum-packed bag. The phone fell from her hands and clattered to the floor. She could hear the faint voice of Kathleen Faulkner saying, "Hello? Hello?"

Annie sunk into a nearby chair and put her head between her legs.

CHAPTER 54

"Hi, this is Annie, I'm out of town, leave a message after the beep."

It was 10 A.M. on Saturday morning and Annie was lying in bed, listening to Jack's voice.

"Out of town? I guess you haven't changed your message since North Carolina. I can't wait to see you tonight. Don't go to too much trouble for dinner, I don't think we'll spend a lot of time eating. Sorry about last night's missing e-mail. I went out with the gang and after my fourth margarita I could barely walk, let alone type. I owe you one."

Click.

Annie watched the phone light start to blink and didn't move. She didn't move for the next hour, despite the growing pressure in her bladder. She just lay there, examining the patterns of light on the ceiling, hearing Kathleen's voice, and thinking about Jack.

She should've known he was too good to be true with his romantic e-mails and his heartfelt assurances. She'd been out of the game too long. It had been more than fifteen years since she'd tangled with the lies of men on the prowl. And she was clearly out of her league with someone as smooth as Jack.

He was good—she had to give him that. Rewriting her past,

calling her his angel, introducing her to his son. She felt sorry for Matthew.

The phone rang again.

"Hi, this is Annie, I'm out of town, leave a message."

"Annie? What do you mean you're out of town? You didn't tell me you were going anywhere. Is everything okay? I'm going to call Laura to find out where you —"

Finally, Annie moved. She reached out her arm and picked up the phone.

"Ma, I'm here. Don't call Laura."

"You sound dead, are you okay?"

"It depends what you mean by okay," Annie said, and then told her mother about Kathleen and Jack.

"Christ almighty," said Joan Hollerman Silver. "First the Gonef, then the Cardboard Box, now the Romeo. You've got worse luck than I do with men. But listen, sweetie, it's better you should know now what he is. And this way, you don't have to worry anymore about telling him what happened in Charlotte."

"Right," Annie said bitterly. Then she told her mother about the *Star-News* reporter who wanted her to spill her guts for the betterment of mankind.

"I've always said reporters make us lawyers look like saints," said her mother. "Anyway, it's out now and that's not the worst thing in the world. Now you can really start fresh. I know the perfect place. Meet me in Atlantic City next Friday. I'm going on one of those junkets. We can share a room; it'll be like old times. You and me on the Boardwalk. We'll eat saltwater taffy till our teeth hurt. Come on, Annie, he's not worthy of you."

CHAPTER 55

Jack called four more times on Saturday and four times again on Sunday. The message was always, "Hi, this is Annie, I'm out of town . . ." The only thing that changed was his concern. At first he wondered if Annie had suddenly gone away on business (was the She-Devil on the rampage somewhere?), then he worried that something had happened to Annie's mother, then he moved on to an entire encyclopedia of disaster scenarios, including kidnapping and serial killers.

When he walked into the newsroom Monday morning his first items of business were clear: call Annie at work, find out if Laura Goodbread had heard anything, get coffee. But before he could implement anything but the coffee part of the checklist, Arthur Steinberg appeared at his desk.

"You wanted to talk about the plagiarism story this morning, remember?" he said.

"What? Oh, yeah. Could we do it later, Arthur?" Jack was about to add, "I've got important things to do," but realized how callous that might sound. He looked at Steinberg's hangdog expression and the latest ugly tie drooping down over his wrinkled shirt. "You're right, Arthur," he said. "Let's talk now."

Steinberg started down his list of plagiarists, explaining in Arthurian detail who had talked and who hadn't and why. When he came to the final name, he said, "I saved this one for last be-cause I think she knows you."

"You're kidding," said Jack. "What's her name?"

"Hollerman."

"What?" said Jack. Steinberg might as well have told him Elvis was dishing out string beans in the cafeteria downstairs. "Hollerman? Annie Hollerman?"

"Yeah. See? I told you. When I interviewed her Friday she asked me if I knew you."

"Friday? You talked to her this past Friday? Look, Arthur, this is important, start from the beginning. Tell me everything."

And that's how Jack learned Annie's secret. He uncovered her deepest trauma—the thing she had tried for so long to keep locked up in the stone tower of her past—from a guy wearing a frayed plaid tie with grease stains. Steinberg told Jack what he'd found out about the *Commercial-Appeal* incident, including some of the details from the *Creative Loafing* story, and described the meeting in Annie's office.

Now Jack knew why Annie had disappeared.

"Anyway," said Steinberg, finishing his story, "she turned me down flat. But I think we have enough people for the sidebar. Don't you? Five should be plenty, shouldn't it, Jack?"

"Sure. That's great, Arthur. Look, I've got an important call to make. Let me talk to you later this morning, okay?"

But his second attempt to call Annie at work was stopped short, too, this time by Laura Goodbread.

"I need to talk to you. Now. It's personal," she said, her lips compressed into two thin lines. The tendons in her neck stood out as if she were steeling her body for a punch or about to de-liver one.

"I need to talk to you, too," said Jack. "Let's go in the confer-ence room. And Laura, don't worry. It's going to be okay."

This assurance didn't seem to make Laura any happier. She looked at him as if he were a virus she didn't want to catch and preceded him to the room with the big table and glass walls.

"Jack," she said evenly, "you're a fucking asshole."

"First of all, Laura, calm down. It's not what you think. I had no idea Steinberg was going to talk to Annie about the plagiarism story. I had no idea that Annie had even worked at a newspaper. She never told me. How was I supposed to know?" He banged a fist down on the conference table. "Laura, I don't care what Annie did twenty years ago. You've got to help me get through to her. Tell her I don't give a shit what happened at the *Charlotte Commercial-Appeal*."

Laura's reaction to these heartfelt words was not what Jack had expected. She didn't smile; there was no softening of the lips. The only thing that changed was the look on her face. He was no longer a virus, but a habitual child molester being questioned by a victims' rights activist.

"I don't give a shit, either," she said. "Steinberg cornered me this morning about his damned 'Thief of Words' story and tried to pump me about it. As far as I'm concerned, it's ancient history. And you know damn well that's not what I'm talking about."

Jack stared at her. He was dumbfounded. "This *is* about Annie, isn't it?"

"Yes, Jack, this is about Annie," she said in staccato, pounding each word as if it were a nail. "Next time you ask me to fix you up with someone, it'd be a good idea to stop fucking Kathleen Faulkner first."

Jack pulled back in horror. "Wh—what are you talking about?" he stammered, feeling his face grow hot.

"Oh shut up, Jack. Everybody knows your little secret. Everybody knows you're sneaking around with her. Shit, Jack, there was even an office pool going last year, betting on who you were boinking. Faulkner was the hands-down favorite."

Jack sat down. He felt like his head was going to explode. "Okay, Laura, maybe we had a thing. I mean, yes. We had an affair. But I swear to you, I haven't seen Kathleen Faulkner outside of the newsroom for six months."

"Oh? How about Friday night at the Plaza? That doesn't count because it was in a different state?"

"No!" Jack practically shouted. A dozen reporters, sitting near the conference room's glass walls, looked up from their desks or stopped in the middle of phone conversations. "You don't understand . . ."

Laura brushed away the beginning of his explanation with a sneer.

"You know, you are a true asshole. It's bad enough to be fucking around with two women at the same time, but to write them the same love letters is beyond despicable. It's weak and hypocritical. How many times have I heard you on your little soapbox preaching the gospel of truth and credibility? You fucking hypocrite. No, I guess you wouldn't care if Annie plagiarized, would you? Tell me, Mr. Snake Slayer, who's the bigger thief of words? You or Annie? You're pathetic. From now on, we're no longer friends. Stay away from me and stay away from Annie."

Laura slammed the door behind her, rattling the glass walls.

Jack staggered back through the Features department red-faced, leaving behind a trail of puzzled looks and whispered conversations. He sat down at his desk, his mind fogged with confusion. Love letters? Snake slayer? Kathleen? It's not possible. He tried to sort it out, hands covering his face. Nothing made sense. It's not possible. It's not possible.

"Jack. You okay?" It was Mike Gray, the Arts editor, at the adjacent desk.

"Oh, man," said Jack. He took in and blew out a couple of deep breaths. "Yeah, Mike. I'm . . . I just need . . . Look, I'm going to walk over to Donna's for some coffee. I'll be back in a bit."

He was trotting across Calvert Street, against the light, when the answer came to him. He didn't know what had happened, exactly, but he knew how it had happened. He turned around in the middle of the street and headed back to the *Star-News* building.

It was the laptop. He'd left the laptop on.

Chapter 56

Kathleen Faulkner was huddled with one of the cop reporters when Jack approached her desk.

"I need to talk to you," he said.

She swung around in her chair. "I'm a little busy. Give me fifteen minutes."

"It's either here, in front of everyone, or in the Metro meeting room." It sounded stupidly melodramatic when he said it, but he didn't care.

The cop reporter coughed nervously. "I'll come back later, Kathleen," she said.

When they entered the meeting room, Kathleen sat down, but Jack remained standing.

"You read my e-mails, didn't you?" he said, leaning over the table toward her.

"What do you mean?" asked Kathleen.

"When I left my room. You read my e-mails, you fucking cunt," he said, straining to keep his voice from trembling. He wanted to lash out at her, he wanted to hurt her, but he also wanted to stay in control.

"Yes, I read them," she said, paling. No one had ever called her that before. "I didn't know what else to do. You shouldn't have left, Jack. You shouldn't have left me there alone."

"What the fuck does that mean? I asked you to leave my room. You wouldn't. So that gave you the right to go through my things?"

"I thought you'd come back so I stayed for a few minutes. The laptop was signed on. Yes. I read some of your e-mails. I'm sorry."

"You're lying," said Jack. "You did more than that. You sent her a message, didn't you?"

"Who?"

"Don't fuck with me," said Jack, his face ugly with anger. "You know who. You sent a message to Annie Hollerman."

"No. I swear. I would never do that."

"You're lying," he said again. "I know it. Tell me now or, so help me God, I will go to your house and tell your husband everything."

Until those words came out of his mouth, it had never occurred to Jack to use their affair as leverage. Would he really have stormed over to Kathleen's house? The answer was probably no, but the tone of his voice said yes. And that was enough.

Kathleen folded her arms against her chest. "She called," she said, through clenched jaws.

"What?"

"The Hollerman woman. She called your room when you were gone."

"My God. What did you say to her?"

"I told her we were there together. I told her I loved your words and I loved you. And that you loved me."

"My God. My God." It was all he could say. He turned away from her and looked out the glass walls of the meeting room. Half the Metro department was looking back at him. Well, he thought, there's plenty of blood in the water today. This will keep the newsroom gossip piranhas busy for weeks.

Behind him he heard Kathleen say, her voice finally beginning to break, "I didn't want to lose you."

He walked toward the door without looking back.

"You lost me six months ago," he said.

CHAPTER 57

It was 11:15 when Jack finally made the phone call he'd been trying to make all morning. It was 11:16 when that call ended.

It hadn't been a satisfying conversation.

Fred had refused to put him through to Annie. There had been
heated emotionality on Jack's side, ruthless efficiency on Fred's,
ending in an abrupt click.

It was 11:17 when Jack made the second call.

"Fred,pleasedon'thangup,Iknowyousaidshedoesn'twanttotalkto
me,butjustgivemethreeminutes—THREEMINUTES—isthat
toomuchtoask?" Jack spoke as quickly as he could make his tongue
move, resulting in one long, blurry sentence. To his relief, there
was no click on the other end.

Then he slowed down. "Just hear me out. Okay? Let me tell you
what happened. It's not what Annie thinks. Three minutes?
Okay? Just enough to tell you the whole story. Then if you think
it's bullshit, you can hang up. But if you don't—and I know you
won't—you have to talk to Annie for me. You've got to get her to
listen to what I have to say."

There was still silence on the other end of the line. A blessed
silence, in Jack's mind. It meant that Fred was, at least, considering his plea.

"Okay," said Fred, finally, "three minutes. No promises, though."

Jack rushed through Friday night's events like a guy qualifying for a NASCAR race. When he finished, Fred responded with a skeptical "Hmmph." In desperation Jack played his one and only ace.

"Look, Fred," he said, "I know this sounds ridiculous, but I can prove it. Those guys I was drinking with, I'll have one of them call you. My boss, Steve Proctor, he was there. He'll tell you what happened."

"Hmmph," Fred snorted again, skepticism intact. "Why should I believe him? You could have coached him."

"I'd never do that."

"Oh?" said Fred, in the voice of a schoolteacher listening to a missed homework excuse.

"If you won't believe him, I'll give you a list of every person I was in the bar with that night. There were at least seven. I'll give you their phone numbers right now, before I have a chance to 'coach' them."

This time Fred's "hmmph" was higher-pitched and contained a note of surprise—but, to Jack's ear, an entire symphonic score of hope. He plowed ahead before the note could change.

"You've got to believe me, Fred. If I were really the lothario-schmuck-asshole everybody thinks I am, would I be this desperate? Would I be on my knees begging?"

There was a ten-second hour before Fred responded.

"All right, Mr. DePaul. I'll consider it. But don't call back again and don't come here. Let's take a week or so for things to settle down."

CHAPTER 58

Annie whammed Sigourney Weaver with a left jab, followed fast by a right uppercut. Just as she snap-kicked the tall brunette into oblivion, she heard the buoyant voice of MaryJo, the fitness instructor at Dupont Sport and Health.

"Wow," MaryJo chirped, lowering the black boxing mitt she'd been holding in front of Annie's gloved fists. "You've really improved your punch. What's going on? You angling for a part in Jackie Chan's next movie?"

"Something like that," Annie said, prancing in place to the beat of "Mambo Number 5."

"Well, keep it up," MaryJo said, moving over to the next salsa boxer in the line. "And did everyone see Annie's last kick?" she said into her headset microphone. "That's just how I want you all to do it."

The face of Sigourney Weaver disappeared with MaryJo's mitt. Now as Annie jabbed, punched, and kicked, she watched the mirrored wall in front of her as a line of women assaulted the air with varying degrees of ferocity. The Monday night salsa boxers came in all shapes and sizes. There were chubbies and skinnies and some in between. There was Deneen, the process server, who looked like she belonged in a *Playboy* spread ("Women of the Justice System"); there was a pregnant woman from Russia (Ivana?

Svetlana?) who always looked angry; there was Lala the lawyer, a short Hispanic woman with the sinewy arms of a rock climber. And there was Annie the literary agent, a slenderish redhead, with a strong desire to maim tonight.

Annie watched herself along with her sisters in salsa. Okay, so she didn't have the smooth hip-glide thing going that MaryJo and Lala had, or Deneen's exuberant breasts, or Svetlana/Ivana's alabaster skin. In fact, there were plenty of things she didn't have. But at age forty-four and three-quarters, Annie decided it was time to stop categorizing herself by her have-nots.

She'd spent an awful few days thinking about Kathleen Faulkner and all the things she had that Annie didn't: long legs, good thighs, a strong jaw, an important job, Jack. It didn't matter that she'd never seen the woman. Laura had told her she looked like Sigourney Weaver and Annie's imagination filled in the rest.

It'd taken Laura's blunt words to shake her out of it. "You're such a dope," she'd said last night over burritos at Wrapworks. Laura had come down to D.C. to take Annie out to dinner—and to apologize for fixing her up with Jack. She'd even sworn never to mention good asses again.

"You remember the Sigourney Weaver part, but forget the turbo-bitch part," Laura said. "Faulkner doesn't have a friend in the newsroom, Annie. They call her Captina Queeg, for Christsakes. Plus, she's got piano-stool legs, so you can erase *that* from your mind. Believe me, she's not half the person you are. Would you like me to list the ways?"

"Yes," Annie had said.

As the beat slowed down for ab work, Annie thought about Laura's list. Funny, smart, kind, determined, small waist, great hair, willing to pee outdoors, and beautiful. She knew the last one was just a best friend's bias (and major guilt for fixing her up with such a schmuck), but she'd let the others stand, dammit. She was measuring herself by her haves now.

Her abs began to burn and she was about to give up. But the same resolve that kicked in Saturday morning, after an hour of moldering in bed torturing herself with Kathleen's words, kicked in now. She went into ab overdrive, clinching so hard with each rep that she felt like coiled steel. She was ready for another twenty crunches, when MaryJo popped to her feet and started swinging her fists again. "Okay, boxers," she yelled, her amplified voice bouncing off the mirrored walls, "let's give it all you got. You're Mike Tyson and someone just smashed your new Mercedes. One, two—jab, punch, kick. Three-four—imagine a crumpled door— kick, punch, jab . . ."

Annie started attacking. A new face came to her with each swing. Kathleen; Jack; that *Star-News* reporter with the dirty tie; Andrew Binder; her old city editor, Mark Snowridge; her fourth-grade teacher, Mrs. Wenzel, who failed her in fingernail check; her former boss, Greg Leeland, who had issues with strong women; and finally herself—for overreacting, as usual.

Jack was free to sleep with whomever he wanted. They'd known each other less than a month. They hadn't even hinted at the L word. They'd had great sex and great e-mails, but that didn't mean he owed her exclusivity. In fact, he didn't owe her anything. It wasn't his fault that she'd taken it all to heart. She hadn't under-stood till Saturday morning, when she was burning holes in the ceiling with her stare, just how needy she'd been when Jack DePaul entered her life.

"I was so ready for romance he could've recited me the god-damned alphabet and I'd have been planning our wedding," Annie had told Laura the previous night. "And that fantasy he spun—that he could rewrite my past—well, shit, I never had a chance. He might as well have hooked me on crack cocaine."

What Annie didn't tell Laura was this: she'd thought she'd fi-nally found the one. Jack DePaul, with his crooked teeth and banty cock chest. She'd thought she was his muse; he was cer-tainly hers. For the first time in twenty years, she couldn't wait to get in front of a keyboard again to see where her fingers took her. She'd loved the mysterious way words tumbled out of her mind and onto the screen. It was alchemy. But she'd stopped writing after the *Commercial-Appeal*.

No, she didn't tell Laura any of these things. She was too embarrassed.

"What're you going to do if he keeps calling?" Laura had asked.

"He'll stop. He's got Ms. Piano-Stool Legs back and that's clearly what he wanted. He was probably just using me to make her jealous—and it obviously worked. Who knows, who cares? I've told Fred not to even tell me if he calls, not that he's going to. I have no desire to talk to him. What would I say? 'How many more snake slayers are there, Jack?'

"It's over. And this way, I don't have to deal with him about the *Commercial-Appeal* thing. Anyhow, this rewriting-my-past stuff— it was great while it lasted, but it's time to put that to bed. In fact, it's time to put my past to bed, period. I've got a present to think about."

"Jab. Punch. Kick! Go girls. Yeah!" yelled MaryJo, exhorting them to new levels of pummelment. Annie followed ferociously, her T-shirt soaked through with sweat. MaryJo whipped her head Annie's way and said, "Don't mess with Annie. She's on fire tonight."

"Yeah, I've killed all my enemies," Annie said with an uppercut to the air.

"That's why we're here," MaryJo shouted into her headset. "That and this," she said, slapping her taut butt. "Okay, last set. Let her rip. Let's go."

By the final jab, Annie wasn't sure she could remain vertical. Her legs were wobbly, her arms shaking. She joined the other salsa ladies in a whoop of relief and joy when MaryJo finally clapped her hands together and said, "Good job. Time to eat."

Before heading to the showers and sauna, Annie assessed the woman before her in the mirror. Did she look like someone whose Mr. Right had just turned into Mr. Schmuck? No. She looked tough and sweaty. Maybe a bit battered, but not beaten.

In a way, Jack DePaul could take some credit for her resilience. She'd loved falling in love and Jack had made it so easy. He was good, no question about it.

But that dream was shattered, and, surprisingly, she didn't feel like retreating to her pile of books. She felt like trying again. Jack had made her hungry. Given her an appetite for more.

"Hey, Annie," it was Lala, a towel around her neck. "You going straight home?"

"No, I'm not. Want to go for a smoothie? Maybe there're some cute guys at Jamba Juice. And if we're lucky, they like girls."

CHAPTER 59

Just about the time Annie was uppercutting her way to self-actualization, Jack was slumped in front of the Mac, still on the ropes, still reeling from the day's body blows.

He'd spent the afternoon ignoring the curious looks and the buzzing newsroom. He chose, instead, to wallow in editing details and self-pity. "But it's not my fault" was his mantra as he sat at his desk hunched like a hedgehog under attack. A little after five, Arts editor Mike Gray suggested kindly that, maybe, Jack should leave early.

"I'm not going to ask what's going on," he said, "but I think you and your little black cloud need to get out of here. Go to the gym; go get drunk; go. Do you want me to meet you at Sisson's later? We can order boutique beers and watch the Lakers."

"Thanks, Mike," Jack said. "I think I'll just go home. There's some stuff I need to do."

Stuff. Like trying to get to Annie. Phoning was out of the question, intermediaries were out, too—Laura would sooner help Pol Pot than Jack DePaul—and a direct assault didn't seem wise. He briefly considered driving to D.C., but he was afraid she'd slam the door in his face or, worse, call the cops.

E-mail was his refuge. It had gotten him into this mess, maybe it would get him out. But what could he say? Just telling his side of the story wasn't going to be enough. He could hardly believe the events himself, and he'd lived through them. How could he explain Kathleen Faulkner in fewer pages than *War and Peace*?

He knew that, somehow, he had to woo Annie all over again. But what words, what message, could soften a heart that must by now be as impervious to him as titanium? And the most important word of all wasn't available. If "love" suddenly appeared, it would only make him look like a desperate con man hitting below the belt.

Jack sat in front of the screen absently eating popcorn. How can I make her believe?

To <u>ahollerman@aol.com</u>
From <u>jdepaul@aol.com</u>
Subject: The truth
Annie,

You've got to read this e-mail. You've got to give us a chance.

Nothing that happened Friday night in New York is what it seems. It was like a bad student film mixing slapstick and soap opera. It involved a jealous, lying former lover, an unlocked hotel room, a laptop left on, and incredible naivete on the part of the hapless protagonist—me.

I need to tell you the whole stupid saga in person. You'll see in my face that I'm telling the truth. But until you let me back into your life, these words will have to do: I'm not seeing anybody else, I'm not having an affair with anybody else, I have never betrayed you or your trust in any way. The only woman I want in my life is you.

The only woman I want in my life is you.

I never realized how true those words were until now. Jack and Annie, Annie and Jack. It's too good, it's too right. We can't let it be destroyed by an evil spirit from my past.

The past seems to be haunting us both. I don't care about the Annie of the past. The Annie of New Jersey or North Carolina. All I care about is the now and future

Annie. From now on, let's create tomorrows, not yesterdays. That way, we can make them come true.

I want to make a lot of things come true. The list can be as long as our lives together. A trip in October. Close your eyes, you can image every scene. . . .

We fly to Santa Fe and rent a car. We drive north to Colorado and west to Utah. From the Abajos, where the leaves of the aspens are as gold as Spanish doubloons, we turn south. Somewhere on Cedar Mesa we pull off onto an old fire road and drive through junipers and pinyon pines to the edge of a canyon. We stop, put on our backpacks, and climb down switchbacks toward the canyon floor about 400 feet below.

The sun is high; the rocks warm to the touch. The air smells dry and sharp. It's clear, though a few mares' tails brush the western horizon. The trail ends in a tricky stretch of slickrock so we slide on our butts the last 30 or 40 feet to a big juniper tree and climb down it to the canyon bottom.

It's easy hiking there on hard-packed sand. You take the lead and I follow your voice like a trail. By late afternoon we're far below the mesa top. On either side of us, the walls rise nearly straight up so, while the rims still burn orange and bright sienna, dusk arrives early to the trail.

A side canyon comes in from the right. Up against the sandstone monoliths that guard the confluence are the remains of an ancient pueblo. With its stony crenellations and empty windows, it looks like a tiny castle. Above the remains, a faded white disc is painted on the sheer sandstone cliff. Inside the disc are two circles the color of the rock beneath. The ghostly remains of a painted face.

We climb up a talus slope to the ruin and explore its seven tiny rooms—how small the builders must have been. On a flat spot that commands a view of both canyons we sit and watch the fading day and say something like this:

Jack: "They sat here, too."

Annie: "Who?"

Jack: "The Anasazi. Eight hundred years ago. If Matthew were here, he could tell us all about them."

Annie: "I wonder what they would think of us."

Jack: "They would look at your hair, fall down on their knees, and worship you as a goddess."

Annie: "Or eat me for dinner."

We camp below the ruin. The temperature plummets at night, so we build a small fire near our tent and huddle by it, wrapped up in our sleeping bag. We sit so close to the flames my hiking boots start to smolder.

A pot of water boils all evening and from time to time we snake our hands out from the folds of the bag just long enough to make another cup of instant cocoa.

I recite you poems by Pablo and we play the explorer game. You say that if you had discovered Australia, you would have named it Koalaland. I vow that, if you give me the last swallow of cocoa, I'll name it Annieland.

Mummied together in the bag, we watch the stars cataract between the canyon rims. We crawl into the tent before 10 o'clock and let the fire burn itself out. Somewhere an owl hoots.

In the middle of the night I awake out of a dream with your insistent hand on my shoulder.

"Jack," you whisper, "there's someone up there."

"Huh?"

"Up at the ruin. There's someone up there."

"What?" I whisper back, still half asleep.

"I was about to get up to pee—all that cocoa—when I heard some rocks falling. I looked out and saw somebody climbing to the ruin."

I pull tent flaps aside. The moon, now high over the rim, is a fingernail paring away from full. "Jesus. It's so bright out. Where is he? Can you still see him?"

"Look to where we were sitting at sunset. See—that black shape. That's him."

"Who is it? Who would hike around here in the middle of the night?"

"Maybe it's . . ."

And then we hear someone singing. A man's voice, deliberate and repetitive. Each syllable strikes the cold air like fingers against a drum, but they beat out no words that we can understand, just melancholy rhythms. We listen, arms around each other, afraid to move, afraid to break the spell.

The big moon climbs; the song goes on. And when it finally stops, maybe a half hour later, pieces of it seem to linger in the shadows. We look outside the flap. Above the ruin, the ghostly painted face glows in the reflected light—a little brother moon—but the dark shape of the singer is gone.

In the innocent brightness of the next morning, it's hard to believe in the moon, let alone chanting in the night. When I wake up, you're already outside. I stick my head out of the tent and see two fires to warm me. One is heating our pot of water; the other, lit by sunrise, is your hair. You've tied it up with a cotton band, about an inch and a half wide, woven in bright threads of green, turquoise, and red.

"That hair ribbon is beautiful," I say. "Why haven't you worn it before?"

You give me a curious look. "I haven't worn it before because I just found it."

"Found it?"

"This morning. It was looped around the center pole of our tent."

In a magical canyon, moon meets moon and a woman is crowned by a singing spirit. Do you think this is just a fanciful story? It's not.

Don't give up on us, and we can make it real. This story and a thousand others.

Please call me. Please message me.

Jack

CHAPTER 60

When Annie woke up Tuesday morning, her legs were screaming, "No," her arms were shrieking, "I hate you," and her stomach? Well, her stomach was frozen in an Edvard Munchian wail of pain.

In that first moment of morning fog, Annie Hollerman couldn't figure out why she felt like she'd gone ten rounds with Mike Tyson. Then she remembered.

"Oh man," she groaned as she hobbled to the shower, "no more salsa boxing."

An hour later she walked into her office, limped past Fred, and held up her hand to silence him.

"Don't even ask," she said. "I got a little carried away last night."

Fred nodded and pretended to work. Under normal circumstances he would have called her Wonder Woman, told her to take up ballroom dancing, and perhaps quoted something pertinent from Shakespeare. But he knew she was hurting on a much deeper level than the muscular, so he remained silent.

Annie had gotten home late last night. She and Lala had talked for hours. Given Annie's recent phone call with Kathleen Faulkner and Lala's difficult divorce, the carcass of the male species had been picked clean.

Usually Annie checked her e-mail before turning in, but last night she went directly from her front door to her bed. And now there was payback in the form of forty-six new messages.

Had Annie been expecting to see something from Jack? Maybe. Probably. Yes. But that didn't stop the sizzle of current that jolted her body when she saw jdepaul listed in new mail.

She looked at his name and for a split second she forgot about Kathleen and New York. For a split second, she was Annie the snake slayer of Hemet, California, ready for another trip to their past.

"Annie, are you alright?"

It was Fred, bringing her back to the present.

"He wrote me," Annie said.

"I'm not surprised," said Fred. "That is what he does, you know. By the way, I know you told me not to tell you, but he called yesterday. He was very distraught."

"Maybe Kathleen dumped him already," Annie said.

"Are you going to read it?"

Annie's hands were poised over the keyboard, the same way they'd been poised over the keyboard a month ago while she fretted about responding to Jack's first e-mail. This time, however, instead of the send button, her finger hovered over delete.

She wished she could just press the damn key and send it to cyber trash or, better yet, let it rot in her mailbox. She imagined Jack's no doubt beautiful, but lying, words decomposing there, so that when she did finally open it in, say, sixty-seven years, the letters would crumble before her eyes, leaving a pile of black dust at the bottom of her screen.

But who was she kidding? She had no more willpower now than she had thirty years ago when she was singing "Let it please be him" to a silent blue Princess telephone.

"Annie, he sounded quite upset yesterday. Read the e-mail. I think you should hear him out."

"Maybe. Maybe tonight."

CHAPTER 61

To jdepaul@aol.com
From ahollerman@aol.com
Re: Words
Jack,

I read your e-mail. It seems Kathleen and I could agree on at least one thing—you are good with words.

You know the expression "Words are cheap"? I disagree. There's nothing more expensive than the wrong word, sentence, or paragraph. Just look what it cost me. Almost an entire life of hiding and regret.

And now I have your words again, trying to lure me back into something that probably should never have been. Jack, we went so fast and built everything on the wrong words. Lies. Certainly mine. Maybe yours. Maybe Kathleen's. There've been so many words, it's hard to know which ones are true.

I agree it's time to move away from the past, but not to the future. I've got the present to think about. I think it would be best if you didn't write again. Save your words for your next partner in time travel. I'm sure she'll love them. We all do.

Annie

CHAPTER 62

"Mom, I can't find Mr. Planters."

Annie was wearing black jogging shorts and an old Outward Bound T-shirt frayed around the neck. It was Friday afternoon and she'd just run half the length of the Atlantic City Boardwalk and back. She was playing hooky for the day but excused herself on the grounds that it had been a horrible week and that it would be a treat for her mother to see her daughter twice in less than a month. Her mother had been so excited when she'd said yes, she'd meet her in Atlantic City, that she'd agreed to Annie's one condition: no mention of the name Jack DePaul.

Annie needed a Jack DePaul–free weekend. Because no matter how hard she'd tried to push it away, his name kept bubbling back into her thoughts all week. Telephone calls helped—momentarily. Conversations with Fred kept it at bay—for a few minutes. But the quiet in Annie's office left too much open space in her brain. Was he lying? Was he telling the truth? Either way, she'd been an idiot.

What she needed was sensory overload, what she needed was Atlantic City, a place that would drown out all her thoughts about Jack DePaul. A place that would chase away her humiliation.

"Forget Mr. Planters," said Joan Hollerman Silver as she slipped four quarters into the poker machine in front of her. "He's gone. Like most of my money."

"Don't blame me," said Annie. "I asked you to come with me. I would've walked instead of run. But you had to win back the two hundred dollars you lost last night."

"Now it's five hundred. Here, sit and play." Annie's mother handed her a fistful of quarters.

Annie wasn't much of a gambler. Yet another of her mother's genes that hadn't attached itself to Annie's DNA ladder. When she was a kid, she'd worried that she'd been adopted. One more thing to set her apart. It was bad enough that she had screaming red hair and her mother was the only unmarried woman on the block—back then she was called a divorcee, pronounced in the French way—div-or-SAY—to imply wantonness. But to be adopted, too?

Both her parents had black hair and olive skin and on more than one occasion she'd heard people say, "Where'd you get the little carrot top, Joanie? The milkman?"

For the longest time, Annie imagined the milkman dropping off a baby with fuzzy red hair, along with the three quart glass bottles. It wasn't until an afternoon at Sid Gold's, an expensive dress store on Haverford Avenue in Philadelphia, that Annie heard two of the most comforting words in her life: recessive gene.

Annie and her mother were in Philly for the March of Dimes dinner honoring her grandmother. Her grandmother didn't like the dress Annie's mother was going to wear to the dinner dance, so they went to Sid Gold's. One of the salesladies made the milkman joke to Annie's mother. Sid, a squat woman with a deep voice who'd been dressing Annie's grandmother, Bea Gerber, since she was a young woman, said, "Oh, can it, Delores, Bea had the same hair color until she went gray. Rose Schwartz told me hair and eye color can skip a generation. Her husband's a doctor and she said it's something called a recessive gene."

Recessive gene. Just one textbook phrase and a whole childhood of feeling like she didn't belong—uncomfortable, as if she were wearing a scratchy wool sweater against her skin—was booted out the window. Kapow! Right there on Haverford Avenue on September 28, 1966, at 3:15 P.M., Annie Beth Hollerman first felt the power of words and started her love affair with the English language.

"More," Annie said, reaching an open hand her mother's way.

"You've lost that already? You're obviously my daughter. Here."

Over coins slamming against metal, the *ding, ding, ding* of winning machines, and the piped-in Muzak of the seventies and eighties, Annie and her mother played video poker and talked.

"Don't you miss it?" Annie said.

"Miss what?"

"Atlantic City," Annie said. "I mean the real Atlantic City. Mr. Planters. The dressed-up ladies. The Sodamat. The rolling chairs, when the seats weren't faded. Don't you miss it, Mom?"

Joan Hollerman Silver stopped feeding the machine. She tilted her head from side to side, weighing past against present.

"Miss it?" she said. "To tell you the truth, those weren't such good times for me. It's better this way. Now when I go on the Boardwalk, what I see is all new. Maybe not good new, but new. So the Peanut Man is gone and hardly anyone even speaks English here anymore. Used to be the closest thing we ever heard to a foreign language was Harry Adler from the Bronx.

"Not to bring up a sore subject—and I know I promised I wouldn't, so I won't say anything else about him—but it's a little like the Romeo and that thing he was doing with his e-mails, changing your past. When I come here and walk down the Boardwalk and there's nothing left from the way it used to be, it almost feels like that old time never happened. That the Joan Hollerman who worked for fifty dollars a week keeping books and fought with your father in court never was. And that's fine by me."

Annie nodded and put her hand on her mother's shoulder. All those years yearning for floor wax. She wished she could have realized, back then, that it was harder being a "divorsay" than a daughter of a "divorsay."

She looked at her mother's perfect hair and perfect nails. At the way her jaw jutted out each time she put another four quarters in the machine, as if daring it to cross her. She wore the same expression in court when she cross-examined witnesses. Imagine that: her mother had gone from a job as a fifty-dollar-a-week book-keeper to being one of the most successful attorneys in Greensboro.

So Annie hadn't gotten her mother's hair, skin, or chest genes, she'd gotten the more important ones.

"Nope, Annie. I don't miss it one bit. And to tell you the truth, the girdles and the spike heels—good riddance."

Annie had stopped playing while her mother had been talking. A big mistake in Atlantic City.

"Are you using that machine or not?" barked a white-haired woman in a walker.

Annie stood up. "It's all yours. But it's a loser, I'm warning you."

The woman sat down, lit a cigarette, and started fishing quarters from her plastic Caesar's cup. Annie turned to her mother and said, "I'm going up to the room to shower and change. After that, how about a stroll down new memory lane?"

"We'll see," said her mother. "Now I have five hundred and fifty dollars to win back—thanks to you."

CHAPTER 63

There had been a 10K race early Saturday at Fort McHenry, so when Jack met Matthew at One World around nine that morning, the coffeehouse was overflowing with runners wearing numbers and carrying plastic sports bottles.

It was a mild day, though blustery. The two of them waited outside for fifteen minutes until a table opened up. Plenty of time for Matthew to learn about the Annie–Kathleen disaster and to offer an opinion.

"Dad, you're a knucklehead."

"Look, son . . ." said Jack.

"Dad, you're an imbecile. A moron."

"Well . . ."

"My father, a retard."

"Okay, Matthew, I get the picture."

"But I really liked her. She was great. I can't believe you let this happen."

"I didn't exactly 'let it happen.' It wasn't my fault."

"Oh?" said Matthew. "Like Kathleen Faulkner is not your fault." Up until then, he'd been bantering. But this remark, with its sharp edge honed by divorce, suddenly brought the conversation to the edge of hurt and resentment.

"That was a very complicated situation," Jack said in the severe tone he used with reporters who missed deadlines. "And it's not something I really want to talk to you about. Besides, it was over nearly a year ago."

Matthew almost replied, "I've heard that before," but stopped short. Leaning against a wall, he looked down at his father, who was sitting on an outside window ledge. Was it his imagination, or had he gotten smaller and grayer in the past two weeks? The resentment began to fade. Matthew's face softened, he reached down and punched his father lightly on the shoulder. "That doesn't alter the facts: you're still a knucklehead and you've still blown it with Annie. What are you going to do?"

"Nothing, I guess," said Jack. "She thinks I'm scum."

"That's it? You're just giving up? You're not going to fight for her?"

"What can I do?" said Jack with a shrug.

"You could get down on your knees and beg for forgiveness. That's what I'd do."

"Well, you're twenty-two and have no dignity."

"Dignity, my left testicle! From what you've told me, she's the best thing to happen to you in . . ." He was going to say twenty years, but it sounded disloyal to his mother, so instead he said, "a very long time."

Then, warming to his new role as Dear Abby, he grabbed one of his father's shoulders and gave it a shake. "How will she know how you feel if you don't tell her?"

"Okay, smart guy, how do I tell her? She won't take my calls and I've tried e-mail. She blew me off."

"Go to her house."

"That's harassment. I won't do it."

"Coward."

"Maybe. But I won't."

"What about Laura Goodbread? Make her your go-between."

"If Annie thinks I'm scum, Laura thinks I'm something you scrape off your shoes."

"But you're innocent. Explain to Laura what happened."

"She'll stab me with a pair of scissors," said Jack with a grin, then added seriously, "it's hard to have such a personal conversation in the newsroom."

"Well, go to her house and tell her. It wouldn't be harassment with Laura. You work together, you're friends—or used to be. It's Saturday, we could go there right now."

"We?" said Jack, narrowing his eyes.

"Us," said Matthew. "You obviously need my help in this matter. Let's go right now." He ended this last sentence on an upturned note of encouragement.

My son the motivational speaker, Jack thought. He knew there must be good reasons to ignore this suggestion, but he couldn't think of any so he stalled. Still scowling, he said, "Let me think about it over breakfast."

After they ordered omelets, Jack steered the conversation away from the minefield of emotional entanglements to subjects such as the O's, the ten-year anniversary of their trip to Chile, and eventually to the Anasazi, which he figured would occupy his son for at least twenty-five minutes.

But he couldn't steer his own mind from stubborn memories of the confrontations at the *Star-News* offices Monday morning and of Annie's dismissive e-mail that he'd read Tuesday evening. He'd felt dull and passive ever since; every night had been fitful and filled with menacing dreams. Twice he'd stayed up till early morning writing pleading e-mails to Annie, and twice he'd deleted them.

After a week of lethargy, he was embarrassed by his son's pep and can-do optimism. Maybe Matthew was right. If I feel this bad about losing Annie, shouldn't I be fighting harder to get her back? After all, what's more important, dignity or love?

He leaned back in his chair, hands behind his head, and gave out a rueful little laugh, stopping Matthew in the middle of a tangent on the domestication of corn in Mesoamerica.

"What?" Matthew said.

"I guess I'm in love," said Jack to his son and a waitress who'd stopped by with coffee refills. Then he nodded to himself. "Yes, I'm in love."

"Well, duh," said Matthew. "You've only been talking about, writing about, and thinking about Annie nonstop for a month."

"Don't 'duh' me, wretched child. We need to do something."

"Dad, didn't I say this just a half hour ago?"

Jack ignored him. "We should go to Laura's house," he said, a surprised look in his eyes as if he had just been shaken awake. "What do we have to lose?" He started to get up out of his chair.

"We?" said Matthew, with a grin.

"We," said his father. "She won't stab me if I bring a witness."

CHAPTER 64

It was Becky who answered the doorbell. She was wearing a grass-stained soccer outfit; in her left hand was a muffin with a big bite missing.

"Yes?" she said tentatively, clinging to the half-opened door.

"Hi, Becky," said Jack, "is your mother home?"

"Oh, hi, Mr. DePaul," she said. "Yeah, she's home, but you're not exactly her favorite person right now."

Jack hesitated and Matthew nudged him. "Right," Jack said, nodding his head. "I'm sure that's true. Could you just tell her I've come to explain?"

"Okay," she said and, without leaving her post by the door, put her head back and yelled at the top of her lungs, "Mom! Mr. DePaul's here! He says he wants to explain things."

Jack winced. This wasn't exactly how the Make-Laura-Understand scene was supposed to unfold. He had envisioned a surprised greeting, a soulful discussion—preferably over coffee—a dawning realization, and reason triumphant. Instead he was getting the Marx Brothers. He looked past Becky into the house but there was no sign of an adult or the sound of one approaching.

The three of them stood in the doorway silently, fidgeting. Jack decided there were few things more obnoxious than a precocious, smart-mouthed twelve-year-old version of Laura Goodbread.

More silence. Jack felt like there was concrete hardening around his ankles. Finally Matthew spoke up. "Think we could wait inside?"

Becky ushered them in just as Laura came down the stairs to the living room. Her scowl changed to a look of surprise when she saw Jack's son.

"Matthew?" Laura said, then turned toward Jack. Before she could say anything else, Jack said, "I brought him because I knew you wouldn't kill me in front of a witness."

Becky laughed and her mother shot her a look. "Very funny, Jack," Laura said. "Matthew, it's nice to see you again, but your father and I said everything we needed to say at the office. Now if you'll excuse us, Becky and I were just heading out."

"We were?" Becky said. "But don't you want to hear Mr. DePaul explain what happened?"

Laura paused. Jack knew he had to seize the moment before she stormed away or, worse, Matthew jumped in to help. He grabbed his cell phone and held it up. "Five minutes," he said. "Just give me five minutes and a call to Proctor."

"Proctor?" Laura said. "What's he got to do with your little Kathleen drama?"

Jack shook the cell phone at her. "That's just it. There is no little Kathleen drama. There's no big Kathleen drama, there's no Kathleen drama at all. She stole my e-mails, she's the thief of words, not me. That's what I've been trying to tell everybody all week."

"Which one's Kathleen, Mom?" asked Becky.

"She's the bad guy," Matthew told her.

"Just hear me out, Laura. What's the harm?" said Jack.

"Yeah, Mom, let's hear him out," said Becky, wide-eyed at finding herself in the middle of an adult drama. Laura gave her a go-to-your-room-right-now-young-lady glare; Becky ignored it.

"Yeah, Mom," said Jack, grinning. His opinion of precocious twelve-year-olds was changing rapidly.

"Okay, okay," said Laura. "Let's go to the kitchen."

The kitchen table was centered by last night's take-out pizza box and strewn with sections of that morning's *Star-News*. Laura moved the papers aside and sat down, quickly followed by Matthew and Becky. Jack sat opposite Laura and, ignoring the fact that two referees under the age of twenty-five had been added to the scene, plunged ahead with his story.

He started with the knock at his hotel room door and his surprise at seeing Kathleen, then he marched through all the major points of that Friday night: walking out on Kathleen, leaving the laptop on, Annie's phone call, Kathleen's treachery. He told her everything, including how many drinks he'd had with their boss.

"This is where Proctor comes in," Jack said. "Kathleen told Annie I was there when she called. In fact, I was nowhere near that hotel room when Annie called. I was getting shitfaced—excuse me, Becky—with my fellow slime-sucking editors. And Proctor can vouch for me."

Jack dialed a number on his cell phone and waited a few moments. "Proc? It's Jack, I'm sorry to call you at home on a weekend. No, everything's okay. But I have a favor to ask you. I know it sounds crazy, but I'm at Goodbread's house and I need you to tell her where you were last Friday night from nine till one, and where I was. No. No. I'm serious."

Jack handed the phone to Laura, who, before she could even say hello, heard Proctor say, "Goodbread, what the hell's going on? Are you guys on drugs or something?"

"Proc, it's too complicated to explain the whole thing right now," said Laura. "I promise I'll fill you in first thing Monday. But in a nutshell, Jack thinks you can save his sorry butt. So, what did happen last Friday night?"

"Nothing happened. Except we got smashed," said Proctor. "A bunch of us decided to go for drinks. We got to the bar a little after eight, Jack joined us about nine. We closed the place down. Left about one, one-thirty in the morning. Does this have something to do with that blowup at the office with Faulkner?"

"Kind of," said Laura. "Thanks, boss, you've been a big help."

After Proctor hung up, Laura handed the phone back to Jack.

"Well?" asked Jack. "What did he say?"

Laura scowled at Jack for a moment, then she slowly turned it into a reluctant smile. "Okay, I believe you," she said.

Jack let out a sigh of relief.

"I guess I'm sorry," said Laura.

"No need to apologize," said Jack. "Just call Annie and tell her. Tell her everything. In fact, tell her I'm on my way over to her house right now."

Jack, nearly overcome with relief and the prospect that Laura would get him out of this mess, was about to jump up and throw his arms around her broad shoulders when he noticed she wasn't smiling anymore.

"I wouldn't start celebrating right now if I were you, Jack," she said.

"Huh?" said Jack. "Isn't everything cleared up? You believe me, you just said so."

Laura shook her head, and for the first time in her life felt actual pity for an editor. "Sorry, Jack. It's not going to be that easy. First of all, Annie's in Atlantic City with her mother. I'll call her there and tell her everything, but don't get your hopes up. There's a lot more to Annie's vanishing act than Kathleen's nasty trick. Kathleen was an easy out for Annie. That way she didn't have to face you after Arthur appeared in her office asking all those questions about what happened at the *Commercial-Appeal*. She can't forgive herself for what she did, so how can she expect anyone else to?"

"But I don't care about her past!" Jack shouted.

"No one does. Except her—and a group of circle-jerk editors looking for a story where there isn't one," Laura said pointedly.

"How was I supposed to know Annie was on Arthur's list?" Jack said. "I'm no mind reader—if I were I'd know what to do now. Do you have any ideas?"

Laura shook her head, and the little entourage gathered around the kitchen table fell silent. Jack stared at the pizza box. Laura stared at Jack staring at the pizza box. Matthew and Becky held their breath waiting for someone to talk. Finally it was Jack.

"Maybe I should follow my own advice for once," he said, pushing around a piece of pizza crust with an index finger. "How many times have I harped on you that when you get stuck writing a story, it's because you need more information. That's what I need, more information. So, what exactly did happen in Charlotte?"

CHAPTER 65

Jack got up from the Mac and arched his back. It was nearly eight in the evening. He'd been writing and polishing since early afternoon.

The idea had come to him when Laura was in the middle of her Annie Hollerman history lesson. By the time he returned to his apartment, he had mapped out the entire e-mail. The most important e-mail of his life.

Before Laura had begun her tale, she'd shooed Becky and Matthew out of the house. "Go to the Towson Mall," she'd ordered them. "Buy some CDs or something." Then she'd put on another pot of coffee.

"I'd been at the *Commercial-Appeal* for six months when they hired Annie. We were friends right from the start," Laura said.

She told Jack how Annie beat out all the other applicants— even the Ivy Leaguers with their upper-crust pedigrees—and how she felt pressured from the beginning. "The editor told her to make page one in three weeks; she made it in two and half." Jack heard about Annie's meteoric rise to stardom, her relationship with fellow wunderkind Andrew Binder, how they were nicknamed A-Squared and were expected to be running the *New York Times* in ten years. He heard about her downfall and how Andrew left her soon after, about her abject shame at being a plagiarist, and how all of it led to a dismal marriage and an increasingly lonely middle age. Laura told him how, after twenty years, Annie still flinched when she heard the word "plagiarist" and how amazing it was that she finally gave in to Laura's pestering and agreed to go on a date with a journalist.

"I'll call her after you leave," Laura said when she'd finished, "but like I said, don't get your hopes up. You think I'm stubborn? Annie makes me look like a pushover. What're you going to do if she won't listen to me?"

"I don't know," said Jack. But by then, he did. He was already fine-tuning the idea, which had flashed into his head nearly fully formed as Laura described the day Annie was fired.

Jack looked down at the final lines on the computer screen. The last time he'd written her, she'd told him to go to hell. "Save your words for your next partner in time travel," she'd replied. He couldn't let that stop him. Words and imagination had won her once. And, like Cupid's little arrows, words were all he had left in his arsenal. Besides, it was a lot harder to hang up on an e-mail than a phone call.

He sat back down. "There've been so many words, it's hard to know which ones are true," Annie had said. These are true, Jack thought, as true as I can make them. Then he made a plea—a prayer, if truth be told—to whatever fates or gods there are: Please make Annie believe what I've written.

He scrolled to the top of the e-mail and read it through, stopping here and there to change a phrase or cut something extraneous. When he reached the end it was complete but for the last sentence. He had avoided writing it during the rough draft stages, wanting to save and savor the moment. With a bit of a flourish he wrote it, hesitating a moment over the final keystroke. It was just three words.

He leaned back and looked at it for a moment, head askance. Then he smiled.

CHAPTER 66

"Well, he used to be funny on Johnny Carson," said Joan Hollerman Silver. She waited as Annie walked through the door to their hotel room, then double-bolted it.

"*Don Rickles?*" Annie said, flinging herself dramatically onto the bed. "What were you thinking? I can't believe I let you talk me into going to see him. What's on for tomorrow night, Soupy Sales?"

"I think he's dead. But Fabian's at Trump's. Remember the crush you used to have on him? Okay, so the show wasn't great, but it's better than you brooding all night. Ever since you talked to Laura you've been a pill."

Annie's mother walked to the desk and opened the laptop. "Check your e-mail, I'll bet you he's written. And stop looking at me like that."

Annie flipped over and buried her face into the puffy mauve bedspread. Her words came out muffled. "You have no money left to bet and you're breaking your promise."

"Promise, schromise, what's your password?"

Annie jumped from the bed and bolted to her laptop.

"Oh relax, Annie, I wasn't really going to do it. But you can't keep going around like an ostrich. I'm going to take a bath now so you and your computer can have some privacy."

Annie's mother gathered her night things and walked to the bathroom. She went in, closed the door, and came right out. "I know, I promised, but one last thing, then I'm finished. The happiest I've ever seen you was when we were in Asheville. And it wasn't because you were with your mother. Annie, this Jack DePaul makes you happy, and I've waited a long time to see that. Second chances don't come along every day. You were on a winning streak with Jack and you should never quit while you're winning. He didn't do anything wrong, Annie, give him a break. Okay, now I'm finished, not another word."

With that, Joan Hollerman Silver closed the bathroom door behind her and lit a Virginia Slim.

Annie hovered by the computer, waiting for her mother's final, final last word. When the mirrored bathroom door stayed shut for five minutes, Annie figured it was safe. She signed on and saw, sandwiched between offers of cheap printer ink, a message from jdepaul, entitled "Proposal."

When she read his opening paragraph, she laughed. A laugh that quickly became a knowing smile. If Joan Hollerman Silver had been spying on her daughter—which, surprisingly, she wasn't—she would have seen a number of other expressions color Annie's face as she read Jack's message: understanding, appreciation, fleeting melancholy, happiness, and, finally, a kind of bewildered relief.

Annie closed the laptop and walked to the bathroom door. She knocked, opened it a crack, and said, "Ma, you better come out now or you'll end up a prune. I'm going for a walk. Don't wait up."

Before her mother had a chance to list all the horrible things that could befall a lone woman on the Boardwalk at night, Annie was out the door.

CHAPTER 67

Annie didn't notice the sea air's tang or the sliver of a moon with a bright star at its cusp. She didn't hear the soft thumping of the waves or the clip-clop of shoes against the Boardwalk's planks. She didn't see the neon lights flashing "Jackpots Here!!" or the rolling chairs carting white-haired ladies from casino to casino. She was deep in memories of her life before and after Jack DePaul.

A month ago—had it been just a month?—he'd written her that he felt like a stranger to himself, like the wind blew right through him. That's how she'd been feeling for twenty years. Who was that woman masquerading as Annie Hollerman? But with Jack, she remembered.

And it felt good to be the old Annie again. Jack made everything seem possible, even a new past. But she'd been deluding herself. The visit from the *Star-News* reporter proved that. Now she was back to the other Annie, the woman masquerading. And it didn't feel good.

She walked slowly past the Sands casino, oblivious to a crowd of teens watching a guy juggling butcher knives. Why couldn't she let go?

She grappled with the question for a while but gave up. It didn't seem as important as it used to. Maybe it wasn't the right question anymore. She looked up and, for the first time that

evening, noticed where she was. Ahead of her were the colored
lights of Steel Pier.

Now it was filled with Tilt-a-Whirls and other amusement
rides, but to Annie it would always be the place where she
watched the diving horses. She closed her eyes and imagined
what the riders of those horses must have felt right as they leapt
from the platform down forty feet into a small pool of water.
The fear, the adrenaline rush; how everything must have disappeared except the heart-stopping question: Will I land safely?

Will I land safely?

Those riders always did. And they were jumping horses off a
platform. All she was trying for was a second chance. It was her
turn on the platform now—behind her were all the trepidations of
a life made miserable by one mistake. In front was Jack DePaul,
the welcoming pool of water.

She ran back through the exuberant lights of the Boardwalk to
Caesar's and her hotel room. Her mother was asleep, or pretending to be. It didn't matter. Without hesitation, she took the leap.

To jdepaul@aol.com
From ahollerman@aol.com
Subject: Diving horses
Jack,

   If a red-haired woman comes up to you at 3:00 this
Sunday afternoon at the corner of Boardwalk and Park
Place in Atlantic City and says, "There are storm clouds
over Lisbon," don't be alarmed. It's her way of saying,
"I've been a fool."

   Love,
   Annie

CHAPTER 68

Jack walked to One World Café with the Sunday *New York Times* stuck under his left arm and the *Star-News* sports section rolled up in his right hand like a baton. It was the kind of bright June morning that indulged petunias in flower boxes and flattered Baltimore's brick row houses. The kind of bright morning you might find in the lede of a feature story by J. R. Thelman.

Jack flicked the sports section back and forth as if he were conducting a sprightly march. He was feeling good. He made a mental checklist of his fifty-year-old self and found everything in working order. Lower back—check. Hamstrings—check. Career—check. Emotional state—well, he'd done everything he could. Jack made a backhand swing with the sports section. The ball was now in Annie Hollerman's court.

He ended up sharing an outdoor table with a twenty-seven-year-old stock analyst who talked about his time-share in Cabo San Lucas. By the time he got back to the apartment it was after ten. He considered ignoring the e-mail possibilities that lurked inside his computer, but signed on anyway.

In less than fifteen minutes from the time he clicked on the message from ahollerman, he was in his car heading to Interstate 95 and Atlantic City. An overnight bag was tossed into the backseat, the windows were rolled down, and the radio was turned to the oldies station.

Jack gunned the Pathfinder up the on-ramp singing "Last Train to Clarksville" at the top of his lungs.

He arrived at the Boardwalk at 1:30. Plenty of time to fret about Annie's message. It was an invitation, right?

The afternoon was lightly overcast and, as he walked along the dark gray planks, the bright gray background made the colors of the signs and storefronts pop out like neon. After an hour's meandering, he headed to Park Place, where he found an empty place on a bench next to an old lady selling knitted cat figurines the size of small Christmas ornaments. A dozen of them were arranged on a blanket spread at her feet. Her face was tanned to leather.

The figurine lady didn't make any sales. For starters, she had even fewer marbles than teeth, and her sales approach lacked finesse. When any tourist veered to within ten feet, she would dangle one of her items from a finger and shout, "Hey, look here!"

It took imagination to picture the Atlantic City that Annie had described to him. That place from her childhood was full of Eisenhower innocence. Sandcastles and saltwater taffy by day, mink stoles and spike heels by night. This modern-day Atlantic City had no Heinz Pier, no one giving out little samples of relish or pickles; there was no Planters Peanut store, let alone a Peanut Man tipping his hat to fine ladies in elegant dresses. Platform sandals and T-shirts with sequined dice represented current Boardwalk fashion.

Only a few things seemed to have survived the tide of slot machines and ninety-nine-cent sunglasses. The rolling chairs were still rolling, Fralinger's was still selling saltwater taffy, and the Boardwalk fortune-tellers were still reading palms and looking into crystal balls.

Madame Chanel's had caught Jack's eye, with its white plastic chairs and purple paisley cushions and wind-up dogs yipping from a corner table in the souvenir shop next door. Madame Chanel, according to her sign, promised to "Solve all problems," "Answer questions," and "Reveal the future."

He thought briefly about getting a reading—it was only $10—but Madame Chanel, who was filing her long fuscia fingernails, seemed to be more in touch with her inner manicurist than the spirits. He decided to pass on her vision of the future.

The minutes passed by, and so did the endless parade of pedestrians. In the next half hour Jack saw more old men with thin white mustaches than he had seen in his entire life. Eventually the figurine lady departed, to be supplanted by two middle-aged women in lilac pedal pushers, who were in turn replaced by two senior citizens eating cherry water ice.

Jack didn't see her until she was only thirty paces away. It was as if she'd materialized out of the gray background. She was walking along the sea side of the Boardwalk, behind a family with four kids all under the age of ten, all wearing identical blue T-shirts. The ocean breeze riffled Annie's hair and she combed it back with her fingers.

Jack stood up.

Years later, when Jack would tell this story, he would say that it felt like time nearly stopped at that moment. That the signs, the sunglasses, the fortune-tellers—the whole tawdry mosaic—disappeared from the Boardwalk, leaving only Jack and Annie and a sun-dappled, Irish Spring ending, where the happy couple floats toward each other in slow-motion joy and the world dissolves in a kiss.

But the real story was better.

Jack stood up. Annie saw him above the four fat, T-shirted kids. They walked toward each other and met by a plaque honoring Charles Darrow, the inventor of Monopoly. They both tried to keep from breaking into silly grins. They both said, "Hi, I'm sorry that . . ." at the same time. They laughed, started again, and stumbled over each other's words again. Then Annie put her hand up and said, "Wait, stop. I've got to say something first." Jack waited, the silly grin bubbling up despite his best intentions. Annie put a hand on his shoulder and said, "Are there storm clouds over Lisbon?"

Jack didn't answer, he simply pulled her to him. And the world dissolved in a kiss.

CHAPTER 69

They sat with their backs to the surf and ate orange saltwater taffy from a two-pound box Annie had bought as Jack's initiation to Atlantic City. They talked and kissed and kissed again. Once, Annie choked back some tears, and when Jack hugged her, his face was buried in her autumn-colored hair. As the sun began to drop, Annie took Jack's hand and led him through the casino maze at Caesar's to find her mother.

"Your hair is grayer than I expected," said Joan Hollerman Silver with a smile. She was playing video poker.

"You're much younger-looking than Annie told me," Jack said and hugged her. Then the three of them huddled around a single machine, playing until they lost another $75.

"Enough of this," Jack said. "Joan, come on, let me teach you to play craps. We'll turn what little we have left into millions."

Annie caught Jack in her arms. "Craps?" she said. "You're going to teach my mother how to play craps? Don't encourage her. She'll wind up broke, living in a cardboard box. Anyhow, you promised me a rolling chair ride the entire length of the Boardwalk."

Jack looked at Annie's mother. "It'll cost a hundred dollars, but she's worth it," he said.

The three walked outside and Annie hailed the first empty rolling chair she saw. The chair pusher, a young man who spoke with a thick Eastern European accent, slapped a rag across the faded blue cushion and Jack and Annie climbed aboard. But before they embarked, Joan Hollerman Silver leaned in and touched her daughter on the shoulder.

"So, I have to ask, what was it in Jack's e-mail that made you change your mind?"

"Let's just say it was persuasive," said Annie.

"Let her read it," said Jack.

"Yeah, let her read it," said her mother, looking at Annie.

CHAPTER 70

Joan Hollerman Silver watched the rolling chair man weave his way down the Boardwalk. She waited until he and his cargo disappeared, swallowed up by the obstacle course of tourists and tired gamblers.

She walked back through Caesar's, making up a song with Annie's password in it, so she wouldn't forget. "Worms, worms . . . I'm gonna go eat worms," she hummed to herself. She thought of Annie, age eight, digging in the front yard collecting earthworms for the earthworm zoo she made out of a shoebox.

In the room, she turned on Annie's laptop and called up Annie's e-mail directory. She clicked on the message entitled "Proposal."

To: ahollerman@aol.com
From: jdepaul@aol.com
Subject: Proposal
Dear Ms. Hollerman,

I'm looking for an agent. Laura Goodbread suggested I contact you to represent my book. She says you understand journalists.

I've been in the newspaper business for 30 years and I am Laura's editor at the Baltimore Star-News.

My book, "Thief of Words," is about second chances and the malleable nature of memory. But mostly, it's about the possibility of happy endings. I know they're old-fashioned, but I think we're all looking for one, don't you?

The story goes like this: A middle-aged couple meets over lunch. Both are divorced; both work in writing and publishing; both are willing to take another chance at love. They seem like a perfect match. But it's hard to start over, especially because the woman is troubled by secrets from her past.

Inadvertently, the man stumbles onto something that may save them. In a series of e-mails, he rewrites the woman's past, this time starring the two of them together. With each of these new memories the bond between them pulls tighter.

But the bond may not be strong enough. Someone from the man's past comes back to haunt them both, just as the woman's secret closes in on her. And the woman refuses to believe the man doesn't care what happened 20 years ago, that he loves her for who she is now.

I don't have any special qualifications to write this book. I'm just a guy working in a comma factory. And I don't know if it's a salable story, but it's honest and true and from the heart.

I realize most writers send you the first chapter of their books. But what follows is the last chapter. It's highly unusual, I know, but I think you'll be particularly interested in how the book ends—or could end if you take me on as a client.

I look forward to hearing from you,
Jack DePaul

THIEF OF WORDS

(final chapter)
by
Jack DePaul

The curtains were slightly parted, letting the morning sun paint a bright median strip across the bed. Annie lay there, on her side, with Jack spooned against her. She could feel the rhythmic rise and fall of his chest.

Annie looked over at the clock. It was 9:35 A.M. She slid out from under the covers, walked to the window, and pulled the curtains wider apart.

"I like the view," said Jack. "And I don't mean outside the window."

Annie turned to see Jack awake, head propped up on one elbow.

"I love your body," he said.

She pulled the gauzy inner curtain over her nakedness, with exaggerated coyness.

"Come back to bed," he said.

The next time Annie noticed the clock it was 10:35.

"I'm starving," said Annie, running an index finger down Jack's thigh. "If I don't get something to eat soon, I'll start chomping on your arm."

Jack leaned over and kissed her on the nose. "Food later," he said. "First, I've got a little job for us. Where'd you stash your laptop?"

Annie pointed to the closet. "Next to your shoes," she said.

Jack got up and returned with the computer. He put it on Annie's lap and snuggled in beside her.

She looked at him curiously and before she had a chance to ask, he said, "Annie, I've been talking about the power of words for thirty years. But it wasn't until I started writing you these e-mails that I really felt it." He put his hand over his heart as if he were giving the pledge of allegiance. "It's like we've been together since we tumbled down the face of that sand dune. But now it's time for the most important rewrite of Annie Hollerman's life. You type. It starts like this:

"If you like rooting for the underdog, Annie Hollerman would have been a fine choice . . ."

They debated a couple of the details—Princeton belt or Yale? Toyota or Honda?—and soon they were deep into Annie's new past and racing to the future.

". . . 'Wow, great hair,' was Jack DePaul's opening line. He blurted it out as Annie Hollerman walked past his desk on her second day in the newsroom. It had been a long time since Annie had heard anything that inept, but she didn't mind, this was Jack DePaul, the brash young features editor the paper had hired away from the *San Diego Tribune*. Her hair had stunned him into an incomplete sentence.

The next afternoon, he came over, sat on the corner of her desk, and suggested she go after a story about a chicken farm inspector. Nobody on his staff would touch it, but he was sure it was a great yarn. In the right hands, he said, it could read like a detective story.

Annie snapped at it like a hungry trout. Before Jack DePaul had returned to his desk, she'd made two phone calls. Twelve days later it was done. An eighty-inch feature she'd worked on between daily assignments and polished up late at night.

The day before the chicken inspector story ran—above the fold on page one—Jack DePaul came by her desk again. "Up for an adventure?" he said. "Always," she said. That night, they got in his '72 VW Bug and drove twelve miles to cross the state line, where they ate fried perch and hush puppies at Bueley's Fish Camp in Rock Hill, South Carolina. They talked until LaFontaine Bueley, the seventy-two-year-old owner, turned out the dining room lights. The next night, he took her to Country City USA, where they learned to line dance.

Within weeks they were known in the newsroom as DeHollerman. They were wunderkind bookends, full of talent and drive. Friends could picture Jack running the *Washington Post*'s style section and Annie reporting from the White House. DeHollerman could picture it, too, but their newsroom pals would have been surprised to learn that the wunderkinds had other, far different, dreams as well.

One Sunday over lox and bagels at the Park Road Deli, they read a *New York Times* Magazine story about Peace Corps volunteers helping street kids in Ghana. The next day, they called the New York office for applications. They imagined trips all over the world. Jack wanted to take Annie to Nepal. Annie wanted to take Jack on a train ride through countries thick with jungle. Jack read Annie some poems by Pablo Neruda. Annie, fired by the words, decided they had to make a pilgrimage to Chile.

They made love on Annie's secondhand sofa halfway through a late-night broadcast of *Goodbye Columbus*. An hour later they made love on the rug by the couch. An hour after that they made love in Annie's bed.

Then came an uncharacteristically cold spring day in the Queen City of Charlotte, North Carolina. The kind of cold day that makes the shiny red tulips lining the city's main streets shiver.

Annie got to the paper at 9:15. First she stopped at the cafeteria, where she bought coffee and joked about the cold weather. She seemed even more buoyant than usual. If the cafeteria ladies had thought to ask her why, she might have told them about the night before, when Jack, being a man who liked ceremony and flourishes, bent down on one knee before her and asked if she would move in with him.

Her second stop was the desk of city editor Mark Snowridge, where she apologized for not bailing him out with a last-minute column. "There was no way I could finish in thirty minutes," she said.

"Don't sweat it," replied Snowridge. "What's another license plate story? It's all just next day's birdcage liner anyway. You'll have something for me next time, Hollerman. You're still the aces."

She arrived at her own desk around 9:30. There on the keyboard of her computer was a small box. Taped to it was a note, in Jack's handwriting, that read, "Open me." Inside, resting on a pillow of white cotton, was Jack's house key. "For you, Annie," the note said. "Always and forever."